The Dying Gaul

David Jones

Photograph by Julian Sheppard

THE DYING GAUL
and Other Writings

DAVID JONES

edited with an Introduction by
HARMAN GRISEWOOD

FABER AND FABER
London & Boston

First published in 1978
by Faber and Faber Limited
3 Queen Square, London WC1
Reprinted 1979
Printed in Great Britain by
Ebenezer Baylis and Son Ltd.
The Trinity Press, Worcester, and London
All rights reserved

British Library Cataloguing in Publication Data

Jones, David, b. 1895
    The Dying Gaul, and other writings.
    I. Title II. Grisewood, Harman
    828'.9'1208   PR6019.053

ISBN 0-571-11067-3

Contents

Illustrations

Introduction

The second collection of David Jones's prose may be thought of as a companion volume or sequel to *Epoch and Artist*, published in 1959. But the differences are greater than the resemblance. Though I collected and arranged the items for the earlier volume, as I have for this, David himself made the final selection. It was he who chose the title and did his best by careful supervision to see that the contents illustrated and exemplified a train of thought in the mind of the reader which the title was meant to provoke. But David has died and there is no comparable mind to decide upon a dominant theme for this second volume; there is no comparable authority who can interpret the author's intention concerning the inclusion or revision of any particular item. Moreover, this book, by necessity, is miscellaneous in character, whereas its predecessor was carefully planned. *The Dying Gaul* is a collection of nearly all the prose pieces found among David's papers which were not included in *Epoch and Artist*. Some could not be included because they were written after 1959; some were left out because David had forgotten them, or had lost them; some he probably consciously rejected because he felt they had been superseded by subsequent articles or by changed opinions. And some he may have thought not good enough or too trivial.

I have included all that I could find in a finished state except for two or three pieces which were merely repetitious or which I knew David would wish to omit. So the second collection is a supplement to the first, and the two books taken together comprise pretty well all the prose pieces which David completed.

We do know that David wanted a second volume to appear. He was thinking about it two years or more before he died and early in 1972 he wrote to Peter du Sautoy, chairman of Faber's, to say that he hoped the book would include three already published pieces. All three were written after *Epoch and Artist*. They were: 'The Dying Gaul', 'Use and Sign' and the Introduction to *The Ancient Mariner*. He explained that he hoped to write an auto-biographical essay specially for the new volume. After his death a large number of foolscap sheets were found representing David's frustrated but persistent attempts to accomplish what he had set out to do.

Fortunately, a friend of David's, Peter Orr of the British Council, rescued the writer from his predicament. He persuaded David to record some of what he had written and to add a good deal. This material was transcribed, and after David's death some of the recorded material was published in *Agenda* (Winter–Spring 1975).

It is thanks to the initiative of the British Council that this volume can begin as David would have wished with some part at least of what he meant to write at greater length. I have given it the title which David had chosen: '*In illo tempore*'. These are the words used in the old Latin Mass to introduce the Gospel. They are commonly translated: 'At that time' or 'In those days'. The next three pieces are so placed because each has some autobiographical interest.

Though the items found in this volume owe their place to circumstance rather than to editorial deliberation, their order is not haphazard. I have tried to arrange them so that the reader will get the best out of the book by reading it straight through, considering each piece in the light of what has gone before. The contents looked at sequentially and as a whole will, it is hoped, afford an encouraging introduction to the work of David Jones for a new generation who had heard nothing or very little about him in his lifetime. Like G. M. Hopkins in the 1930s, David Jones needs to be 're-discovered' by those who are at some distance from the time in which he wrote. For David, though greatly concerned with the past, was a prophetic writer. What he has to say is more relevant to those who are to endure the conditions which he foresaw than it was for those who admired his foresight at the time he wrote. Understood aright, his insight, for anyone who nerves himself to love the truth as David did, will provide a unique interpretation of the epoch which is taking shape.

The first four items, then, are meant to give the reader an impression of David's tastes and beliefs and of those influences which he chose to follow or reject. 'The Dying Gaul' comes next. The reader who at this point has understood how strong was the attraction of Wales for David Jones as poet and painter will, through this fifth item, begin to appreciate how complex was the nature of that attraction. Wales was the focus for what David in this essay calls 'Celticity itself'. What makes his Welsh sympathies interesting and what for him as a creative artist made them fruitful, is the encounter between 'Rome' and 'Wales'. 'Rome' is not only the historic Rome. It is also the large, conquering, imperial power of money or of military might, wherever in history it is found. And though his devotion to Wales was indeed real and heartfelt, 'Wales' is not only the British Principality but is also any small, self-conscious, oppressed and oppositional, historic group. That encounter and its consequences are in David's work as actual and significant for today and tomorrow as they were when the Gauls climbed the Tarpeian Rock, or when Llywelyn the Last was murdered in the woods at Builth.

The essay itself is reticent and slight compared with the strong feeling which animates it. That I have chosen this essay to give its title to the whole collection is because nowhere else in his prose does David make so far-reaching a statement of what lay at the root of his concern for Wales and for the larger world of the oppressed of which Wales is part.

The role of the conquering hero is well known in literature and art. Poets and painters do most often respond affirmatively to success whether of power or fashion. No matter if the fashion is 'protest' or 'the drop-out', the artist knows how to make the fashionable underdog into a 'success' even if it is only a *succès d'estime*. But David's keenest sympathies were with defeat, and with the efforts of the defeated to survive. Achilles was never a hero to David. His heart was with Hector in the dust.

'The Dying Gaul' is about defeat—and resurrection. But in the course of the essay David turns aside from the main theme to make some observations about a particular art form which shows what he calls an 'essential Celticity'. He characterizes this element as 'intricate, complex, flexible, exact, and abstract'. Following this observation, I have placed next the two pieces which are about art in relation to national characteristics: 'An Aspect of the Art of England' and 'Wales and Visual Form'.

After these come two other essays related to the theme of the dying hero. Each of them will, it is hoped, have more meaning for the reader than would be the case if he had not read 'The Dying Gaul'. The two essays which then follow, 'The Welsh Dragon' and 'Welsh Culture', are also connected with themes which have been discussed in 'The Dying Gaul'. These shorter pieces too will, I believe, have more significance for the reader who has thought about the implications of the previous essay.

Those who at this stage in the book have been wondering what David meant by 'art' and 'artist' will, no doubt, have realized he uses these terms with meanings which are not commonly met with. The large-scale essay 'Art in Relation to War', written in 1942 and 1943, will go far to explain his views on this fundamental subject. It should be read in conjunction with 'Art and Sacrament', written eleven years later (*Epoch and Artist*, p. 143).

If David had never written a line of poetry nor painted a single picture, these two essays would give him some claim upon posterity as a thinker. In the second essay he explains that the essential character of sacrament is also the essential character of art so that you cannot have one without the other. 'No artefacture no Christian religion', he says in the Preface to *The Anathémata* (*Epoch and Artist*, p. 127). And in the earlier and complementary essay on art and war he explains that the practice of art in some sense is an essential attribute of our humanity. He might have summarized his argument by the phrase: 'No artefacture, no human being.'

In the next two essays David develops points which grow out of 'Art in Relation to War', though these were written after 'Art and Sacrament' and are more closely related to that second essay than the first.

Introduction

This book ends with the *Ancient Mariner* Introduction. This was the last substantial piece which David wrote. Writers' typical last pieces, written when they are past seventy, are usually résumés or reflections upon what they have previously expressed. But in the *Ancient Mariner* commentary David breaks what is for him altogether new ground. In no other essay does he discuss the themes of personal guilt and personal redemption, though it is obvious from his poetry that he thought a good deal about them. He allows Coleridge to lead him to introduce such themes as the redemptive role of a woman in a man's life which he would not, I think, have taken up if left solely to his own initiative. The scope of the essay is nothing less than the journey of a man throughout his earthly life and for that reason, if for no other, it is a fitting ending to this posthumous volume.

HARMAN GRISEWOOD

Acknowledgements

Thanks are due to the Trustees of David Jones's Estate, Mrs. Elkin, Mrs. Wright, and Mr. Hyne; to the British Council and Mr. Peter Orr; to Mr. René Hague; and to the editors of *Agenda*, *The Catholic Herald*, *The Listener*, *The London Magazine*, *The Tablet*, and *Wales*, and to Mr. Douglas Cleverdon and Clover Hill Editions, who first published some of the writings in this volume, for permission to reprint them here.

The worth of this book has been greatly enhanced by the scholarship and care of Miss Catharine Carver. Most of the pieces included were found among David Jones's papers in a number of different versions; to decide what text he would have chosen for publication called for a most sensitive discernment and much painstaking research. Miss Carver's work on the texts has I believe fulfilled the likely wishes of the author as closely as any of David's friends could hope for and could not have been bettered by anyone else.

H.G.

I am in no sense a scholar, but an artist, and it is paramount for any artist that he should use whatever happens to be to hand. For artists depend on the immediate and the contactual and their apperception must have a 'now-ness' about it. *But,* in our present megalopolitan technocracy the artist must still remain a 'rememberer' (part of the official bardic function in earlier phases of society). But in the totally changed and rapidly changing circumstances of today this ancient function takes on a peculiar significance. For now the artist becomes, willy-nilly, a sort of Boethius, who has been nicknamed 'the Bridge', because he carried forward into an altogether metamorphosed world certain of the fading oracles which had sustained antiquity. My view is that all artists, whether they know it or not, whether they would repudiate the notion or not, are in fact 'showers forth' of things which tend to be impoverished, or misconceived, or altogether lost or wilfully set aside in the preoccupations of our present intense technological phase, but which, none the less, belong to man.

So that when asked to what end does my work proceed I can do no more than answer in the most tentative and hesitant fashion imaginable, thus: Perhaps it is in the maintenance of some sort of single plank in some sort of bridge.

DAVID JONES, in a statement to
the Bollingen Foundation, 1959

In illo tempore*

I was born in the evening of 1 November 1895, the Feast of
All Saints, in Kent; son of James Jones and Alice Ann (*née*
Bradshaw), on my paternal side of wholly Welsh blood. My
father was born in 1860 in Treffynnon, of a family from
Ysgeifiog, in that north-east corner of Wales that had, historically,
been a continuous cause of contention between the earls of
Chester, backed by the Crown, and the princes of Gwynedd.
James Jones had come to London in about 1885, which he
referred to as 'the year of Gordon's death at the stairhead'.

I suppose my first remembered thing was in 1900, or about
1900. I was tucked up in a cot next to my mother's bed, but an
unfamiliar sound from the roadway outside impelled me to creep
out as cautiously as I could and make for the window, to look
between the slats of the venetian blinds; and what I saw and
heard was a thing of great marvel—a troop of horse, moving in
column to the *taratantara* of bugles. It was in fact a detachment of
the City Imperial Volunteers on a recruitment ride through the
outer suburbs for the war in South Africa of which I was, as yet,
in blissful ignorance. But to me, those mounted men were a
sight of exceeding wonder, and I said to myself: 'Some day I shall
ride on horseback', a desire never to be realized, to my continued
regret to this day. Anyway, I had but very brief joy of the
equestrian column and the inimitable sound of steel-shod horse

* Most of this essay is taken from transcripts of tape recordings made in 1973
by Peter Orr, Head of Recorded Sound at the British Council, though it
incorporates autobiographical material from other sources as well. It was first
published, as 'Fragments of an Attempted Autobiographical Writing', with an
introductory note by Mr. Orr, in *Agenda*, vol. 13, no. 1 (Winter–Spring
1975), and is reprinted here with occasional insertions of additional material
from the transcripts.

hooves, and the sight of white dust rising, and the metallic sound of bugles; though I thought I had been very careful, those damned venetian blind-slats had evidently betrayed me, for in an instant my mother appeared and without a word swiftly lifted me back to the cot, covering me with an extra blanket.

'How many times have I to tell you that once I've put you to bed and drawn the blinds, that's where you stay. Cot's best for you at this hour, now go to sleep.'

'But Mother, what were those men on those beautiful horses, and why did they blow those trumpets?'

'Go to sleep, you'll know soon enough, but for now be off to sleep.'

'But Mother, are there Guardian Angels like Miss Best says, but which Daddy says can't be proved from the Bible, but that someone called Dr. Pusey got it from what he calls Papists?'

This was a little awkward for my mother, but after a pause she said, 'Not for little boys who won't do as their mothers bid them. Now no more of this. Matthew, Mark, Luke and John bless the beds of all of us. I've told you that rhyme often, but even they expect little boys to be obedient. Now goodnight and don't let me hear another sound, you understand?'

'Yes, Mother.'

After her leaving me with the gentle command to sleep, I lay some time wondering who, in fact, were those strange horsemen. I had heard my sister saying something about 'the vats of Luna' and the 'yellow Tiber', but nothing of 'in harness on the right' or the Great Twin Brethren, or certainly I would have supposed they were making for, perhaps, Keston ponds to serve for Lake Regillus. But who were they, and why had Mother been so guarded in answer to my question about angels? Before I fell asleep I heard, much farther off, the bugles' renewing *taratantara*, but from very far off indeed, and beneficent, I thought, as from a detachment of the heavenly armies—so they were angels after all. Well, I could still hope to ride some day on horseback, but I knew I could never be an angel. At least I knew that much.

I make these recallings here solely to indicate how complex and tricky is this business of 'sources' and 'influences' in any work.

Of course research and perceptive analysis often disclose connections not previously apparent and throw light on unexpected liaisons, but beneath all that there remain 'unshared backgrounds' that make the 'sources' far further back than would appear likely, even to the writer himself. For example, in writing *In Parenthesis* (begun in 1928, but not entitled till the late 1930s), I toyed with the idea of calling it *In Harness on the Right*, without at first connecting the title with the incident described above, at the opening of the twentieth century. And in *The Tribune's Visitation*, first published in 1958, the Tribune compares the 'sour issue tot' (the vinegar-like wine of each Roman soldier's ration) to 'some remembered fuller cup from Luna vats'. I wrote quite unconsciously and without hesitation, as though Luna was the only place in Italy for wine of good vintage, again a direct recalling of 1900 or 1902. And again, in part 7 of *In Parenthesis* (p. 163), my reference to 'Peredur of steel arms', though quoted from Edward Anwyl's translation of the *Gododdin* fragments, also recalled the childhood glimpse of the strange riders seen through the slats of the venetian blinds, and the *At tuba terribili sonitu tarantara dixit*, many years before I heard of Ennius.

* * * * *

My mother was born in the year of the Crimean War, of a Thames-side family, so spent her childhood when the Pool of London was at a peak of mercantile importance. There was an Italian strain on her maternal side. My grandmother was an old lady when I first remember her, but had those symmetric features and what I believe is called an 'olive complexion' and very dark eyes, such as we tend to associate with the Middle Sea, nor was it difficult to understand why she had been known as 'the beautiful Miss Mockford', or why my mother's father had desired her as his bride. All that side of the family were of Thames-side stock. If Uncle Ben was a marine engineer, cousin Fred was something or other with the Royal Victualling people (always pronounced 'Vit-lin'), while another was wholly concerned with 'sight drafts' and 'bills of lading'. These were terms frequently used when elderly relations visited the house in Kent, which was rapidly becoming part of the suburbia of Greater London. They meant nothing to the child-years of David Jones, but decades later, in the 1920s, when I first read in 'The Fire Sermon' of *The Waste Land* the line, 'C.i.f. London: documents at sight', the poet evoked for me an echo dead central to all that world, a real bull's-eye and no mistake.

My grandfather was a master mast- and block-maker, which involved competence in all that belongs to a ship's carpentry. Which float of Norweyan from the mast-pond? Keel-elm for those caps aloft by the hounding? Best Indies lignum vitae to resheave those heavier running-blocks?

'The virtue of art is to judge'; 'Art is a virtue of the practical intelligence'. Bradshaw knew nothing of these definitions but, unknown to himself, he practised them. By a happy chance Joyce, according to Gogarty, declared boat-building to be comprehended in practical life as 'art', no less than the making of a poem. It was no accident that the bardic poets of Wales called themselves *seiri cerdd*, 'carpenters of song'.

Such as I know of my grandfather was gleaned over the years, mainly from my mother, but also from my father, for there had been a great affection between the very English father-in-law and his Welsh son-in-law, in whose arms he died of some sudden heart-attack.

Like Samuel Pepys, Ebenezer Bradshaw was 'up betimes' (round about 5 a.m. in the summer, and not much after 6 in the winter), casting accounts, it seems, of his small business and reading the Book of Common Prayer and, it would appear, much of Milton, before breakfast with Ann his wife, and then down to his yard to see how things were going there. Had Murphy arrived? Though, like John Jones in far-off Tegeingl, he was of the Church of England and a parish clerk, his proudest boast was that his name was the same as the first signature on the warrant that brought 'the man Charles Stuart' to his decapitation by the 'bright axe' brought especially from the Tower to White-hall for that memorable scene. Indeed, he went further, and without any supporting documents whatever, claimed to be descended from the family of Justice Bradshaw, the regicide.

In illo tempore

Years later, in suburban Kent, I used to sit under a pear tree on a small log of Ganges teak, brought there as an act of *pietas* by my parents along with some blocks and dead-eyes and other tackle and tools of ship's carpentry, just as reliques to recall the skilled artifex in his Thames-side yard.

*   *   *   *   *

From about the age of six, I felt I belonged to my father's people and their land, though brought up in an entirely English atmosphere. So it was natural that when, sometime in the first decade of the twentieth century, I was taken to Gwynedd Wen, with the taut sea-horizon on the right, and to the left the *bryniau* and west, and further off, the misted *mynyddoedd* of Arfon, I felt a Rubicon had been crossed, and that this was the land of which my father had spoken with affection and suppressed pride—for James Jones was not given to voicing his deeper feelings. As the saying goes, he did not wear his heart on his sleeve!

However that may be, this initial visit made an indelible mark, not to be erased. There were, of course, subsequent visits, but it is fair to say that the first of these remained the most fixt in my heart and mind. This was, at a guess, in 1904 or thereabouts.

My father was, at the time of my birth, a printer's overseer and that meant that I was brought up in a home that took the printed page and its illustration for granted. It is conceivable that this may have had some influence on my early preoccupation with drawing. My mother had drawn well as a young woman, but such activities were given up long before I was born.

However, I had decided by about the age of six that when I grew up there was only one thing that I would do. By which I do not mean that I was possessed of some special sense of vocation. I merely mean that I cannot recall a time when drawing of some sort was not an accustomed activity and one which I supposed I should pursue later in life. For one thing, I was so backward at my lessons that I regarded drawing as a counter-weight to my deficiency in all else. To attempt to convey on paper this or that object seemed to me as natural a desire as, say, stroking a cat, and I couldn't understand why my brother and sister had not the same compulsion. I think many children have this inclination towards drawing, but either it fades out as they grow older, or they are discouraged by their elders, who fear that this obsession—as it certainly was with me—will make them backward in those more serious studies which are necessary in our sort of society.

Animals were what I usually drew, and the dancing bear, a drawing from the window in 1902 of one of those brown bears that used to be brought round the streets and roads by keepers seeking to earn a pittance, is still, I think, my favourite drawing. There was no doubt in my mind that somehow or other, when I grew up, I would become what is called 'an artist'—even if it was a pavement artist.

My mention of pavement artists here is by no means without its recallings, for my mother used always to slip something into the suppliant hand or cap of any pavement artist we passed—and there were many more such in those days than there are today. I asked her why they all got a few pence, irrespective of the merit of their work, but she only smiled and said, 'Well, that's my business, and anyhow they are very poor men and we are told to give what we can to the poor.' I discovered later that she feared I would end in the gutter if I gave my entire attention to drawing and remained so backward at my lessons.

Looking back, I think this has a very medieval feeling—something in some way analogous to what the Church calls the 'store-house of merit'. If such and such acts of charity are persevered in with some specific intention, it may be that some seemingly likely and even well-deserved fate will be averted.

*   *   *   *   *

There were, at that time, establishments that I should guess were perhaps the descendants of those 'dame-schools' of a far earlier epoch, though that was the last thing evoked by the place I'm thinking of. It was run, I think, by two young women for a handful of small children, and one of the two had two long plaits of peat-dark hair, a very white skin and a smile that would do justice to Creirwy of Llyn Tegid, the love of Garwy Hir—though

I was not to know of them for many years. But I hastened in the morning, even Monday morning, so as not to miss whatever the enchantress might be able to effect with regard to my deplorable inability in the matter of spelling and reading, for I was becoming most painfully aware that I must somehow make out what those black lines of print meant for myself. I couldn't rely for ever on my sister to read to me *The Knight of the Sparrowhawk* in the 'Books for the Bairns' series, and much else, even though I could draw bears and lions, and even the horse in the green-grocer's stable next door which I could see through a break in the brick-course, better, I told my mother, than Rosa Bonheur. But the black shapes on white paper remained for me what the notation of the Chant meant for Archbishop Ullathorne, when some Sequence or Preface proper to the day was held for him to see which of the modes and what tonic note he must use: 'Take it away, boy, take it away, those black things mean nothing to me.'

But I was in no such condition of independence as that remarkable and very English eccentric *sacerdos*. Somehow or other, I must make those lines of black things mean something to me. And some small progress was made, and in a few days quite a bit. Was it by enchantment? Was Two Plaits a camouflaged Creirwy *tegkaf morwyn o'r byt*, and had she summoned the aid of the proverbial wisdom of Garwy Hir her lover and the magic of Keritwen her mother or of Fferyllt, son of Maia, Pentret Andreas apud Mantua, the greatest word-master in all the world, and lord of metamorphoses as, say, David cum Sibylla? I don't know, but by whatever craft, at least some measure of the metamorphosis was achieved, in that the printed page began to mean something, and it was no longer a case of 'those black things mean nothing to me'.

But when it came to the simplest imaginable sort of arithmetic no *hud a lledrith* enabled me to have by heart what I believe was called the twice-times table. I could not relate the concrete, tangible and desirable with the formal and conceptual.

'Come now, just suppose I wore my hair in a bun, like Miss Hopkins, would that mean a plus or a minus in plaits?'

'I don't know, but I do know that you would look as horrible as Miss Hopkins, even though she is Welsh like my father.'

And then I cried and cried.

'Never mind, but you must never speak of Miss Hopkins in that way; but it's time to go home now. We'll try again tomorrow.'

And we did, tomorrow and tomorrow and tomorrow.

But the time was passing, and soon the establishment closed, and I vaguely understood what was meant by 'minus two plaits'.

Many, many years and decades later, in writing of the Roman *viae* that grid our island and which the men of the island would not have built but for Elen of magical beauty, I suggested that there is always a Virgo Potens to direct the *via*.

* * * * *

But with the years there came a time when I found myself having to plead that I wanted only to pursue the practice of the visual arts and to go to an art school. We know from the story of the importunate woman in the Gospel how importunacy can some-times achieve its end, and it would seem that my requests became sufficiently tedious and I was allowed to get away with it, and attend an art school, not with 'the bottoms of my trousers rolled', but in schoolboy's knickerbockers.

Hence, when I should have been having Latin declensions and the elements of Greek knocked into me, aside from other *disciplinae* of various sorts, I was, in fact, making drawings of plaster casts of such works of classical antiquity as the Aphrodite of Melos (that most serene and gracious of works in the academic tradition), or that confounded Disc-Thrower, or the Boy and the Goose, or the Dying Gaul from Pergamon, with his typical oblong Celtic shield and his torque. I naturally liked him, for he epitomized for me so much of Celtdom, or what little I knew of it in 1909–10. At least I sensed a continuity of struggle and a continuity of loss. I could not recall hearing of works celebrative of victory, but only of relentless resistance culminating in defeat. But from each defeat came the living embers to feed the fires of resistance yet to be. That plaster copy of a Roman marble, copy of a Greek bronze from Anatolia, in some way was a *signum* for me of much that I had not yet more than a very shadowy knowledge of; but years later the facts gave substance to the shadows.

After a while I was allowed to draw from life. At first, the living nude was considered not suitable for a boy of fourteen in the year 1910. But it was still animals I most wanted to draw, still the cat-tribe, and wolves and deer, and that partiality has remained throughout the years, especially marked in the late 1920s and early '30s. But these fragments are not intended as a discourse on my work: that must speak for itself.

At the outbreak of the First World War, in 1914, I had been a student in a London art school for some years, and I was beginning to wonder what sort of shape the future might have for an artist of no particular qualifications when he left the art school.

In January 1915, being in a battalion of the Royal Welch Fusiliers, as part of the 38th (Welsh) Division, I found myself once more on the coast of Gwynedd, this time doing squad drill on the esplanade at Llandudno. But soon the Division was moved for extensive training in the neighbourhood of Winchester and, early in December 1915, embarked from Southampton for France.

The various units of the Division were taking up positions astride the Estaires–La Bassée Road, in that short section of the front where the meandering forward trenches ran through battered remains best known to soldiers of the British front— Laventie in the north, through Richebourg l'Avoué and Festubert to Neuve Chapelle and south to Givenchy.

Units of the brigades that formed the Division, and the four battalions that formed the brigades, would take what was known as a 'tour in', and would switch from one sector to another. It was mostly as regular a routine as possible: so many days in the front-most trench, so many in the support trench (if there was one), so many days in 'reserve', which was less attractive than it may sound, for you could count on endless fatigues when in 'reserve'. Of course, this 'regular routine' was easily disrupted by all manner of happenings: heavy shelling, or raiding parties, or 'gas alerts'. A false alarm that gas was being used by the enemy could cause commotion right back at Divisional H.Q., or even over a whole Army area.

There the Division remained from about Christmas 1915 to early June 1916, when the long, long march south began, from the watery flats of Flanders to the wide undulating chalkland of the Somme.

It was those first six months in the trenches of the forward zone that I chose as the period and subject-matter in writing *In Parenthesis*, partly because it provided a convenient beginning and ending and demonstrated the varying pattern of our lives, and partly because those first six months could most easily be recalled in some detail, whereas later periods became much more muddled and less intimate, more wholesale and repetitive.

On 10–11 July, in a confused attack on Mametz Wood, I was, along with many, many others of my unit, wounded and was evacuated to England. When I returned some few months later— in October 1916—I found my unit was occupying positions on the extreme north flank of the British line, just north of the Ypres Salient.

I can only register a very considerable change of feelings and conditions on my return in late October: the piling-up of shells for guns of various calibre, with little attempt to camouflage them, and the bringing forward of heavy platformed howitzers, made one wonder. For one thing, continuous fatigue work was in progress, and defences were very evident, as though an impregnable line of sureness against an enemy attack, almost like German 'defence-in-depth', was in the mind of those in command. What it actually was, was the careful planning for an offensive against the enemy on a big scale. Anyway, the increased use of mechanical transport, and mechanization in general, made the whole 'feel' very different from the war I had known in the months before the Somme battle.

Sometime after the assault on Pilkan Ridge we were withdrawn and again sent south to a part of the front as astonishing in its quietness as north of Ypres was for its continuing and methodical activity. It was called the Bois Grenier sector: the communication trench had convolvulus and other floral creepers lending the revetment frames a positively festal feeling. A small French boy used to come along the road blowing a little metal horn of some sort, with packages of French newspapers such as *Le Matin* (now, I believe, extinct) for anyone who wanted to buy them.

So, through the best part of the autumn of 1917 (apart from sudden violences of considerable intensity from the German artillery, and other disturbances), we remained, until January or February 1918. I missed the astonishing German offensives of March and April, because ill with severe trench fever. It felt like the worst imaginable type of 'flu.

*   *   *   *   *

I used to stay in a house at Portslade, near Brighton. It was one of a row of stone-built bungalows which my parents occupied each year for some months in the 1920s; the bungalows were remarkable in that they were built literally on the sea margin, so that if the weather were at all rough, surf and spray broke on the seaward balconies, and I made numerous watercolour drawings looking waveward. I always think of Calypso gazing on an empty sea from a chair on a balcony, and associate that with the balcony at Portslade. In 1928, at this bungalow in Portslade, I began to write down some sentences which turned out to be the initial passages of *In Parenthesis*, published some ten years later.

This was a beginning of another sort. I had no idea of what I was letting myself in for.

1966–73

On the Difficulties of One Writer of Welsh Affinity Whose Language is English*

All works, whether of written poetry or of the visual arts, but especially of written poetry, depend to some extent upon the images used being drawn from the deposits of a common tradition, by virtue of which their validity is to be recognized by reader or beholder. True, the beauty of form and line can be appreciated without this common background, but, especially in the case of written poetry, if the allusions are outside the comprehension of the reader or listener, clearly a sense of what is said is immeasurably blunted.

In the case of very great poets, such as Milton, the sound and feeling may well be appreciated, but without some sort of acquaintance with the classical images and the biblical deposits I fail to see that it can mean much more than great beauty of sound, together of course with *general* concepts, I mean concepts general to mankind: anger, pity, love, hate, and so on. Well, all that's pretty obvious and is hardly worth saying; but it serves as a reminder of the difficulties we are considering in relation to persons of Welsh affinity, blood or tradition, whose medium is English. In so far as such persons either quite consciously, or partly so, or perhaps hardly at all, are the heirs of an anterior tradition, a tradition very much of this island, but the deposits of which are in a language which is no longer their language, and the

---

* A typescript of this unpublished essay, undated but apparently written after 1952, was found among David Jones's papers. It was originally entitled 'Some Notes on the Difficulties . . .'.

traditions of which have *not* been assimilated into the English tradition, they are made aware of a hiatus between the soil of the language they use and their own roots. Even if they are Welsh-speaking, yet write in English, the same difficulty remains: the appalling difficulty of using images (especially perhaps involving proper names) in a linguistic tradition that is quite other than that of their—or their forebears'—*patria*. The matter is far, far more complex than people think.

Perhaps I had better speak only for myself in this matter; otherwise there is a danger of generalizations, and they are useless, especially to the artist, who, of his nature, deals in the contactual and the particular.

I am a Londoner, brought up entirely in an English setting. But my father was a pure Welshman, but a Welshman of that generation—he was born in 1860—whose parents were determined that he should be as English as possible. Consequently he had only a rather feeble grasp of the Welsh language, knew virtually nothing of ancient Welsh tradition, but was deeply religious, and, I *know*, 'felt' extremely 'Welsh'.

From about the age of seven, I myself, for reasons that I suppose only psychologists could fathom, 'felt' Welsh also. But it happened that my bent was towards the visual arts. I was more than ordinarily stupid at lessons, so that even elementary French was beyond me, let alone mastering the extremely difficult language of my father's land. Yet, mainly via the English translation of *The Mabinogion*, Giraldus Cambrensis, the Arthurian cycle, the works of John Rhŷs, John Lloyd, and others, I maintained, and, I think, with a deeper understanding, an enthusiasm for the Welsh heritage. But there remained the barrier of language, and, also, the barrier that separates, since the sixteenth century at least, the Welsh of the early centuries from the Welsh of recent times.

Hence, when, far later in life, I attempted to *write* (previously I had *only* been concerned with drawing), I experienced the full difficulty of somehow making viable the things of Wales in the only language I know—English.

If one writes the proper name 'Aphrodite', because a general

31

understanding of the classical images has been, at least until recently, part and parcel of the English tradition, the undertones and overtones of that name incant *something* for the English reader. But supposing one used the proper name 'Rhiannon'; what then? Not only has it no meaning at all for the average Englishman (educated or otherwise), but little meaning (so I have discovered) for the average Welsh-speaking Welshman.

This is but one glaring, simple and obvious example of the well-nigh insurmountable difficulties confronting the poet, who, though drawing upon the ancient deposits of the Welsh race, has only English as his medium.

It is the *materia* that presents the main difficulty. But it is precisely from the deep *materia*, with the asides and allusions and implications deriving from a virtually lost tradition, that the poet may wish to draw.

For the poet or the artist the 'past' is much what 'nature' is for him: it is the raw stuff which he uses. But when that 'past' is virtually forgotten, and available perhaps, as in the Welsh case, in another linguistic tradition, and moreover a tradition separated from us by centuries of a contrary tradition, then the *poeta* is in a real jam. I don't pretend to know what the answer is. But I do believe that this is the main fundamental difficulty (there are others) for the Welshman, or the half-Welshman, writing in English.

The name 'Rhiannon' is a very good symbol of what I am trying to say. The name means a very great deal to me: it means as much as some classical name or some biblical name; but when one writes it down one *knows* that, not only will the reader be unable to pronounce it, but its connotations, the Celtic Mother Goddess, 'Rigantona', the 'Great Queen', the woman who did penance at the horse-block, and so much more, will be *wholly* lost on the 'English' reader and, alas, on many 'Welsh' readers also.

It is this break with a whole extremely complex cultural, religious and linguistic tradition that is the real problem for those of us who, while able only to use English, have our deepest roots, in some way or other, in the Welsh past.

I expect this is the reason why part-Welshmen, such as myself, have drawn so much on Malory and the English–French Arthurian sources. For there alone is a connecting link between the tradition of Wales and that of England. But this is far from satisfactory. For one thing the 'Arthurian' material has been vitiated by a kind of Tennysonian romanticism, which is so very distinct from Malory, let alone from the Welsh deposits.

Some few English historians are now beginning, owing to the fairly recent development of Celtic studies, to evaluate more reasonably the importance of the Welsh (or Brittonic Celtic) tradition during the Dark Ages to the history of Britain as a whole. So that today even some English public-school boys have at least heard of *Y Gododdin* and other Welsh classics; but on the whole that would apply only to specialists in Dark Age history; it has precious little general effect, and maybe now never will have.

There is the same process of decreasing accessibility in early English literature from *Beowulf* and the other Anglo-Saxon poetry to *Piers Plowman*, *Gawain*, and even Chaucer. There are centuries and centuries of cultural metamorphoses standing between that Old English and Middle English tradition and modern Englishmen. For example the grey wolf, Fenris, that sits on the 'throne of heaven' in Northern myth, is just about as meaningless to people today as Rhiannon or Ceridwen or the Twrch Trwyth or Olwen the daughter of Yspaddaden Pencawr.

When I write these names in my work I try to make them come naturally, because by accident I've for long been interested in what they signify in English translations of Welsh stuff, but I realize that they mean *virtually nothing* to the reader. That is why I thought it necessary to append all those notes to *In Parenthesis* and *The Anathémata*. But I'm becoming more and more doubtful as to the validity of this way of carrying on. It's not just *names* or being able to pronounce them: it involves a whole complex of associations. So far classical allusions and biblical ones and (in my case) liturgical ones still *more or less* work, but only more or less, because the whole of the past, as far as I can make out, is down the drain. The civilizational change in which we live has

33

occasioned this. For a writer who relies on this *materia* for his stuff this is a bit of a facer. People think one is being deliberately obscure or affected, but the fact is that one 'thinks' in those obsolete or becoming-obsolete terms. This all sounds as though I thought that poetry could not be written (in English or Welsh or double Dutch or what you will) without this reference back. I don't think that at all; I mean only that *for me* it gets difficult if people don't know what Aphrodite, let alone Rhiannon, *signifies*.

The deep things of Wales belong to the past (there again I don't mean that they have no future), but, as I see it, the difficulty, or the *main* difficulty, for the Welshman writing in English is but a further extension of the difficulty faced by all for whom the past means a great deal; the added difficulty being of somehow conveying, in English, what, at its subtlest and best and most incantational, is locked up in the ancient tongue of Britain.

I have mentioned only some of the excruciating difficulties of the situation. I see it as a civilizational situation—of traditions wholly or partly lost—of linguistic changes that can't be overcome. And, after all, all 'artists' or 'poets' of whatever sort can best work within the civilizational or cultural setting in which they find themselves. They are not responsible for the particular circumstances into which they were born. So I suppose the most that any of us can do is to 'show forth' the things that seem real to us and which we have inherited by this accident or that. It does not matter much whether it's appreciated at all. What does matter is that one feels oneself that it is *valid*.

A London Artist Looks at
Contemporary Wales*

F irst of all I must say that I speak as one whose father was a
Welshman. For his parents the normal means of communication was the Welsh language; yet they 'discouraged',
to use no stronger a word, the use of Welsh in their eldest
son.

This was in the '60s and '70s of the last century and in the
'80s he came to London, where by one of those bitter ironies
that may play tricks with any one of us he was offered a job
in Fleet Street which happened to require competent type-
setting and proof-correcting in the Welsh language: needless to
say his command of that language was insufficient.

Thirty-five or so years later he laughed good-humouredly
when he told me about this but *I* found it hard to share that
amusement then and I find it even harder now. For I am an
English monoglot, born, bred, and for practically all my life,
have lived near where Thames runs softly.

These things considered, I doubt whether it has been very wise
of me to take advantage of the freedom extended to a Guest
Speaker and to have chosen as my subject the matter of Wales as
seen by a Londoner whose life has been mainly occupied with
what are sometimes called the 'arts of form'. As was so well
understood by the author of Ecclesiasticus, chap. 38, such persons
are best left to the perfecting of their own works.

So you see that is another reason for my being more than a
little doubtful about this broadcast.

* A talk as Guest Speaker, broadcast on the Welsh Home Service of the
BBC, 20 April 1959; first published in *Wales*, May 1959.

A moment back I used the word 'chosen'; I think I should have said 'impelled', for it is the continuous nagging of my own thoughts touching the present predicament of the Cymry that inclines me to speak to you, who are the Cymry, of your own affairs.

There is a well-known saying, attributed, I think, to St. Augustine of Hippo, which seems to me as true in content as it is concise in form: *Amor meus pondus meum*, 'My love is my weight'. Anyway, I am sure that it is only the weight of love for the deeper things of the Cymry that can be of avail now.

If this Latin saying *is* from the pen of the author of *The City of God* then it was written down in Roman Africa by a passionate man who, though so very Roman in culture, betrays a warmth of feeling for his Carthaginian *patria* and ancestry.

Now just at that same time, far off, at another frontier of the Roman world-state, that is to say here, in Britannia, among the ancestors of some of us, events were moving towards the beginnings of certain territorial divisions that in course of time were to become nerve-centres of Welshness and to remain so.

Theodosius the Great was as yet ruling from the New Rome on the Bosphorus and St. Ambrose was preaching in Milan. The hour was very late, and as someone truly said: 'It is always later than you think.'

Less than a century after the Celtic rhetoric of Ambrose had been heard for the last time in his cathedral in Transpadane Gaul or Cunedda and his associates had accomplished their foundational task in Venedotia, the thing we call the Roman West had a decidedly new look.

Any day now, as you or I read the newspaper or listen to the news there is sufficient to indicate that our own times afford some interesting parallels with that fourth-century world.

The Welsh language had not yet stemmed from Brittonic Celtic, just as the French language had yet to stem from the Latin of Gaul when Cunedda came from Clyde to Clwyd.

Thus it comes about that the only continuous living link with antiquity in this island is the language which those of you who are Welsh-speaking have the honour to be using today.

Don't neglect it; for once lost it will not be easily recoverable, and your children's children may suffer the pain of loss. And here, at least, I can speak from experience and with feeling.

I remember Hilaire Belloc saying somewhere that 'names have power to bind and loose material things'. Welshmen certainly should know this to be true of many names.

Our actual, personal, memories may lack the concrete and happy double image of Hywel ab Owain Gwynedd who was able to associate the foam-bright margin of Cantref Meirion with the white arm that had been his pillow by that sea-margin; but at least we can say, with him (if you will be lenient with my attempted pronunciation), *Caraf morfa Meirionnydd*.

We need not have been there, the eye of the mind is sufficient for us to love, with him, the sea-flats of Merioneth; always providing we have at least an inkling of the weight of content which that name bears.

Such names have power to bind and loose; if we did not believe at least something of that sort we should, I think, have to regard our dealings with *cerdd* or *poiesis* as a convenient marriage with whimsy rather than, what I hope it is, a committed love of the Muse.

Hitherto many names have signified for us the things of this land of our fathers, because they were the names of some specific locality of that land. But now, at this present time, we are aware of a new anxiety, a cloud in our minds when we make a recalling of those same bright names, such as Arfon, Eifionydd, Llŷn, Penllyn, fertile Ynys Fôn and green Dyfed.

I say we are aware of an anxiety and a perplexity and a fore-boding. I do not, myself, see how we can very well side-step these emotions. We know now that even the loveliness of lovely Gwynedd will avail her nothing and that Mona Insula whose grain-yield has, since the earliest times, made her proverbial as the mother and nourisher of Wales must now be thought of as best fitted for industrial sites necessitating an influx from the English Midlands. I am in no position whatever to comment upon the real or supposed exigencies which, I imagine, dictate such schemes; but when it comes to a consideration of what those and other developments may bode for the future of the Welsh heritage, then, perhaps one can say something.

It would seem to me that by all the accidents of history and every attendant circumstance the placeless cosmopolis of the technocrats which more and more conditions us all, whoever and wherever we are, hits the things of Wales where it most hurts.

One is sometimes charged with a romantic rather than a realist attitude to these matters. But it is certainly no want of realism which makes one assert that the things of the Cymry are intricated in a rather special way with an historic language in an historic terrain.

This boundary stream, that mound, the scattered vestigial enclaves and their speech forms . . . this lime-washed, sacral enclosure; these dunes at the river mouth where no vestige remains but where once stood the *llys* at Aberffraw—'the principal seat': so far by means as fragile, vulnerable and scarcely tangible, or wholly immaterial, as this and these the elusive things of Wales have, in a tattered and fragmentary sort of way, been tabernacled for us.

Can this be so much longer? I don't know.

About a year ago [i.e. 1958] Wales was described, by a Welshman, as an industrial country with beauty enough and to spare. What disturbed one most about this statement was the implication that there was plenty of elbow-room, whereas it is the very circumscribed nature of Wales and the ever-shrinking perimeters of Welshness within that narrow space which occasions part of our anxiety.

As has already been indicated, it is a commonplace that our technocracy tends in all lands to be at odds with the older locality-patterns and that this sets up a measure of dichotomy in *all* of us, whether we belong to France or to England or Wales or elsewhere. But for Wales this dichotomy poses some particularly hard dilemmas.

It is quite evident that the specific heritage of the Welsh is in a very vulnerable position indeed with regard to the new civilizational pattern.

There is the perilously balanced linguistic situation, there is the whole tie-up of very ancient duration with site and locality, whereby terrain and nomenclature and the web of history are so intermixed as to be hardly patient of separation, even in the mind.

What 'the Abbey of Westminster' calls up for some of us may, in Wales, have a partial correspondence in a given configuration of the actual land itself, but with this crucial difference that the tract in question may be an enclave harbouring a community of living men and women with a living language and tradition linking the Britain of now with that of the earliest deposits.

Those who read the 'Stanzas of the Graves', the *Englynion y Beddau*, will understand how an actual topography, being commemorative, becomes inviolate, like a shrine. Perhaps Cymru has no shrines because she *is* one. And it may be no accident that her highest hill is called, in Welsh, the Great Burial-Place.

Throughout her long past the things of Wales have been destroyed or lost by weakness from within and hostilities from without, and though no doubt more of this pattern remains than some would admit, nevertheless I believe the main headache now is more owing to a general civilizational trend.

I do *not* mean that Welsh people with their talents are in the least likely to be at a disadvantage compared with others in this new and rapidly newer world of the technocrats. In fact, contrary to what I once would have argued, their intelligences seem rather suited to it. Moreover I am certain that the artistic genius of this people will make itself felt, whatever the shape of things to come. But this is somewhat aside from what is meant by 'the things of the Cymry' as conceived in this talk.

Alas, I am no hand at stating simply and briefly what is of its nature very, very complex. I don't pretend to have an answer to the questions I have raised, nor have I much right to offer advice. I would end rather with a confession: It so happens that I am, by this chance or that, mixed up with, involved in, or at least I wonder a good deal about, three things: the arts which I try to practice, the tradition of the Cymry, and the continuance of any sort of *sacramental* religion. And, as far as I can make out, by how things feel to me, all these three phenomena are in much the same predicament *vis-à-vis* today, and the technocracy which, so it seems to me, makes today other than yesterday.

Still, I try to continue to say *Dewi Ddyfrwr, gweddïa dros Gymru*, 'David the Waterman, pray for Wales', and even if you don't hold with the invocation of saints, I ask you to make this exception. Or, if you can't run to that, then remember Augustine's (if it was his) 'My love is my weight'. For whether your heart's love is *Cymru Fawr* or something or someone quite other, those words, being true, can do you no possible harm to contemplate.

1959

Notes on the 1930s[*]

First perhaps it should be said that I was in a somewhat peripheral position to the major 'movements' of that time. Perhaps 'complex' or 'ambiguous' might be a better adjective than 'peripheral' to convey my position *vis-à-vis* certain well-known and defined trends, I don't know.

There were a number of converging reasons for this. For one thing I had, and have, something of an antipathy to groups with stated aims. This does not mean that I regard such groups as bad or serving no purpose, or that I have not been influenced by the various intentions that caused those groups to be. It means more that I have felt that group labels are too arbitrary and also have observed that what sets out to be an assertion of values, which some academism has for long occluded, itself quickly develops an academism of its own. It is a thing that can't be helped—any clearly seen and passionately felt need to assert (or re-assert) this or that principle, as against some long accepted convention is always in danger of isolating a truth. Indeed it is that single-eyed concentration on some such truth *in isolation*, to the exclusion of all else, that lends vitality to the works of the initiators of such movements. The same isolation of something which it was very necessary to assert can subsequently produce works that are far from vital, as the absence of the excluded truths begin to cry out for recognition.

Something of this sort, a nagging sense that however much I agreed with the, so to say, 'manifestos' of some congenial group (and however much I may have been influenced by their works) there remained a lot unaccounted for in such manifestos, and I

* First published as part of a symposium, 'Looking Back at the Thirties', in *The London Magazine*, vol. 5, no. 1 (April 1965).

did not wish to be committed to truths that, however valuable, were not the whole truth.

This, as I write it, sounds somewhat pompous, self-conscious and deliberate. It sounds as though I had been forced into a position in which such choices had to be made. That was not the case, and I am trying only to express a state of mind in which, while stimulated by the works of this or that artist or this or that movement, I had reservations of all sorts. It was not the assertions but the implied (and sometimes explicit) denials that bothered me.

Perhaps a concrete example will convey more my attitude than all the foregoing paragraphs. The use of the term 'abstract art' was much in vogue in the 1930s. I suppose I myself first heard it used sometime before going into the Army in the 1914–18 War. I seem to recollect a Post-Impressionist Exhibition round about 1912, but it was not until after demobilization and my return to the life of an art student in 1919 that I have any conscious recollections of an awareness, or the beginnings of an awareness of the *implications* inherent in the Post-Impressionist *theory* and the insistence on 'the abstract' in the arts.

This to me, the more I considered the matter, came as a key, of sorts, which opened a large number of locks. I can't here recount the very varied and extensive matters which, for me, this notion affected. In any case I have done so in various connections elsewhere. It must here suffice to say that it provided a, so to say, 'code word' indicative of the factor which unified not only any given work but all those multifarious products of man that we call 'the arts'—the *poiesis*, 'making', call it what you will, that man has indulged in—from remotest pre-history onwards.

I would emphasize that I was and am thinking more of what was implicit in the notion of 'the abstract' and the term 'Post-Impressionist' than of the works, some abiding and great, some of more ephemeral interest, some mediocre or worse, which were made under the influence of that movement.

Perhaps the most concise (and I find conciseness extremely difficult) indication of my own attitude is to be found in a letter published in *The Listener* on 3 August 1950. It was reprinted in a book of selected bits and pieces, articles, etc., of mine published under the title *Epoch and Artist* (1959). But for your convenience I will quote the relevant passages, which read:

> Those of us whose work no one, I imagine, would call 'abstract', know, nevertheless, that it is an abstract *quality*, however hidden or devious, which determines the real worth of any work. This is true of Botticelli's *Primavera*, of the White Horse of Uffington, of the music of Monteverdi, of *Finnegans Wake*, of the 'Alfred jewel', of the glass goblet I am now trying to draw, of the shape of a liturgy, of the shape of a tea-cup. The one common factor implicit in all the arts of man resides in a certain juxtaposing of forms.
>
> In theory 'abstract art' is no more than a conscious assertion of this truth. It is then the assertion, in isolation, of a real, and indeed a first, principle. The least 'abstract' work (in the contemporary sense) could not be made apart from this principle, for without it a 'thing' having integration and a life of its own, could not be. Therefore without it the arts could not be.

I go on to indicate that with this 'clearly understood' we are in a better position to consider the possible aridities and impoverishments that may be latent in the practice of what is today (i.e. 1950) called 'pure abstraction'. I then go on to say that this, like all else, must be considered in its historical setting, and that it cannot be an accident that a preoccupation of various forms of abstract art has developed among us, and I conclude by saying:

> Remembering that our time is that of a 'late civilization', in which severe stress as to what direction is bound to be the lot of most serious artists, Blake's poignant and apposite question 'Do you, sir, paint in fear and trembling?' might also be asked of critics with regard to their trade.

(The letter was written apropos of what some critic had said about something.)

Well, I cite this 1950 quotation as a pretty fair indication of my personal attitude, which could just as well have been written in much the same terms in the 1930s.

It was the 'cornering', the restrictive use of the term 'abstract' that I felt to be regrettable because misleading. It is always difficult when one can see certain developments have come about by a complex of historical causes and the validity of which one can recognize, but the 'labels' or 'aims' of which, even while asserting *a* truth, are restricted to a particular approach and one suspects that this will, in turn, be used as a surrogate for sensitivity and genuine creativity, as ersatz, in its own way, as the banalities of any decayed academism.

But this is, no doubt, in the nature of things. It is probable that this wearing of blinkers may be necessary in order to pursue some single aim, the solution of what appears to the artist contactually involved as a new problem. That intense preoccupation certainly lent strength to many of the artists whose work I found most stimulating.

But if there was, and to some degree there always is and should be, this feeling of 'newness' for the artist struggling to resolve some problem of form and content, there was in the 1920s and becoming more obvious in the 1930s an objective 'newness', not brought about by, or from within, the activity we call 'the arts', but from a civilizational change, causing, I should think, a greater metamorphosis than any historic or proto-historic change known to us.

Now, in the mid-1960s, even the most imperceptive person is aware of at least some aspects of that ubiquitous civilizational change, for none of us can escape something of its implications. Needless to say the artist cannot.

That this change had been developing for a very long time before the periods under consideration is of course true, but I'm speaking of its onward and rapid acceleration in our own times.

The technocracy in which we live is of its nature concerned with the purely utile, with what functions. This of necessity demands a preoccupation with the analytical, with formulae that have as their end the furthering of devices that serve a definable

44

purpose and are in no sense made as *signa* of something other than themselves.

As the artist is concerned precisely with making things that are *signa* of some otherness (no matter what) his works would appear to have no essential and crucial place in such a situation were the matter carried to its logical conclusion. But as things stand at present, 'the arts' are regarded as serving a purpose—as part of something called 'cultural activities'; they are regarded as psychologically necessary, part of the 'amenities', of 'entertainment value' if you chance to care for that sort of entertainment.

The bearing of all this on my own meandering attempt to speak of the situation in the 1930s is that while one had some notion that the main civilizational trend was for a complex of reasons running counter to the presuppositions of 'man-the-artist', nevertheless there was a feeling of hopefulness and I think one could say of exhilaration, and a feeling that though the general weather-situation and the behaviour of the sea did not seem propitious, yet the vessel was in fairly good trim and holding to a course that was not without promise.

The immediately post-war years of the 1920s had, one way and another, been a period of a good deal of stock-taking and assessments and re-assessments, of very considerable vitality in various of the arts and these stirrings and re-awakenings had (I speak here for myself and some of my friends and acquaintances) a converging effect, by which I mean that the 'findings' or 'soundings' on the waters of the visual arts tallied with those of the aural and oral arts and these together had correspondences with certain works of scholarship. For example it was no accident that Tom Eliot's poem *The Waste Land* should have had for its main inspiration Jessie Weston's treatise *From Ritual to Romance*. Nor was it an accident that many of us were especially interested in various sections of Frazer's *Golden Bough* and less monumental but more recent anthropological, mythological and archaeological studies.

It is obvious, but none the less a matter of great interest, that James Joyce, an artist of unique qualities and of enormous

stature, though so 'cosmopolitan' a figure and highly 'contemporary' and *thought of* by many as 'a rebel' destructive of
standards of all sorts, an enemy of tradition, etc., was, in reality,
the artist who more than any other, not only employed as his
materia poetica all that which those historical, mythological,
anthropological, archaeological, etc., studies had to offer, plus
the new researches into psychology of Freud, Jung, etc., plus the
abiding influence of the medieval scholastic modes of thought
inseparable from his early years under the tuition of the Fathers of
the Society of Jesus in Ireland, plus a complete familiarity with
the popular devotional practices of a peasantry *and* those practices
transferred to the streets, slums, saloon bars, etc., of the city and
port of Dublin, but also the artist who, more than any other, for
all the universality of his theme, depended upon a given locality,
for no man could have adhered with more absolute fidelity to a
specified site, and the complex historic strata special to that site,
to express a universal concept. It was from the *particular* that he
made the *general* shine out. That is to say he was quintessentially
'incarnational'.

Now that again has a considerable bearing on the 1930s, at all
events for some of us. We saw, with varying degrees of clarity,
the trend of which I have spoken above, I mean the technological,
scientific advances which, one way or another and whether
beneficent or otherwise, were destructive of immemorial ways of
life, of rooted cultures of all sorts and of erosions too numerous
to mention, at all sorts of levels. We saw also that there was an
inevitability about all this. But, as 'artists' of various sorts, we, I
think, at least a number of us felt that come what may our job,
the making of things which were significant of something other,
that is to say *signa*, was a job, an activity wholly in keeping with
the kind of activity which had characterized man from his first
emergence, whenever that may have been, and had characterized
him at some periods and in some cultures to a superlative degree.

In certain stages of society, in tribal communities especially
among some peoples, the *poeta* not only had a recognized status
along with the makers of other necessary works, but occupied a
special position essential to the structure of that society, for he

was the official 'rememberer', and continuator of the tradition of that tribal organism. Early Ireland and Wales provide examples of this within our own historic past, and examples can be found in still existing societies in parts of the world.

It is obvious that our civilizational phase is totally removed from any vestige of that kind of society. None the less, *one* of the functions of those bardic artists has remained to be shared by poets, painters, or artists of any sort in all epochs: that is, a carrying forward of the making of works that are 'significant', that (unlike the, often superb, contrivances of our technocracy which have as their end pure utility) can be justified *only* as signs of something other, are evocative, incantative and have the power of 're-calling', of 'bringing to mind'—are in fact one with that whole world of sign or sacrament, whether it be the flowers sent to Clio on her birthday or the profound intention of the art of the man at the Altar, the work known as anamnesis, 'an effectual re-calling'. One does not have to subscribe to a given religion to see this point; it should be obvious to anyone, seeing that we all in our ordinary lives, however unconsciously, act 'sacramentally'.

In the 1930s such was my view of the artist's position and nothing that has occurred since has, as yet, caused me to change that view, but a great deal has occurred which would seem to intensify the difficulties in practice.

The difficulty of making what I have called, for convenience, *signa* that were one with the whole past and yet valid for 'now' was less apparent in the 1930s. One was conscious of the difficulties, heaven knows, but they were, for a number of reasons, more surmountable, or less blatant.

The artist (in whatever media) has certain difficult-to-express problems, the nature of which are not, in my view, by any means widely appreciated, even by many who are exponents of the arts. While, as Jacques Maritain, I think, put it, 'art abides on the side of the mind', the same writer, along with classical and medieval philosophers, understood that the practice of the arts did not belong to the 'speculative' but to the 'practical intelligence'.

That is to say the artist has to make 'things'. He cannot make them from nothing, nor from pure concepts, he can 'make' only from what is contactually known to him. But that 'what' may be his in a thousand and one very differing ways. For examples at the extremes, that 'what' which is contactually known to him, may be like Van Gogh's chair, a visible, handled, used, commonplace object, made in a phase of our civilization when such utile objects were humble products of the same world of human artefacture to which the painter himself belonged. Vincent Van Gogh's achievement was to so make that chair under the form of paint as to give to us an abiding image of all 'chair-ness', and moreover to raise that rush-bottomed chair to the status of the *sedes*; one of those thrones which stand before us, with such solid reality, in gleaming Byzantine mosaics.

Or, at the other extreme, that 'what' which is available to the artist, may be no more than a street name familiar to the artist but which affords liaison with a whole complex of layers and strata of centuries. Such was Suffolk Place in Dublin for James Joyce.

The Norse who occupied Dublin in the Viking age and who called their assembly by the common Teutonic term, *Thing*, were very remote from Joyce, but Suffolk Place enabled him to give us the extremely evocative line in the Anna Livia Plurabelle fragment of *Finnegans Wake*, 'Northmen's thing made southfolk's place'.

In the 1930s there was, I think, a feeling that liaison with the whole past of man-the-artist was still possible however 'contemporary' the images employed.

It is, of course, extremely difficult to assess with much exactitude the subjective and objective matters of a period of one's life when one was three decades younger than one now is in 1965. But taking that into consideration, I still feel that the notions I have tried to outline have a validity.

As to what present practitioners of various of the arts who are now in 1965 of the same age as I was in 1935, think of as the essential function of the arts I am in no position to speak.

I would add that while I am not unduly disturbed by not perceiving the beauty of certain contemporary works, though I can, in most cases, see the impulse and the, so to say, genesis of them, I am often disturbed by what seems to me to be a lack of something anthropomorphic.

I had occasion to write in the Preface of a book first published twenty-eight years ago a passage with reference to the war techniques, high explosive, poison gas, and the like, of World War I; it read as follows:

> That our culture has accelerated every line of advance into the territory of physical science is well appreciated—but not so well understood are the unforeseen, subsidiary effects of this achievement. We stroke cats, pluck flowers, tie ribands, assist at the manual acts of religion, make some kind of love, write poems, paint pictures, are generally at one with that creaturely world inherited from our remote beginnings. Our perception of many things is heightened and clarified. Yet must we do gas-drill, be attuned to many newfangled technicalities, respond to increasingly exacting mechanical devices; some fascinating and compelling, others sinister in the extreme; all requiring a new and strange direction of the mind, a new sensitivity certainly, but at a considerable cost.
>
> We who are of the same world of sense with hairy ass and furry wolf and who presume to other and more radiant affinities, are finding it difficult, as yet, to recognize these creatures of chemicals as true extensions of ourselves, that we may feel for them a native affection, which alone can make them magical for us. It would be interesting to know how we shall ennoble our new media as we have already ennobled and made significant our old. . . .

That was written in 1936–7 and a very great deal has happened since then, profoundly affecting the lives of all of us. But I do not think there has been any radical change in direction but rather a vast extension and unprecedented acceleration of the technologies referred to, which leaves the dilemmas of the artist much the same, but intensified.

25 February–1 March 1965

The Dying Gaul*

I t used to be part of the normal curriculum of art schools that
before one drew from the living model one had to draw from
the Antique. It depended upon a number of accidents whether
one found oneself faced with the immense stillness of the
Aphrodite of Melos or the uninspired forms of the Disc-
Thrower. Thus, one of my first recollections of the Antique
happens to have been a plaster cast of a Roman marble copy of
a Greek bronze, which was labelled 'The Dying Gaul'. That was
in 1909.

It was many years before I was to know that the original
bronze had been erected at Pergamon by an ally of Rome, King
Attalos I, to celebrate his victory over groups of Celts operating
in Asia Minor in the third century B.C.—the forefathers of Paul's
'bewitched' Galatians.

In a book published last summer [*The Celts* (London, 1958)]
Mr. T. G. E. Powell, a Dubliner and a Cambridge archaeologist,
gives us a most able, lucid and concise analysis of the Celts, their
origins, their arts and something of their chequered story.

Among the many admirable plates that illustrate this attractive
book is one of the Dying Gaul. By a most rewarding perception,
the author had this work photographed from above, whereby its
full significance is, at last, well seen. Our thoughts and feelings are
many as we gaze, either actually or with the eyes of the mind
only, on the prostrate form of this Galatic *uchelwr* or 'high-man',
naked except for his torque, collapsed upon his oval Celtic war-
shield and the narrow, curved Celtic war-trumpets cast down.

---

* A talk broadcast on the BBC Third Programme on 24 April 1959; first
published in *The Listener*, 7 May 1959. Some passages omitted for the broadcast
have been restored in the version printed here.

Two centuries later Caesar was to hear these bray across the surf on a Kentish foreshore, and twelve centuries after Caesar, an Angevin archdeacon, Sylvester Gerald de Barri, was to hear them in the wooded defiles of Wales. He says that when the Welsh attacked the sound of their deep-toned trumpets mingled with their harsh cries. You see the Dying Gaul was going west, slowly.

Now together with the typically Celtic objects portrayed on this statue, there is something which strikes the eye as being very un-Celtic. I mean the curved quillons that form the cross-guard of his thrown-down sword. That is no Celtic *kladobio*, 'claymore' or *cleddyf*; it has the wrong feeling entirely. Is it there, as some have suggested, to indicate loot? Possibly, for the association of Celts with loot was a received opinion of the Graeco-Roman world.

There is also a commonly received opinion among the English, expressed in the rhyme 'Taffy was a Welshman, Taffy was a thief'; but for this now to have any kind of factual equivalence with its classical antecedent we should have to suppose the sack of London by Welsh tribesmen as late as the end of the eighteenth century. A comical thought indeed, but I will explain:

Little more than a century and a half previous to the erection of the statue of the Dying Gaul at Pergamon some very much alive Gauls had crossed Apennine, taken Clusium, destroyed a Roman field army at the Allia River and were free to violate the Urbs herself. But, at this crucial point (and here one is reminded of events in later Celtic history), the Gaulish leaders hung about, time was lost, and the defence organization was able to victual and munition the urban fortress on the Tarpeian Rock and to partially evacuate the city, which the Gauls eventually entered and sacked. A few months later they disappeared over the mountains just as they had come.

That the Gauls received danegeld from the Romans is suggested by the familiar story of how Brennus tossed on to the already unfairly weighted scales his long, straight-bladed, two-edged, early La Tène, iron great-sword; while the treasury official (a tribune), standing in the urban desolation, an exemplar of the

Roman virtues of patience and fortitude, lodged his formal protest against the falsification of weights and measures, even by exultant Celts.

The quick recovery of the Urbs from this calamity is said to have been a surprise to her neighbours and not, for all of them, a pleasant one, but neither Rome nor Italy nor antiquity as a whole was ever to forget that in the Year of the City 364 a cackle of geese may have saved the Capitol but that nothing had saved the city from the realities of that Celtic raid from over the mountains. And that was nearly four centuries before the decree went out from Caesar Augustus that all the world would be taxed.

Thus, this raid, already ancient, gave to Virgil, in the age of Augustus, a chance to give to us in these latter days of the West a description of some of the personnel of a Celtic raiding party; 'gold clad' Gauls he calls them. But he adopts a most ingenious device in order to describe them and the nature of the ground as they begin their night assault on the south-western escarpment of the Capitoline Hill.

This he does by reference to a wonder-shield, smithied by Vulcan for Aeneas, on which were shown forth the things of Italy and the triumphs of Rome. So, on this prefiguring shield (which, by Virgil's art, is for us a shield of anamnesis) we are shown the glistening figures of Gauls in their striped plaids as they slip from their assembly positions in the thorn-brake. The night's dark is a gift for them, and under its camouflage will they reach their first objective, the shadowy glacis of the dark hill within which, spell-bound and earth-bound and gold-bound, the maiden sits? For we must not forget that is what Tarpeia and her rock meant for them. They were assaulting the stronghold of a female earth-spirit, as well as the hill of Saturn and the mound of the buried head—and of course, also, a virtually impregnable military position.

But as for Juno and her sacred geese, well, they were upstart and newfangled on this height of ancient under-dreads. Perhaps that is why the cackling did the trick; for it is the continuing fate of Celtdom to be betrayed by the gods of the newer culture-phase. A fate which had not begun to show itself at that date, early in the fourth century B.C., but which later was to develop. This was in part derived from their war-techniques being increasingly outmoded. You will remember that even in Caesar's time, although the Celts of Gaul had already abandoned the use of war-chariots, the British Celts still used them and the Irish Celts were using them centuries later still. Yet this chariot-fighting had had its heyday long since, among Canaanites and Israelites, centuries before the Macedonian wedge had become the vogue, let alone the 'cohort formation', the *triplex acies*, that was now conquering the world.

But of course there was much more to it than techniques of war. Later again this sense of fighting a losing battle was to find expression in a kind of defeat-tradition which is part of the texture of the poetry of the peoples of the 'Celtic Survival' in the first millennium A.D.

There was a 'Second Heroic Age' for the Celtic West in the sub-Roman and post-Roman periods. It was now that the Welsh language stemmed from Brittonic Celtic just as the French and Spanish languages stemmed from the Latin of Gaul and Iberia. It was the birth time of the Welsh nation. The earliest surviving poem in the Welsh language, a poem as it were celebrative of that birth, does in fact celebrate the death of three hundred horsemen, armed, it would seem, in the late-Roman manner, but all wearing gold torques like Virgil's Gauls, and like my Dying Gaul in the suburban art school. Much the same might be said for the succeeding stratum of poetry which is concerned with the loss of Pengwern (Shrewsbury) and the burning of the Hall of Cynddylan and the death at the Ford of Morlas on the River Llawen of the last remaining of Llywarch's twenty-four sons. The Gaul dies daily. Next are the *Englynion y Beddau*, the 'Stanzas of the Graves', so you see the birth-poetry of Wales makes continuous anamnesis of the Dying Gaul.

Now this tradition, with newer calamities piling up in plenty to give the old saws their modern instances and to intensify the feeling in differing localities of the Celtic West, developed, centuries later still and under the influence of a European-wide movement, a romantic conception of Celtdom, whereby, as we all know, if you want a minstrel boy it is 'In the ranks of death you'll find him'. So again the Gaul dies, this time in Ireland, to be sung in the drawing-rooms of the English-speaking world. But, to be fair to the Romantic Movement of the eighteenth and nineteenth centuries, it must be observed that one hardly has to bend over backwards in order to find in the authentic early deposits the requisite material for the romantic to use.

But to get back to the Gaulish assault-party of 2,349 years ago this summer, 1959: Virgil notes the milk-white necks and the gold torques round the necks and the golden-hued hair. He conveys the feeling of necks and heads and shoulders bent forward to the assault and he notes the gleam of iron weapons. The scene is familiar. Take away the gold and add some rusted wire and there you have it. He notes that their shields are of the longish Celtic type and that each man has in his hands two heavy, iron-headed, Celtic javelins. Thus Virgil makes Vulcan to have been a most ingenious and observant artist and archaeologically almost as much in the know as Sir Mortimer Wheeler. But that, after all, was only good classical theology, for a Vulcan–Hephaestus figure was, with an Athena–Minerva figure, tutelar of all art-works. Thus do Virgil's living Gauls bring us back to our Dying Gaul.

I wish now to speak of a carving in soft stone of a man's head. (It is Plate 2 in Mr. Powell's book.) It is broken off at the neck but sufficient remains for the torque to be seen meeting in two large bosses under the strangely elongated chin. It is a native Celtic carving found in Bohemia and now in the National Museum in Prague. In date it is roughly contemporaneous with the Pergamon bronze of the Dying Gaul. Apart from this contemporaneousness they could hardly have less in common. For the one is a fair example of how a Celt appeared from the outside, to an artist employing the idealized realism of the classical academic tradition, whereas the other is Celticity itself, seen from the inside. In this fragment (less than ten inches high) we get just a glimpse of what sculpture in the round could accomplish among the Celts of the La Tène culture, and a hint, perhaps, of possible further developments—but which the Muse of History decided could not be.

This stone head is a work illustrative of the continuous characteristic Celtic tendency to transmogrify observed objects (in this case elements of the human face) by the use of stylized motifs which none the less retain a powerful representational significance within a dynamic abstract form. But apart from the aesthetic interest there was another and quite separate thing that riveted my attention: the face itself was strangely familiar. This puzzled me for quite a while and then I recalled a photograph which I had seen a year or two back in an obituary notice of a representative figure in recent Welsh religious and Eisteddfodic circles. His was the face called up by this highly formalized cult-object of the Celtic warrior-hegemony of Middle Europe of twenty-three centuries ago. It seems a far cry indeed. This was a personal impression only, yet one which was dramatically confirmed later by a friend, who taking one glance at the photograph of the Celtic cult-figure said the two words 'Elfed Lewis'.

I record this for what it is worth at a time when I see that in various circles the very idea of a common Celticity is regarded as being a figment of eighteenth- or nineteenth-century English romanticism.

I would now invite you to glance for a brief moment at the latter end of Celtdom as an institutional entity, and for that we must look across the narrow Celtic Sea to Holy Ireland. The last Gaelic overlordship in Ireland to be made valid at a stone of inauguration seems to have been as late as 1592, whereas in Scotland the practice had ceased nearly three and a half centuries earlier. I can recall no evidence of its survival among the Brythonic Celts of Wales, for though the Welsh codes tell us about the king and his officers and the status of his bands, as far as I am aware they cast no light on the forms used at his inauguration; which is a nuisance, because this ceremony at the stone of inauguration provided a direct link, through Celtic antiquity and Indo-European practice, back to the men of the megalithic culture.

At the stone the names of the chieftain's ancestors were recited and his own identity confirmed in the presence of the people, rather as today at papal burials the *Rogito* is recited by the Notary of the Chapter and the *Eulogium* by the Secretary of Briefs to Princes. Listening last autumn to the broadcast of the interment rites of a Pontifex Maximus, and hearing, for the first time, those confirmatory and identifying data recited by the Notary, my thoughts shuttled back to the stones of inauguration where the chieftain died to his former status and put on the new life of kingship—New Grange Tumulus and the twelve-columned undercroft of St. Peter's, called the Confession, had met; Capitoline Hill and Tara Hill had kissed each other.

Another essential institution that survived was that of the bardic academies whereby the collective memory of the community was safeguarded. A pivotal figure of the Celtic West, St. Columba, had himself seen to it, at the Synod of Drumcet, that the bardic schools should not be jettisoned, thereby securing, side by side with the institutions of the new Judaeo-Hellenistic cult of Christ, this heritage of pagan Celtic antiquity.

Thus that particular Dying Gaul was, by Columba's insight, saved—anyway among the Goidels, for another thousand years. For the Synod of Drumcet was in 575, and by 1575, or rather a decade later, the 'sage and serious Spenser' was writing: 'If they be well followed one winter, ye shall have little work to do with them the next summer.' The twin target was Irish revolt and Irish Catholicity. As we know well, those terrible twins both survived. But the full weight of fire intended for them fell with deadly effect on something behind them, and, to use an Irishism, something far older than either of them. What was brought to its term was a hieratic pattern of society which had survived as a functioning organism from pre-history: something which had at one time been influential from Denmark to the Aegean but which already, by the third century B.C., was representative of an older order.

We have to go back behind Celtdom itself to understand how it comes about that things as widely separated in both time and space as the Mahabharatan epic of India and the poetry of Homeric Greece find an echo in our own early Welsh and Irish

The Dying Gaul

material. Once upon a time this common culture had given to us the sky-gods, the 'vedas', the 'bright ones', whether Varuna in Mother India, or the Heavenly Twins in Middle Sea, or Camulus or Mabon in our own Lear Sea.

But, as Mr. Christopher Dawson especially noted in an early book of his, *The Age of the Gods*, there is duality, a dichotomy perhaps, in the Celtic thing. The warrior-aristocracy had its sky-gods but beneath it were peoples of earlier cultures, different in physical and psychological make-up, for whom the Mother Goddess and various chthonic deities were tutelar. Druidism itself appears to have been taken over by Celtic-speaking groups from earlier peoples.

The Welsh may be dark and short, but are linguistically Celtic and in their literature the figures have golden hair and wear gold collars just as do Virgil's Gauls. A very reliable witness has told me that when, at Cardiff Arms Park, England meet Wales, it appears that fair-hued men are opposed to men of dark hue, but that when France meet Wales it is the Welsh who appear the fairer. You may say, but is not the French nation well known to be on the dark side? Perhaps, but dark or no, the French are the direct descendants of Caesar's fair-haired Gauls with the addition of supposedly still fairer Nordic Franks. Perhaps the theory of a steadily increasing nigrescence is right, or in more colloquial language: what's under works up. Or is it that the Great Mother is coming into her own?

To return to sixteenth-century Ireland: it was the surviving westernmost peripheral remnant, of the ancient pattern of Celtdom that failed to survive the justice of the Faerie Queene. (It will be recalled that in Spenser's allegory the Lord Deputy of Ireland was taken as the model for a figure called Artegal, symbolizing Justice.) To put it quite simply and as an aid to our memories, we could say that the Dying Gaul did die in 1603, the same year as 'Sidanen', 'the silky one' as Elizabeth Tudor was called in Wales, the year of the death in Rome of Hugh O'Neill, Earl of Tyrone, the last really great chieftain of an authentically Celtic society. It is strangely congruent with the thread of frustration and betrayal that runs throughout the

Celtic story that the Tudors, with their attenuated Welsh connections, should have been instrumental in destroying what was left of the ancient pattern, first in Wales and then in Ireland.

It need hardly be stressed how in other ways and divers manners the Dying Gaul is not dead yet. Especially so, when the most creative literary genius of this century, using English as the *lingua franca* of a megalopolitan civilization, developed an artform showing an essential Celticity as intricate, complex, flexible, exact and abstract as anything from the visual arts of La Tène or Kells or from the aural intricacies of medieval Welsh metric, an art-form in which the Celtic demands with regard to place, site, identity, are a hundred-fold fulfilled. An art forged in exile by a man of our placeless cosmopolis, yet an art wholly determined by place, *a* place, an exact site, an art which, for its *materia poetica*, employs stuff from all the strata and the flux, from before and before again, to weave a word-web, a sound-web, round the 'Town of the Ford of Hurdles' as Dublin was called by the Goidels.

It is impossible in recalling the Dying Gaul not to recall James Joyce. And impossible in that recalling not to recall the words from the Dublin street-ballad: 'Bedad he revives! See how he raises!'

These are some few of my own vagrant thoughts as I contemplate this famous antique, which I encountered for the first time just fifty years ago, having then but little, or rather no, idea of what significance it was to hold for me, or of how it would condition my feelings in all sorts of contexts, both personal and impersonal, from then till now.

17 February 1959

An Aspect of the Art of England*

The name by which these islands were known to the Greek geographers, to Strabo and to Diodorus of Sicily, was the Pretanic Isles, and the Romans got their 'Picti' from the same source—the Old Welsh *Priten*, the Old Irish *Cruithin*, the speckled, mottled, variegated, painted men. So it would be Pretania had not Julius Caesar (it is surmised) by a misunderstanding decided that it should be Britannia, after the Britanni of Gaul.

It was a pity, because Pretanic or Pictish describe us well. Not only is our land a most mottled, dappled, pied, partied and brindled land, but so is our character, and so is the physical structure beneath and determining the surface of the land (one of the most interesting, geologically speaking, in the world, I believe), but so also in a curious way is our art, at least one of the characteristics of our art.

When one tries to conjure up an image signifying this distinguishing quality, a fretted, meandering, countered image emerges. And when further it is remembered that *the* one art which has taken its name from us, is that kind of needlework called 'Opus Anglicanum', we get a further hint, and another in the unique character of the early English miniatures, as those of Nicholas Hillyarde (1547–1619). We see very plainly how that deeply native poet, G. M. Hopkins, when he wrote his 'Pied Beauty' was expressing an intensely native feeling. As for the fragments most remembered from the English poetry of the middle ages, again and again the thing evoked, the image lifted up, is a flowery, starry, intertwined image. I speak of only one of

* The manuscript of this unpublished, undated essay was found among David Jones's papers after his death.

59

a number of characteristics—opposing characteristics. It suffers from time to time almost complete eclipse, both the Apollonian order of 'classicism', and the drama of 'romanticism' can over-power it, and numerous theories put it in a strait-jacket, but then again it asserts itself and can be detected sometimes peeping out unexpectedly from the work of people whose traditions are consciously and frankly 'foreign'. The Wilton Diptych is thought, I'm told, to be French work, but has often seemed to me to be 'English' in feeling, and as was pointed out to me by my old friend Mr. A. S. Hartrick the wings of the angels are gulls' wings, or at least wings of wave-birds—this seems a very appropriate English 'conceit', and an extremely interesting one.

The mood of this flexible, delicate, chequered art is on the whole rather gay, and is very observant of nature. It is linear rather than an affair of masses, and in this later respect it shows some affinity with the abstract work of the Celts of pre-history. As the whole of our culture, lock, stock and barrel, is but a part of West European culture and has, historically and at each turn, taken its cue from continental developments (I speak of main trends and not in detail), it follows that our native genius has had to express itself within those developments. Some have been more patient of native modification than have others, some have given us great opportunities, some have been very unsym-pathetic to our particular genius, and of course, other matters, religious, political and economic have profoundly affected our freedom or lack of freedom in this respect, our chances of being most ourselves.

It is a matter of the greatest possible complexity, and it is not at all easy to say for instance what period of architecture we have found most patient of being imprinted with our insular feeling. Perhaps certain moments in Gothic—if only because Gothic was itself more of its nature flexible and adaptable. Be such questions answered as they may, for many reasons we have to look, in the case of England, not at the main style (which is derived from Europe) but at what has been possible within the succession of styles. For instance even in William Blake, who is about as fantastically 'English' as anything could be, the *superficial* form is wholly the neo-classical of the eighteenth-century academies. He is more superficially 'classical' than Reynolds. But whereas we feel hardly an inkling of this particular native characteristic which we are discussing in Reynolds (an English enough painter in other respects), in Blake it declares itself, though in him there is a dynamism which overrides and is apart from, this specific native feeling. He indeed could not possibly be anything other than an English artist, but whatever his blood or soil he would have so set fire to whatever tradition he worked in as to be quite a unique figure within that tradition. The extraordinary thing about Blake is that he is one of the few absolutely 'great' English geniuses in the domain of art, and we all recognize him as mostly intensely of this island, yet how utterly unlike the spirit of England as observed and appraised by other nations. It is partly the 'price of empire' that the most inner and most valuable and most living artistic feeling of a people should not be the representative feeling as far as other peoples are concerned.

It is often discussed how it is that, speaking very generally, English artists express themselves better in the medium of water-colour than they do in oils. I think this too is not unconnected with the quality we are considering. The English are not heavy-weight champions in the art of painting. On the whole the freer, lighter, more tentative, in some respects more spontaneous (though this word may be misunderstood in this connection), more tractable medium suits them best. Also their feeling for the linear is more readily allied to watercolour. It would be very false, and convey a quite untrue impression to say that the English are in general not good 'technically'—they have been magnificent craftsmen, but for some reason or other exceptionally few have ever mastered, in the grand manner and on the great scale, the techniques of oil painting as compared with some other peoples. Not infrequently oil paintings by contemporary English artists give the feeling that they would have 'come off' better in the other medium. But these are wide generalizations and must not be taken as more than generalizations.

It is said that the 'cottage garden' is peculiar to this island, and that is not without interest—for the dappled complexity that makes the unity of those small gardens (there are fewer than there were by a long chalk)—especially after sunset, when each colour and each form is distinct and like an embroidery and as complex as an embroidery—is very much akin to the quality I mean; also it is fair and cool. Fairness, a kind of blondness (except that the word 'blonde' has an altogether wrong association), belong to this characteristic of English art.

This is meant to be no more than a note on one aspect of English art—a few related aspects have been mentioned only in passing. Others, very markedly such as the interest in the delineation of character and a certain homeliness, have not even been touched upon—these too are important. But here we are only concerned to point out that 'Glory be to God for dappled things' which the English Jesuit of Welsh affinity sang about, is not only evoked by the thrush in the tangled hedges of the island, but has been reflected also by artists of the island—whether, or to what degree or in what manner, such 'pied beauty' can survive the arid and uninviting sub-cultures of today and tomorrow remains to be seen. But whatever should be our destiny, and whatever the characteristics of the men of tomorrow, it is worth noting that this quality which I have attempted to state, this dappled fairness, was once not wanting in us. I expect it will crop up in some form or other, come what may.

Wales and Visual Form[*]

The following is an attempt to put down a few thoughts with regard to a subject which I feel deserves some consideration. In most respects they are the thoughts of a layman, of an amateur, and my reason for presuming to embark on this enquiry at all is that by the accidents of my work I have been compelled to consider somewhat this matter of visual form. I speak solely and exclusively as a person who has tried to practise one or more of the arts. To practise any one of the arts, demands (at least in some of us, and from time to time) a consideration of them all and their relationship to each other and the relationship of other things to them, both now and in the past.

Many passages in the two recent articles on architecture which have appeared in *Wales*[1] and particularly perhaps Dr. Peate's amusing but tragic anecdote concerning the 'Welsh writer' and the 'magnificent' chapel, inevitably draw the reader's attention to the many questions which concern the history of the visual and plastic arts in Wales: what sort of history have those arts had; what have been their ups and downs, what kind of evidence have we with regard to them? Peoples and groups of men within certain areas are so largely to be understood by the characteristic perfections and failings of their art-forms, of their works, that the questions raised are of some importance and certainly interesting. The formidable saying: 'By their works ye shall know them', although said with reference to man as a moral being and with

* The manuscript of this unpublished essay is undated, but internal evidence indicates that it was written in March 1944.
[1] Clough Williams-Ellis, 'Problems of Reconstruction', *Wales*, no. 2 (Oct.–Nov.–Dec. 1943), and Iorwerth C. Peate, 'A Note on Architecture', *Wales*, no. 3 (Jan.–Feb.–Mar. 1944).

regard to his Last End, can be, and in fact is, also applied by analogy to man as artist.

The word 'Roman' has scarcely escaped our lips but what we see in the eyes of the mind, the lucid forms of the Latin alphabet—which means that whatever sort of people—disagreeable or admirable—we think 'the Romans' to have been, their aesthetic with regard to the making of incised inscriptions was so felicitous that the Roman name is linked in our minds with that particular perfection. For this reason we desire visual, material, contactual evidence when we would consider the culture of any group of people—such evidence is worth cartloads of descriptive writing—just as a glance at the formidable lines of a trench-mortar tells us more about the temper and feeling of the Forward Area than many pages of print.

The famous 'Battersea shield' (in the British Museum) of bronze and red enamel is similarly, though a single object, of enormous value towards an appreciation of what kind of people 'the ancient Britons' were and in itself illuminates and extends Caesar's partial descriptions. That shield, like the Roman inscriptions, and for the same reason, tells us something—something quite limited, but something of absolute certainty: the men who made it, whoever and whatever else they were, were complete masters of abstract form of a certain kind. It is this kind of limited, particularized, dead-certain evidence that archaeology has given to us—hence its satisfactory character. It may say little and in a quiet voice but what it says is, in itself, true. It by no means follows that what we deduce from it will be equally true. Now it is entirely with this kind of evidence that we are here concerned. What, in short, do the material, visual remains of past centuries tell us with regard to what sort of 'artist' the men were who lived in what is now called Wales? 'There's nothing like a good bodily image' (or words to that effect), says 'the man in black', in Borrow—there most certainly is not when it comes to judging the aesthetic of a past civilization.

Now those who look for evidence left by the successive and highly complex culture-waves which have broken on the Welsh hills from the dawn of time until recently, sometimes suffer disappointment. The disappointment is largely due to a mis-understanding, but I incline to think that there may be a modicum of justification in their disappointment. The more we genuinely love a thing the more we wish to find in it evidence of those qualities which we happen to admire, and when we do not find as much evidence as we had hoped we are apt to be disappointed and even in some danger of allowing our imaginations to fill the gaps.

The misunderstanding referred to above resides in our not fully realizing the position of Wales geographically, its con-struction geologically and its consequent historical situation in relation to the successive vital movements which have spread from various centres in prehistoric or historic times. If it can be said of Britain that she has been at the periphery of those move-ments (and it is widely true but with certain reservations and amplifications) then one would suppose that the Highland Zone—the more westerly parts of Britain—would for a number of reasons feel the impact last and in a more fragmentary fashion. This supposition is, in the main, borne out by archaeological evidence; see for instance Wheeler's *Prehistoric and Roman Wales* (1925) and the clear summary of the main trends and their consequences in the recent Pelican Book *Prehistoric Britain* by J. and C. Hawkes (1943).

So that by and large we can suppose that the art-forms em-ployed in Wales would naturally tend to be those which had already seen their main efflorescence in Europe, or if not on the mainland then in the lowland and more prosperous parts of this island, for from the very beginning the economic factor was of very great importance. We must not forget of course the cross-current from Ireland, clearly influential in the case of Wales;[2] for

[2] The relationship between Ireland and Wales from the Bronze Age onwards well into the middle ages has been often discussed. As we all know, this affected political matters during the Age of the Princes and is said to have affected the arts of music and poetry. I understand that the age of Gruffydd ap Cynan reflected this intercourse in more ways than one. Not only were his Dublin axes effective in battle but certain Irish influences are said to have been felt in the bardic art. It is one of the accidents of history that a closer relationship between Ireland and Wales was not maintained. But politics seem more powerful than cultures and nearness of feeling is overridden by other necessities.

Ireland at certain periods of history and prehistory developed techniques and forms of real importance, and the late Bronze Age Irish gold work found its way into Wales and England and elsewhere.

These currents and cross-currents are complex and cover long periods of time all of which witnessed profound changes of equilibrium, artistically, economically and racially; but throughout those changes and those periods of time it would rather seem that the Welsh area kept in the main its later characteristic of being a recipient of trend after trend of influence rather than a centre or place of development of distinctive forms. By a curious coincidence, as I write this, I pick up *The Times* for today (7 March 1944) and find in it Dr. Cyril Fox's account of the immediately recent Iron Age find in Anglesey. All that he says concerning this most exciting and new evidence, the heterogeneous collection of arms, chariot-fittings, 'currency bars', wands of office, ornament, etc., appears fully to bear out the position of Wales as a recipient of the current manufactures and forms from lowland Britain and from Ireland; as it also bears out the satisfactory nature of archaeological evidence in helping us to see not 'through a glass darkly' as in the case of written accounts, but literally and deliciously 'face to face'. It is surmised that this particular find is to be dated as contemporary with the operations of the 14th and 20th Legions in A.D. 61, the account of which we must all have often re-read in our desire to picture more clearly that scene at the Mona beach-head; and as often to have closed the book feeling how little the writer tells us of what we most wish to know.

Rhetoric about wild-haired women and praying druids and flaming torches is all rich enough as descriptive writing of a conventional nature to convey any general scene of that sort, but it tells us nothing of the particular set-up, nothing of the cultural level of the victims on whom the torchlight shone. The Anglesey find gives us precisely that 'substance and precision to scanty and inaccurate written records'—as J. and C. Hawkes so exactly describe the chief excellence of the archaeological method.

To revert to Dr. Peate's experience in front of the chapel, I saw a letter to the press, recently, which in its own way displayed an English attitude not much less extraordinary: the writer suggested that Westminster Hall was more redolent of Christian and historic significance than all the monuments of Italy!

Englishmen, and intelligent Englishmen, sometimes incline to speak of English Gothic as though it were the major flowering of that great movement and northern expression of form, forgetting in their natural enthusiasm that in strict language there never was in that connection an 'English culture', there was only a European culture with provincial modifications and characteristics.[3] I have introduced this otherwise irrelevant matter as an analogy: the Lowland Zone in Britain has made many noble contributions to these successive culture-waves, and has imposed upon these several trends the strong imprint of this island. We are considering here what the Highland Zone has done.

Here we come to what perhaps we might, within limits, even in the very adverse circumstances of Welsh geography and history, legitimately hope to find: i.e. some sign at some date or dates of a genuinely 'Welsh' imprint upon some particular expression of one or more of these common culture-expansions.

Keeping in mind these general conditions we may turn to more specific considerations. Leaving aside for the moment the question of archaeological evidence with respect to those works of form which can be seen and handled, what can be inferred from the characteristics of the people of Wales in other directions? When all self-congratulatory ideas have been taken into account, it remains evident that the Welsh people have shown themselves to be very far from lacking in those qualities which are prerequisite to 'man as artist'. It has often been said, and I need make no apology for saying it again, that the Welsh are an 'imaginative' people. They most certainly do not lack that

[3] Arthur Gardner, in *English Medieval Sculpture* (1937), comments that it is a superficial view that would regard English Gothic as a mere offshoot of French Gothic. We can concede that much without falling into the opposite error of supposing the provincial splendours to be the major splendours and of forgetting that the whole was a part of a North-West European cultural fusion reaching its grandest expression on French land. One has only to see Chartres to see what 'Gothic' means—at least that was my personal impression.

power to respond which is so essential to the making of a work of art. Further they can be said to be metaphysically inclined rather than the reverse, and what is perhaps more to the point they have shown themselves to be predisposed towards expressing themselves in poetic form, and what is still nearer to the real core of what I am, rather laboriously, trying to say, their poetic forms have been of a peculiarly intricate and constructed nature.[4] All who are qualified to speak on the subject of Welsh poetic forms agree that the severest technical devices have been employed to convey the emotions expressed in the ancient poetry. Indeed the criticism seems sometimes to be that a delight in form has predominated at the expense of content. Of this I cannot speak but certainly that has been the criticism rather than the other way round.

A further consideration and one which even a person unqualified by lack of knowledge of the language and the old metres can vouch for (by reference to any translation of the prose tales or by such pieces of transliteration of the poetry as are from time to time available), is that very marked liking for the visual image and a particular fondness for noting the colour and texture of things. The many passages in *The Mabinogion* which bear this out are too well known to need quotation, but to reinforce the truth of this one may glance for example at the extremely interesting specimens of poetry given in Mr. F. G. Payne's *Guide to the Collection of Samplers and Embroideries*, published by the National Museum of Wales. I will quote one example from that admirable museum guidebook. It is of sixteenth-century date, and so shows how that love of colour and the visual continues:

Bicoloured sheen of Greek embroideries fit for nobles of the Round Table. Veins of molten gold, a work of fire, other veins

[4] So much is this so that an English poet of the last century whose work has only come into its own during the last decade or so—Gerard Manley Hopkins —derived much of his technique and something more than technique from an acquaintance with the intricacies and interior rhythms of that Welsh poetry— this is being increasingly recognized. And is a most exciting example of the unexpected influence of one tradition of form upon another greatly removed from it.

of silver work. Has there ever been such a sight beneath satin-grained velvet in Christendom? A pall as black as that on Calvary, shot through with sunbeams. An acre plaited in silver twigs, in fine lines on a cloth to cover a man. A knight am I, respected by worthy poets. Where in their midst is such a dress to be found?

This is good poetry even in translation and lifts up a clear bodily image. I don't know any more vivid image than that 'acre plaited in silver twigs' to describe the grand garment of a man—especially when we remember that it in fact describes one of those early sixteenth-century doublets.—What a pity there was no Welsh Nicholas Hillyarde! For it is that artist, but in words, and with an extra twist too, for the English miniaturist missed the black pall on the Juda hill—*wybren ddu bryn Iddewon*—when he painted his starry doublets, of whom the passage reminds us.

In passing and with reference to what may be called a metaphysical sense, which, as I have suggested, is far from absent in Welsh expression, it is perhaps worth noting that in the group of English poets called the 'Metaphysicals'—in the early seventeenth century—there is a locality-affinity or a blood-affinity with Wales; in Vaughan, Herbert, Donne there is a Welsh or a Welsh border association. It is conceivable that some element in the meticulous technicality and the use of images in the latter may not be wholly unconnected with this, however attenuated, Welsh connection. But all this is by the way.

These things being so we know that we are not dealing with an uncreative people—no matter how much the accidents of geography and history have created conditions which in turn have imposed certain limitations to the outlets of that creativity. A good example at a late date of some of these possible limitations is suggested by Dr. Peate when he says (*Welsh Folk Crafts*, National Museum of Wales, 1935):

In many ways the last quarter of the seventeenth century may be looked upon as a notable age in the history of British architecture—the period of Christopher Wren. . . . In Wales— far removed from the fount of inspiration and already gripped by the austere discipline of Puritanism—the renascence of architecture was not so discernible. There were geographical reasons too: Wales, as a moorland country, did not lend itself to the types of building which were to become notable in the English plain.

Similar adverse circumstances must be borne in mind in more or less degree throughout all Welsh history.

Having cleared the ground a little we can begin to ask what are the most likely periods when a local, essentially Welsh, feeling might have expressed itself within the common traditions of the plastic and visual art-forms which have successively dominated the western world including this island. Leaving aside the pre-historic period, but remembering its main trends, and leaving aside also the period of the Roman occupation proper (which was for the hill tribes a quiescent continuation of the conditions of pre-history), we come to the sub-Roman, post-Roman, and early Anglo-Saxon epochs, the earlier part of which time might well be called the 'Homeric Age' of the Cymry.[5]

I mean, roughly, from Cunedda (the founder of the royal line of the North Welsh princes) in the time of Stilicho's reorganization of the Province (about A.D. 400) onwards to Urien, Maelgwn, 'Arthur', Cadwaladr, and the rest—the age reflected in the *Gododdin* poems, the age of Llywarch and the earliest literary deposits, the age which is still by far the most potent in the imagination as it was in fact the most decisive in determining the future history of the whole island—the age of similar decisive events in so many other provinces of the Empire.

What do we find when we look for material evidence of the forms of this crucial time? The answer is: exceptionally little. As far as the earlier section of this period goes we have a number of sub-Roman memorial stones, notably that set up to Vorteporix —a contemporary of Gildas and denounced by him—in Dyfed. This then is an object of great interest and there are the other

[5] Not the 'Homeric Age' of the Celts—that was in pre-history, but the 'Homeric Age'—the legend-forming age—of the Cymry, the age which ended in the peninsular between the Bristol Channel and the mouth of the Dee becoming the area called *Cymru*.

stones with ogham and Latin inscriptions, but little else. Some stone crosses from Galloway may date from the time of Nyniaw's fourth-century mission to the Picts. They are undecorated except for the sacred monogram.[6]

The fall of mist and the thunder clap which accompanied the disappearance of Rhiannon and Pryderi together with the marble fountain were not more effective than fate has been in removing the evidence. We shall speak in a moment of the works of the Celtic-Christian revival.

We can of course surmise and deduce from evidence elsewhere, concerning a Romano-Celtic or Brito-Roman, semi-barbaric semi-civilized conglomerate society of this date (fifth, sixth and seventh centuries), but of substantial and direct evidence we have practically nothing. King Maelgwn and his *llys* in Rhôs might have been in the moon for all we know of its or his appearance. We know, again from the literature, that he was *Maelgwn Hir*— the tallest of the kings, that he was a headstrong character, that he took the religious habit but returned again to his robes of king-ship, but we do not know at all the cut of those garments—how far his rig was Roman, how far that of his Celtic ancestors.

There is one other object from those ages which I have recalled to mind, the lovely Capel Garmon 'fire-dog'. That is to say I believe it is assigned to the early Christian centuries, or a little earlier. There is also the sixth-century find in Anglesey of the silver fibulae from the hut settlement. These are described as conforming to a Scottish type and according to Dr. Fox must not be taken as necessarily typical of the mainland of Wales because of the peculiar position of Anglesey with regard to Goidelic (as later, to Viking) influence, from over the Irish Sea. We know also that in the full Roman period, from such finds as the bronze mirror from Harlech and one or two other isolated fragments, there was a continuance of native Celtic forms with some Roman modification in the hill forts and hut settlements, during the actual Roman occupation and so previous to the epochs we are now considering. No doubt that fusion continued.

Dovetailed as it were with this epoch or rather these epochs

[6] See Gardner, *English Medieval Sculpture*, p. 28.

(for we are covering in a most cursory manner a longish and changing period of history), there was an important religious movement which was very much a Celtic movement—one might call it the last great effective movement associated with Celtic-speaking groups of men—only this time it was not as previously a movement of war leaders in their splendid paraphernalia such as characterized Celtic activity in pre-history. This time it was a zeal for the Christian religion that provided the incentive.

Following upon this monastic and evangelistic enthusiasm there was a considerable artistic resurgence, affecting to various degrees almost the whole of the British islands. It will not do at all to refer to this plastic outburst as 'Celtic'—it was not only very mixed in its expression, but the derivations of the motifs used are complex and connect up with forms found from the Adriatic to the North Sea. The intermixed racial strains and the motley of tribes used, and gave their own feeling to, forms common to all that world.

Few art-forms have been the subject of hotter debate among specialists, theorists and students. But at least it is safe for the lay person to say that he can observe some of the identities in the derivation of the outward forms and at the same time be very aware of the divergences of feeling in the employment and modification of those forms, though he might be a bit chary of saying to which locality or racial group any one of those divergences of feeling belonged. However, I think anyone can presume to say that the inner feeling of some of the illuminations in the Book of St. Chad (at Lichfield, but once possessed by Llandaff, though not it is said of Welsh workmanship[7]) is decidedly 'Celtic' rather than 'Teutonic'—or let us say more 'Irish' than 'Anglo-Saxon'. Similarly some of the drawings in the Lindisfarne Gospels look already to have a little of the feeling— a kind of 'humanism'—which we rather associate with later 'English' draughtsmanship.

[7] See J. E. Lloyd, *History of Wales*, vol. I (1911), pp. 222–3: 'though the Book of St. Chad was for a considerable time at Llandaff and was then known as "Efengyl Teilo", it came there by purchase and may well have been produced by Irish art.'

The motifs, the ingredients of the decoration may, in a given work, derive in part from as far away as Ravenna or Syria, and the Angle who made the given work may have learned to handle his tools in a Celtic monastery, but the Angle imprint may very well be on his angels none the less. And the Goidel who gave to some particular work a feeling which we recognize as Irish-Celtic may very well have been under the tuition of a master whose stock-in-trade of motifs was derived from the same or similar sources as the Angle craftsman—but with very different results. There were no doubt many tendencies at work and this movement or movements included in its effective influence such masterpieces as the Book of Kells, the Lindisfarne Gospels, the great crosses of Northumbria and elsewhere in Britain and Ireland (these latter are said to be of later date).

Wales shared to the full the religious enthusiasm, and the earlier part of this period was the great age of the Welsh saints. In Wales too are numerous remains of carved stone crosses from such centres as Margam, Llantwit Major, Llanbadarn Fawr and elsewhere; and the carved cross at Carew included in its design the name of the craftsman who made it—Meredudd of Rheged.[8] Counting the many fragments of these Welsh crosses and stones it is evident that the original number was considerable. Further the tradition continued, for at St. Davids, as late as the end of the eleventh century, a stone was set up of the same general 'Celtic' character, with Latin minuscule inscriptions. Professor J. E. Lloyd says that over thirty carved stones have been discovered in Glamorgan alone, and about a hundred in Wales as a whole.

It is impossible to make aesthetic judgements of any sort when one has not seen with one's own eyes the objects in question. And even the memory of the sight of certain of them, either as photographs or in reality, is not sufficient; for one's memory needs refreshment. I am therefore unable to express a secure

[8] Does this refer to the district of Rheged or Reget situated in North Britain? If so then the artist Meredudd came from near that northern zone within which the Anglian or Anglo-Celtic great crosses were erected. It would be interesting to know the exact date of the Carew cross in relation to those in the North of England.

opinion of my own as to the aesthetic of these particular Welsh works.

Comparative aesthetics is of all matters the most tricky and authorities whose impartiality and judgement can be respected and relied upon in other matters cannot by any means be so readily trusted in this respect. So that in citing the opinion of a most careful historian who himself cites the opinion of a writer on Celtic art I do so with a consciousness that their views are subject to the above considerations. Professor Lloyd, in dealing with this matter of Celtic-Christian art in Wales gives as his mean authority the late J. Romilly Allen. I shall quote one short passage from Lloyd's *History of Wales*:

> In Wales the same causes were at work, evolving a native art of sculpture out of primitive and Christian decorative elements, but with less felicitous results. A good deal of carving in the Celtic style was at this period executed in the county; nearly a hundred stones—if fragments be taken into the reckoning—with Celtic ornament upon them have come to light. . . . But it is agreed that the Welsh crosses are inferior in design and workmanship to the Irish ones; spirals are almost wholly absent, there is little figure sculpture, and there is less grace of form. The new style of decorating tombstones was adopted in Wales, but the artists and gravers had not the Irish cunning.
>
> (Vol. I, p. 221)

It will be seen that according to this view the evidence is disappointing. It may be added that no illuminated MSS. have come down to us. One bell of Celtic quadrangular form, from among the few now existing, is decorated, according to these same authorities.

We must here note another comment of Dr. Fox in his Presidential Address to the Cambrian Archaeological Association in 1933. In commenting upon the comparative scarcity of the native remains he says (in dealing with the sculptures or inscribed fragments covering a period of some 700 years in the National Museum):

What they do show in most vivid fashion is the unbroken persistence of the written Latin tongue in the highlands through a period which was in the lowlands marked by a decline into complete illiteracy: they show, that is, continuity as the outstanding feature of the highland culture. The absorption and utilization of every type of decorative art current in the West during the latter half of the Dark Ages is also well shown in the monuments: Irish, Northumbrian, and Scandinavian motifs mingle with debased classical designs.

Now the question is *not* how much has survived, *nor* the skill in workmanship; the amount does not matter, neither does the facility—or at least the facility is very secondary: what matters is whether or not there is evidence of an authentic, characteristic, local feeling for form.

Is there, in short, within this Celtic-Christian plastic, evidence of a form-creating genius peculiar to the area called Wales?

It is more in this direction that we search. So that what we are on the look-out for is by no means brilliance of technique, still less quantity—nor is it anything easily catalogued or, for that matter, described. It is that thing, that very recognizable thing, which can be sometimes felt in a few lines of a song, or, on occasion, in a single sentence of a language, when, in a flash, a whole inward world is given concrete expression.[9] This thing can disclose itself in the most varied connections—humble or grand; in a mere fragment or a great building.

It would seem that it is not easy to say how effectively the Welsh of this period of Celtic-Christian revival marked material with their own particular image.

It may be necessary to say here that I include in the term 'plastic' all art-forms where visual shape is the determining factor.

[9] A single example must suffice: when one's going into a church happens to coincide with the beginning of Sunday Vespers in the Latin Rite, both the opening sentences of the office and the psalm-tone of the psalm *Dixit Dominus* seem to lay bare the whole inner feeling of the Latin Christian tradition. On such occasions—and they can occur in any conjunction, sacred or profane—we need no one to say *Sursum corda*, for our hearts are already lifted up by the *authenticity of the form*.

So that a drawing or a painting belongs as much to 'plastics' as does a statue in the round or in relief—or for that matter a door post, a sword hilt, a tea-cup. All are subject to that genius which presides over visual form. I do so even against custom, in order to keep in mind the shape-creating, texture-making, organization in depth as well as on the linear plane that is common in some fashion to all these visual expressions of form.

We are now well within that long period of the rule of the princes which continued to the times of the Plantagenet kings. We know quite a lot about the mode of life, the aspirations and vicissitudes of the Welsh within that period; we have the Laws, the bardic writings, the Chronicles, the prose-tales, the traditions and by sheer fortune the unique contribution in the twelfth century of Gerald de Barri. Had the latter augmented his acute observation with pictorial illustration (as might have been the case in some other age) we should have a very full record indeed of his particular epoch.

As it is, all or almost all of our knowledge is conveyed in written form—but for the art of letters we should know next to nothing of the state of Wales during those centuries except what could be deduced from oral and folk-tradition and from such folk-methods as have until recently lingered in the construction and layout of farm buildings, etc., and these latter would not help much unless we had the written records to inform us of the kind of society which existed and which determined the forms from which the much later and fragmentary forms derive—or presumably derive, for it is largely a question of inference. We have rather scanty evidence of the inner feeling of the men of those earlier ages as expressed in plastic; we have considerable evidence of that feeling as expressed in writings and institutions. So that again we know little of what the impact of the earliest Gothic forms (those forms and that feeling which dominated all West Europe during the very latest part of the period in question) had upon the Welsh genius.

We know that in the main the native Welsh built in wood and wattle and not in stone. We know even the gradated prices and values of such details as roof-trees, posts, and other constituent parts of buildings. We have nothing at all like the simple and impressive 'priest's cell' from Dingle in Ireland (ascribed to the eighth century) which is said to be a stone version of what normally would be of turf construction. It would seem probable that such buildings were erected occasionally in Wales, but if so they seem not to have survived.[10] Nor have we any such later characteristic things as the Irish 'round towers'.

As the Welsh magnates became affected to this or that degree by feudal conditions and ideas it is obvious that changes of all kinds occurred in all matters of material culture, but we are in the dark as to the precise nature of these changes. It would seem that even the court at Aberffraw—'the principal seat'—remained of wood construction, but in any case the site of the palace appears to have yielded nothing. The most important of the great men in the last phase of our independence—men like Llywelyn Fawr and Llywelyn ein Llyw Olaf, with their English baronial connections and their intermarryings into the noble and even into the royal English families, were obviously, in all material things, likely to be much affected by the current European standards. They too, no less than the Warrennes and the Mortimers, had their stone keeps. If you marry Simon de Montfort's daughter you must, I imagine, bring her home to a court with at least some of the current European amenities. But it is precisely the character of the fusion in material things of the old Welsh and new Norman cultures that escapes us and about which we have little or no evidence.

When Gerald de Barri speaks of meeting one of the princes of South Wales in the latter's 'palace', what sort of, or what degree of, fused Norman-Welsh, Welsh-Norman, building and impedimenta are we expected to conjure up? Or again when he refers in his *Description of Wales* to the 'small coats of mail' and the 'greaves plated with iron' (I quote from memory) as being characteristic of the Welsh, in so far as they wore armour at all, are we to envisage the forms of those things as being identical with the ordinary Anglo-Norman defensive armour of the

[10] I suppose the round 'pig-sties' noted and illustrated in *The Welsh House* (1944 ed.) are related to this same tradition of construction?

middle twelfth century or something of a more local particularity inherited from some earlier culture? It is precisely these details that escape us.

It is the definitive character of the appearance and inner feeling of 'things' that tends so much to elude us over large periods of Welsh history.

We know, as has already been said, quite minute details, from the Laws of Hywel Dda and from passages elsewhere, of the set-up of the prince's court—where each of his officials sat in the *neuadd*, the duties and status of each of them from the foot-holder to the mounted troop of horse. We know the price of clothes, arms, objects of various kinds, but we are in almost complete ignorance of the form[11] and so of the feeling of these listed articles over all this period.

To give way to a mere fancy one almost feels as though those mysterious disappearances and vanishings which are not untypical of Welsh tradition—not forgetting the disappearance of 'Arthur' —have a kind of corollary in historic fact. The things, the objects, fade out, leaving only disembodied memories and vivid impressions orally or in writing, with visual echoes in some of the yet existing building-construction of the oldest farms and cottages, as Dr. Peate reminds us when, in describing the layout of one or more of these primitive dwellings, he recalls that vivid visual image in the 'Dream of Rhonabwy'—the hall of Heilyn Goch. I remember seeing, in Ireland, a very similar interior of the profoundest squalor but which brought back a similar *Mabinogion* flavour. There too was the floor 'full of puddles and mounds' and there too the 'old hag, making a fire' and there too the atmosphere was 'scarcely to be borne' and to increase the *Mabinogion* association, another figure appeared, driving with a billet of wood a red cow; this figure was ragged

[11] It is not without interest that there are, in the Laws, references to blue enamel in connection with shields in Dark Age Wales, and that the blue enamelled shields of the Yorkshire Brigantes were mentioned by a Roman poet; which detail points, as does much else, to a continuation of the common Celtic practices surviving the Roman occupation in all the Highland Zone of Britain. My reference to the unnamed Roman poet (Lucan?) comes from *The Romans in Britain*, by B. C. A. Windle of Toronto University (1923 ed.).

and bare-limbed and wore a red skirt with a very wide hem of crimson velvet, and was a figure of great dignity, with flowing red hair. Moreover there was a red evening sun. The whole scene was very like in colour-relationships to a painting by Mr. Graham Sutherland, and perhaps had something of the same feeling too.

But I must remember Elizabeth Tudor and stick to my text. It was only that Dr. Peate's reference recalled to me that feeling common to the traditions of both Goidel and Brython that I experienced at the doorposts of the white Gwyddelig cabin not far from Limerick in 1918—where the squalor seems not modern but prehistoric, for it was the mingled squalor of beasts and men within one enclosure, and so easily the enclosure might have changed from stone to wattle and easily a spearman might have made his appearance without any incongruity, except perhaps for the 'Lea-Enfield shorts' of my companions.

As the new feudal world of stone-building and the habit of putting great men in stone coffins within the precincts of the new stone churches and religious houses, spread all over the West, the great men of Wales began to follow this usage. There is for instance the empty stone coffin said to be that of Llywelyn the Great, the son-in-law to King John. Perhaps much specialist work has been done recently in tracing possible local characterizations in these Norman-Welsh remains. But as Dr. Fox says of the entire collection in the Medieval Gallery in the National Museum at Cardiff (covering the eleventh to the sixteenth centuries), it illustrates 'the intruding lowland culture rather than the native culture which was gradually driven back into the mountainous core of the country'. He goes on to insist—I think very wisely—that the Norman pressure was not 'a striking example of military and political genius' but rather 'an inevitable primary expansion into the highlands of a novel lowland culture'. And that the Anglo-Norman knights in being the agents of this culture were 'the servants of destiny'. I believe it is very necessary to remember the truth in this whenever we are thinking of Wales. Nevertheless there was the fusion and that must have had an impact on the forms—at least to some degree.

I have, by chance, before me, a guidebook to the church of Cilcain in Flintshire, compiled by the late Mr. Frank Simpson of Chester. In it are a number of photographs of sculptured stone fragments recovered from various ill-usages. (So easily they might yet remain hidden discarded in dusty corners or used face-down as door-steps or what not.) One in particular—to judge from the reproduction—is of great liveliness and character. It is described by the compiler as fourteenth-century work. No one would imagine, from looking at the photograph, so late a date. It is very primitive in feeling—of mixed decorative motifs—the whole pattern and form look to be sensitive and full of interest. It may be that it conforms to a classified local type well known to specialists—of that I cannot judge. My point is that it was only a mere accident which brought this reproduction my way, so that it may be other such works of interest, or perhaps of greater interest, exist unknown, up and down Wales, at least unknown to the general public, but offering some indication of local fused styles and characterizations and showing in fragments a vital plastic sense.

To repeat what has already been said: geography and history must modify our expectations in all these matters in all countries and at all times (less today than at any time for reasons which will be touched on later), and that Wales is far from being an exception to this rule but rather an example *par excellence* of its operation.

We know and understand the set-up and the likelihoods in a general way but I am a little less confident that we have, so far, sifted all the more accidental evidence. I have no doubt that that is being done. It is all and every surviving bit and fragment that will help us. It is precision as to the existing evidence that is most needed. Dr. Iorwerth Peate's carefully compiled factual book on *The Welsh House* is a perfect contribution to this kind of exact information, and aided by the excellent photographs and diagrams is invaluable as far as the folk-tradition of building is concerned. His tracing of the evidence showing the relationship of the still existing 'long-houses' and 'round-houses' with the wooden structures described in the Laws, and referred to in

Giraldus, and the relationship of all this with other common Celtic features is illuminating. He supplies many clues as to the continuity of a native tradition of peasant building. Altogether apart from this tradition with its common Celtic features, he notes an interesting passage from Leland concerning some border architecture as being 'after the Walche fascion' which suggests that in the sixteenth century certain other characteristics, of whatever alien origin, were at all events associated with Wales or rather with the more eastern parts of Wales.

The varying local traditions of decorating floor surfaces is full of interest and the geometric patterns formed of pebbles—the 'pitched floors'—found in Montgomery can be seen from the excellent photographs to be exceedingly beautiful.[12] Incidentally the covering of these surfaces with linoleum, and still worse, the removal of them, is a classic example of that very understandable weakness in human nature—especially when household drudgery is involved—of seeking first utility and the saving of labour. A subject which my friend, the late Mr. Eric Gill, constantly dwelt upon. In it he saw one of the chief causes of degradation in the everyday arts of man.

Another extremely interesting point is the reference to the painted fragment of wall-surface of seventeenth-century type from Penrhyn-coch, Cardiganshire, and the very strange coincidence which connects this site with the passage in Dafydd ap Gwilym mentioning the decoration of walls three hundred years previously. But again and again throughout the whole book we get glimpses of evidence of the shape of things that were, but which now no longer are, nor can be. The appendix to chap. VI dealing with the evidence from medieval literature as to buildings in Wales is also suggestive of the fusing Welsh-English styles as the middle ages wore on. But it is clear, in view of the great and

---

[12] These 'pitched floors' are not exclusively of the Welsh area but this patterning of flat surfaces may be rather typical. I note that Mr. John Betjeman in a review speaks of 'the innate love of surface decoration in all Celtic peoples'. I think there is probably something in it. The revival of interest in quilt-making with its essentially surface patterning may perhaps also be indicative of the same tendency.

sad, however inevitable, passing of the old ways, and especially with the coming of the modern world and the cold douche which modern industrialized techniques have let loose on all the old locality-traditions, that it is now, in the main, a question of inferring and deducing what once was from exceedingly scattered and meagre fragments. But we owe a great debt to Dr. Peate for his labours with regard to this one subject: the construction and form of the folk-builders.

I cannot leave this subject without mentioning the stimulating reference (p. 148) to the passage in the Tristram tale about the stream which passes through Iseult's chamber, and how Dr. Peate shows from factual references that within our own days examples have been noted of similar ducts of water through habitations. I must say, even if it is indulging a dubious racial romanticism, that this whole conception has to me a typically 'Celtic' feeling about it—and a very attractive concept it is, and it is exceedingly satisfying to know that, as in all good 'concepts', the roots are in hard material reality: for then the flowers can be in the stars—then we have imagination and not mere fancy.

The examination of the subsequent periods from the later middle ages onwards offers, no doubt, evidence of all kinds and of every complexity. We see from the references already mentioned in the appendix to chap. VI of *The Welsh House* that there are some literary allusions. Speaking generally we have to guess almost as much about the age of Glyn Dŵr as we do about that of the Princes. Again the evidence is mostly written; the folk-tradition, the records and the poetry remain, but little of the things. Iolo Goch's often quoted description of Glyn Dŵr's wooden house at Sycharth is referred to by Dr. Peate as having 'reflected to a high degree the Norman and English developments in architecture'. And in other interesting references from the poets which he cites we see the same fusion described or suggested. We do not and cannot now know how much 'Welshness' would come through if we could look with our own eyes at these habitations of the leaders. The old *arglwyddi* and the 'good men', the 'high men' were fast becoming the 'Welsh gentry' and soon (as history goes) would become just 'gentry'—

'lesser gentry', on the whole, by English standards—and these were increasingly to be the standards.

And here is a point which has a bearing on our subject. We have now to look for the remains of the traditions in entirely peasant and labouring abodes and circumstances. It was the alienation of the natural leaders that gradually but finally decided the fate of whatever there was in the material culture of a Welsh characterization other than what could be absorbed and given some kind of continuance among the ordinary folk. Once the political and economic native tribal structure was broken down, the end, however long delayed, was certain. When such processes are completed 'the sheep look up and are not fed'. It is then that the delicately balanced corporate way of life, the liturgy and syncretism of the tribal ecclesia, become meaningless, as we see in many 'backward' and primitive peoples in our time; it is then that the 'folk' become 'fellaheen'. And the folk-leaders become identified with the alien culture, and are 'pensioned off'.

As so often, if not always, the disintegration first showed itself in the top stratum.

Strike the shepherd and the sheep shall be scattered. Give the dark king a wireless set and other amenities and his chieftains will not be long in acquiring the same amenities and before long the tribesmen will be sporting sock-suspenders or any other symbol of the higher civilization. The spell of a common culture binding the entire society will gradually but inevitably lose its potency and eventually snap, even though it may have endured for a thousand years as a form-creating way of life. The advantages of civilization will have triumphed but a cultural death will also have to be registered. There is no point in blurring the shape of this situation. It is better to say that the culture is stone dead, than to suggest something analogous to that 'passing on' which is beloved of those people who wish to evade the reality of other sorts of death. I do not imply that the above illustration of the dark king can be taken as fitting the facts of what happened in Wales from the middle ages onwards. That would be most disgracefully unjust to the quality of the true culture which broke down the old ways, and be very misleading in most respects, but though quite dissimilar in kind and quality the *process* was analogous at some points.

Although the first intimation of these coming collapses is very often to be seen in military eclipse[13] and is usually if not always mixed with power politics and its necessities, it is in the domain of material form and the making of the objects that the effects are

[13] December 10th or 11th, 1282, is a date not to be forgotten in Welsh history. I have detected latterly a tendency in some quarters to blur the reality of those events. It is sometimes suggested that the age of Glyn Dŵr saw the real birth of 'Welsh nationhood'. I think this is extremely wrong-headed. It seems to me to confuse the shadow with the reality. It is a kind of Bonny Prince Charlieism. No doubt some Scots have worn the trews or the kilt with a more conscious air since '45, but that does not alter the realities of history. Some Catholics no doubt have been more dutifully aware of Catholicism since the Counter-Reformation but that does not restore the lost unconscious acceptance of the Catholic synthesis. No doubt that most clear-sighted historian F. M. Powicke of Oriel is right when he suggests that Welsh history began anew in the fourteenth century and that Welsh racial consciousness is able to survive independently of political forms. No doubt that is an important truth. Nevertheless that race-consciousness could not restore the lost integrated structure of society under the native rulers and under native law—when race-consciousness was much less in evidence. I know that the laws were to some extent permitted to continue under the Plantagenet settlement, but deprived of the support of the native princes the situation became increasingly artificial. I know that the bards continued to sing under the patronage of the lesser lords and composed eulogies to the leaders fighting for the English factions in the Wars of the Roses, just as they had sung of the autonomous rulers of a real society, but the thing must have become increasingly a charade.

The loss of political independence (however shadowy) means in the very long run the loss of most else. No doubt one can legitimately take the line that there are compensations—no doubt that can be true from more than one point of view—but nothing can affect the reality of the deprivation and the impoverishment of the loss. The laws of a society by a kind of syncretism display and preserve the inner feeling of a society just as do the plastic forms the inner feeling of a culture. And the sole point of political control—a thing unimportant in itself—is the defence against disruption from without. Loss of political power is to this extent a very serious matter indeed, for it affects matters beyond and a thousand times more important than politics, power or nationality. To pretend otherwise is an indulgence—a very fashionable indulgence—which can lead only to further misconceptions and unreality; worse, it is a symptom of intellectual cowardice, or I suppose it can be conscious and deliberate eye-wash used straight from the propagandist bottle.

most final and most complete. There can be a measure of quasi-political and sociological recovery, and every sort of deeply felt revivalism and 'national movement'. Exceedingly valuable as these things are they cannot restore the lost integrated culture and its unconscious expression.

There was the further ironing-out of what remained of the old order under what might be accurately called the '*Gleichs-geschaltung* of the Tudors of Môn'. The religious upheaval itself must have done a good bit to destroy the very sort of evidence which we need, to what extent we shall never know. I wonder what sort of plastic the great wooden image from Llandderfel disclosed when they used it for fuel at Smithfield at the martyrdom of Father Forrest the Franciscan?

Presumably most, or all, of the Welsh churches contained sacred images of some description, 'good bodily images', which would have told us something. Also places such as Ystrad-fflur would possess treasures of various sorts, MSS. etc.—not to be compared with the greater Abbeys[14] of the Lowland Zone, but nevertheless things which in part at least *may* have expressed some local spirit. It may be that specialist historians could refer us to inventories of Thomas Cromwell's agents regarding some of the things confiscated: but even if they could, those files would not enlighten us as to the plastic feeling of the objects in question— and it is only that which concerns us here. The immediately recent centuries which are of such interest to the social historian and which include the inception of industrial capitalism and the beginnings of the world we suffer today are, for a number of reasons—understandable but highly complex—more difficult to assess with regard to our subject. More and more, and affecting in an increasing degree each strata of life, the material culture of the Highland Zone has been dependent upon the material culture of the Lowland Zone. Without doubt the objects and paraphernalia of rural and peasant life, the sleds, the wains and farm implements and farm and cottage furnitures continued in Wales as elsewhere

[14] I believe I am right in supposing that all the Welsh monastic houses would be included in the first suppression, which affected all monastic foundations worth less than £200 per annum—all those called the 'lesser houses'.

in Britain and Europe to show local differentiation, and all that rich variation natural to any pre-industrial society. But it is perfectly plain to anyone that in the main it would be extremely unlikely that a country such as Wales in the eighteenth or nineteenth centuries would show signs of initiative with regard to the resurgence, or development or inception of a true local plastic. As I have said, there were religious revivals, literary revivals, politico-social revivals, revived interest in folk-custom, in literature and the heritage of the language—yes—but nothing which could really affect the making of things in a decisive way. On every ground this would seem unlikely. More and more as to material culture, as to the making of things, the Highland Zone would be distinguished from the Lowland Zone only in being the poorer of the two and the least 'advanced' and in preserving for a little longer some of the ancient local techniques.

An example of this continuance of the older ways can be seen in the survival of a rural woollen yarn industry in Cardiganshire in the late nineteenth century under an economic and cultural set-up which had vanished in England much earlier. No doubt into the nineteenth century local manufacture with a local clientele could still be practised by the agricultural people.[15] In those parts of the year when farming is slack there was the 'making of things' both to keep men more complete human beings and to augment the exceedingly scanty incomes. In spite of the undoubted hardness, narrowness, severity and wretched-ness of the conditions there is a picture of a natural and reasonable economy and way of life—something still approaching a 'culture', something which 'civilization' makes everywhere impossible whether in Wales or Timbuktu.

Finally we have the present situation where both zones have to a large extent and in all essentials a common dead-level machine-culture which in the nature of things can take no regard of differentiations and immemorial ways and tends to be actively inimical to all such, and which quite inevitably causes the hands to lose their cunning and saps the whole integral feeling and

[15] See I. C. Peate, *Welsh Folk Crafts*, op. cit., and Cyril Fox, *A Short Account of the Archaeological Collections* (National Museum of Wales, 1934).

changes the entire rhythm, puts a premium on 'town intelligence' at the expense of 'country understanding',[16] relegates the 'crafts' to the category of things to be 'preserved' or 'encouraged' and to be contemplated in 'leisure hours', for those who like 'old-fashioned ways' while others can enjoy that same leisure in the scenery museums that were once the living countryside. Do not let it be supposed that these contemporary efforts at preservation or encouragement are to be despised any more than are the laudable efforts to preserve 'the scenery' from the vileness of the building contractors—but we *must* understand the true nature of the situation and be under no illusions.

So that we have in that sense no 'culture' now but a number of contrivances of a utile nature which are indeed the product of man and bear his national imprint and show to a marked degree his intelligence, potency, ingenuity and skill, but which have all the same 'inward feeling' and the same outward characterization, whether assembled at Detroit, in the Lowland or Highland Zones of Britain or in any European production area. Prefabricated houses are liable to be as alike as two bombs.

No doubt there are and will continue to be minor differences: partly consciously maintained for this or that reason, partly because, even still, climatic and other conditions determine something, even under machine- and mass-production; but it does not amount to anything very fundamental and does not reflect the determining feeling throughout. It is either a dubious difference, a mere propagandist difference, or something imposed by *purely* utilitarian motives, unintegrated and thin and, of course, peculiarly loveless, though no doubt of the highest efficiency and

[16] The convenient expressions 'town intelligence' and 'country understanding' are Spengler's, or rather Spengler's translator's. I don't know that they can be improved upon as shorthand expressions to convey the *characteristic* mood and approach of the townsman and the countryman, so long as it is remembered that I use 'country understanding' to include a great deal more than what is meant by 'countrified' or bucolic. It includes the whole perceptive, intuitive, instinctual, traditional and contemplative thing in contrast to the intellectualized, entirely cerebral, sharp-witted, uprooted, self-conscious, divorced-from-the-rhythm-of-nature tendency of the larger urban communities. Clearly the norm should be a free exchange between the two.

the product of considerable combined intelligence and most careful experiment. It is very necessary to get this clear in the mind, as it is very clear in the things which condition our daily lives. Such differentiations as the names: Yorkshire, Glamorgan, Denbigh, Kent, may call up, are rapidly becoming, if they have not already become, as obsolete as Wessex, Gwynedd, Deheubarth, Mercia, as far as material culture is concerned.

More and more, throughout the last decades and still more today, any plastic feeling must be looked for not in 'places'—there can hardly be said to be 'places' in that sense: the genii and *numina* of place 'troop to th'infernall jail' in a way Milton never saw. We all are as uprooted as the nation of the Jews and that is why we weep when we remember Sion—the old local Sions with their variants of the form-creating human cultures.[17] We all are of the diaspora now. This is not only a figure of speech, it corresponds to the facts of our kind of civilization; and its realization will help us better to understand the nature of that civilization as it affects the arts, no less in our own country than elsewhere.

Any person, either Welsh or English, in so far as the forms he makes reflect the inner feeling of the localities called 'Wales' or 'England' and in so far as he inherits and reflects the traditional mood of those places, is a man of the diaspora—no matter whether he lives physically within or outside the borders of those places. All who 'are of' the cultures are now necessarily 'of the dispersion', because the cultures themselves no longer exist.[18]

[17] I do not imply that we should have liked to live in those cultures. We should find them extremely horrible no doubt. Our sophistication and the whole orientation of our sensitivities would be gravely upset; but that by no means should prevent us from weeping at the contemplation of their excellence and integration. I append this note for the express purpose of anticipating the thoughts of those readers who will say: 'How would Mr. Jones have liked to live under such-and-such conditions in such-and-such a century?' The question is quite irrelevant. We know that we are altogether conditioned by our age quite independently of our assessment of its values.

[18] This is why I say above that we all are now in a position somewhat analogous to that of the Jews. By which I do not presume to express any opinion on the supra-natural mystery of Israel; but only to say that Jacob's

They have been or are being destroyed by a new type of civilization.

Here a clarification may be necessary: we are speaking *solely* of the material, plastic forms, the visible forms—if you like and if you can be rid of certain unfortunate connotations, the common arts and crafts in the most comprehensive sense: from the making of a building to the making of a spoon or a picture. It is clear that local expression of a social, institutional, religious and, in a somewhat disembodied fashion, aesthetic nature can maintain and assert itself, one way or another, within our present set-up and can display a certain genuine locality-characteristic. This is true—at least for a while. Indeed some of these expressions may be particularly assertive, truly felt, conscious, but above all, self-conscious. It is the visible, material, plastic forms of everyday life that feel the rub, first and most and all the time.

These forms are important, for they touch the daily life of man at more points than all else. They are the forms where man normally and historically most commonly conjoined matter and spirit, and which most naturally and of necessity have borne the stamp of locality and displayed the whole inner feeling of corporate ways of life. The importance, just mentioned, resides in the stabilizing nature of these activities. It is central because in prosecuting them there is necessarily maintained an indissoluble and balanced union between matter and spirit. No matter what other miseries, degradations and impoverishments characterize the men of the culture as opposed to the men of today, in this matter of the making of things it cannot be denied that the balance of his dual nature was more easily and more normally maintained. Because in the responsible fashioning of material

---

trouble is in some sense now becoming our trouble, in that we all are of a dispersion and all are tending to an analogous disembodiment which may perhaps encourage a sharpening of the intelligence and a kind of heightening of the appreciative faculties at the expense of rootedness and locality-feeling. This is an immensely involved subject and requires qualifications within qualifications and requires great patience to get even partially clear, but it is one which involves us all. No knots must be cut here but everything conscientiously untied. Each link must be tested to see what holds and what does not hold.

towards an idea he is protected from becoming sub-human on the one hand and from being disembodied on the other.

To a unique degree this phase of our civilization poses a great problem. For more than any previous civilization it tends to disembody man *and at the same time* compels him to sub-human (because entirely material utile and functional) activities. So that a severe dislocation or cleavage vitiates all his efforts and tends to a most unnatural departmentalizing of his thought and necessarily of his work. The word 'culture' itself then takes on quite a new and far less happy meaning—it becomes debased, for it now connotes something added, something to be encouraged by government departments, something to sugar the pill. Material objects are the greatest give-away of any epoch or place. They, more readily than any other thing, lay bare the state of affairs, and indicate the 'soul' of a period or a culture. For the good reason that in them there is no escape—they compel the maker to disclose his dual nature. Not that other of his activities do not, for without exception they all do; but here in this fashioning of things is the archetype and norm of all the ways and modes by which he signs his name.

It will be evident to all that the signature on the mass-produced forms, whether part of a piece of machinery or any object or gadget you care to name (it may have 'beauty', it may have none —that is irrelevant) tends in varying degrees to be a somewhat different signature from that on what are now called 'art-works' or 'cultural objects'. It is that variation of signature which tells us something definite and important about the nature of our age. That variation is indicative of one of the problems we share as Welshmen, Englishmen, Europeans, Asiatics or whatever we happen to be. The same is increasingly applying to all places from, I nearly said from China to Peru, but that calls up too much the ancient *numina* of place—and 'in both hemispheres' would be too reminiscent of a vanishing geography; I think 'global' fits the case—this new duality is for the first time global.

It is then against the background of a global machine-culture that any contemporary or future feeling for plastic must be seen. It is against this background that any individual, or other than individual, feeling left over from the cultural locality-feelings, must now express itself. In the case of Wales we have a locality within a locality within a locality—i.e. Wales, Britain, Europe. We have suggested the ironing-out process (especially as to the making of things) that is overtaking the larger traditions and the greater localities. It is clear that the smaller ones are subject to the same problems—one would suppose, other things being equal, to a greater degree. Be that as it may, any 'Welshness' expressed in plastic form of any description whatsoever has now and will have in the future (at least unless processes at present hidden change altogether the whole world-direction—and that we cannot profitably discuss) to maintain itself against this megalopolitan background and will have to resolve the same extremely difficult problems which confront the 'arts' all over the world.

I must stress that it is the *plastic forms alone* that I speak of here. As to poetry and music, they too operate within the same general conditions, but owing to their modes of operation they are not so immediately affected; because of being in one way less obviously bound to material they seem to abide more easily 'on the side of the mind' and are perhaps less obviously troubled by the duality we have mentioned. But in the last analysis this also is illusory—they too in the long run are affected, and to much the same degree. The interior structure, the technical devices, the concepts and ideas and all the morphology of the art of poetry can be maintained in all kinds of circumstances—in a world very other from that in which the poetry is written—but even so certain essential lines of communication cannot indefinitely be lengthened, still less severed. For poetry like any other art has to preserve liaison with the actual, the bodily, the visible—and these necessarily involve the contemporary scene.[19] Of the art of music, of

[19] I cannot do better than quote once again the Regius Professor of Modern History at Oxford on this subject of the relationship of the poet to locality and the living expression of locality:

. . . this source of strength which comes from contact with long tradition was in some of our poets a chief source of their spiritual life. We may not perhaps be conscious of the historical sense in the poetry of Keats; but it is there and he was well aware of it. He writes in one of his letters: 'I like,

how the composer operates, I know absolutely nothing at all; but there again, because it is an art of man it cannot be rid of these same conditions, even if more than most arts it may seem sometimes to evade them. When people say music is the purest of the arts, one knows what is meant, but as it stands it is about as sensible as saying: man is pure spirit. For all the arts are of their very nature impure, i.e. they are essentially a conjoining of two things, matter and spirit—that's what it's all about!

In what has been said in the last few paragraphs, criticism of modern developments is not intended, at least if by criticism, judgement is meant or a remedy implied. All that has been attempted is to suggest the kind of background against which, and the kind of situation within which, any local expression, or expression deriving ultimately from the old localities, must now operate—in or from or obliquely of, Wales, England, or elsewhere. There is every reason to suppose that much such expression will, one way and another, continue under these very changed and rapidly more changing, world conditions. The machine age *may* see an intensive productivity in certain specified arts—even for instance painting: that quite well fits the picture; but it will be

---

I love England. I like its living men. Give me a long brown plain . . . so I may meet with some of Edmund Ironside's descendants. Give me a barren mould, so I may meet with some shadowing of Alfred in the shape of a gipsy, a huntsman or a shepherd. Scenery is fine—but human nature is finer—the sward is richer for the tread of a real nervous English foot.' Those of us who love the songs and the drawings of William Blake do not think of him, with his prophetic soul, as a historian, even though he did write of building Jerusalem in England's green and pleasant land. But when Blake was a boy, apprenticed to an engraver, he used to be sent to Westminster Abbey, and locked in by himself, he spent hours in copying the tombs of mediaeval kings and queens and barons; and all through his wonderful work, in the long beautiful lines of his drawings, we can see the influence of the mediaeval craftsman. For men of vision and purpose England has been inseparable from her past—the past has not been antiquity, but part of the present. . . .

(F. M. Powicke, *Mediaeval England, 1066–1485* (1942 ed.))

When that past is altogether divorced from the visible present the poet is in great danger of disembodiment.

painting as a separate 'cultural' (in the new sense) activity. Already we see a great 'interest' displayed in these different 'cultural' activities. The next hundred years or so may be very interesting apropos of this business of technological man and man the artist. It is impossible to say how the spirit of man will resolve the antithesis—including the spirit of man as expressed in Welshman.

March 1944

The Roland Epic and Ourselves[*]

T here is a very important aspect of this translation of the
Roland which I must leave to those with a critical knowledge of the original French. I can only speak of it as a
work in English, and of a few ideas which it evokes. *The Song of
Roland* is one of those comparatively rare writings of which
it can be said that their titles alone open a door for us, and call up
for us a whole order of things. *The Battle of Maldon*, *The Iliad*,
The Song of Deborah, *Piers Plowman*, are all, I think, fair examples
of what I mean. These very dissimilar compositions have this in
common that their titles alone are efficacious in changing some
gear in the mind. Even if we have but a nodding acquaintance
with their contents we sense the world to which they belong;
just as, for instance, by merely calling to remembrance the
Lindisfarne Gospels, the Glastonbury thorn, the Alfred jewel, we
experience a heightening of our perceptions—forgotten things
begin to shape—we sit up and take notice. A writer who takes
upon himself the task of dealing with any such charged material
does so knowing that his readers, whether they be learned or
unlearned, will take up his writing expecting a good deal.

If we have heard with our ears that *The Song of Roland* is a
noble work, this translation corroborates what our fathers have
told us with regard to it. From the opening lines:

> Charles the King, our great Emperor, has been all full seven
> years in Spain. He has taken the high land as far as the sea. . . .
> King Marsiliun was at Saragossa. He has gone into an orchard,
> under the shade. He lies on a bench of blue marble. . . . (p. 1),

[*] A review of *The Song of Roland*, Text of the Oxford MS. with translation by René Hague (Faber & Faber, 1937), first published in *The Tablet*,
24 December 1938.

to the final:

> ... the Christians call and cry out to you. The Emperor would
> not want to go. 'God,' said the King, 'how heavy is my life.'
> He weeps from his eyes, he tears his white beard (p. 141),

there is maintained a direct and objective presentation of the
characters and the world in which they live. The ill-will and
stress common to any march lands is made a hundred times more
intense and inveterate, in that these marches indicate the boundary
situations of two cultures and two religions. The keepers of such
marches, in such an age, necessarily identify themselves with the
keepers of the gulf between heaven and hell. It is not 'poor old
Jerry', suffering a common fate, affectionately regarded, honoured
and fraternized with, that Roland's Tommies looked for in the
Basque no-man's-land, but only black heathens for whose souls
devils wait: '. . . the big-headed Micenes; they have bristles like
pigs on their spines in the middle of their backs . . . they are a
people whose will is never turned to good . . . you will never
hear talk of a more wicked people' (p. 114). (It is true that this
language is similar to that used by some of our friends when
speaking of nations with whom we are at peace—that surely is a
sign of the times—the war of cultures and ideologies has returned,
and, for Boars Hill, Jerry already has a tail.)

It has been often said that one of the marks by which we know
a true writing from a false is to be found in a kind of inevitability
—of both form and content. In a satisfactory art-work we cannot
tolerate a need to ask questions. We expect to be convinced of the
behaviour of the characters—we want no impediment to our
appreciation. In reading this translation, we, who have rather
other ideas of how an Archbishop should interpret his pastoral
powers, accept in Turpin of Reims his 'great battles' together
with his 'fine sermons' as equally becoming a shepherd of the
sheepfold. This is a good sign: that we should become so knit
with the work we contemplate.

It is a precept of our religion that we should 'weep with them
that weep'. It is likewise a certain sign of excellence in an art-work
that it should cause us to identify ourselves with its written or

painted image in some way. Mr. Hague's translation frequently effects this. The economy and choice of his words is particularly successful in such passages as that one which portrays the death of Oliver—Oliver, the Jonathan of our European tradition:

> At that word they have leant one on the other. You see them parted in their great love. . . . Roland sees that his friend is dead, his face against the ground. He began to call his name sweetly, 'My lord companion, your strength was made for death. You never did me wrong and I was not untrue to you. Now you are dead it is my grief that I live.' When he has spoken the marquis faints on his horse, which he calls Veillantif. He is held up by the stirrups of fine gold. Whichever side he leans, he cannot fall (pp. 72–3).

We feel clearly the war-saddle, the supporting stirrups, the stiff paraphernalia of the medieval *miles*, binding rider and horse into a rigid unity (in a manner not known to the stirrupless ancients) and here buttressing and holding erect a man, faint because of his friend dead.

It is this casual but precise observation of workaday accidents, and the employment of that observation in such a manner as to express situations of universal significance, that is so satisfactory. One can imagine the writer who would cover many pages in attempting to convey the poignance of a situation where a mere accident of furniture saves the hero's emotion from publicly overpowering him—here it is done in a single line of quite objective statement, without any disturbance of the narrative.

Then there is the sustained climax of the poem—Roland's own death and that of the Archbishop. From section 154 (p. 74) to section 177 (p. 85) the tightness of the form and the nobility of the content are equally memorable. Even the final chapters of Malory, with Ector's lament for Lancelot, are not more moving; and the reiterated statement of Turpin: 'Sirs, you are set for sorrow,' is almost, for us, too near the knuckle to be read without fear.

'The trees are high, the hills are very high.' How better, or more briefly could the site of that rearguard action in the

Basque valley be expressed? It has somewhat of the terseness we associate with a section-commander describing 'a field of fire'—as well as being good poetry.

Afterwards we have the return of the King.

Roland is dead. God has his soul in heavens. There is no road nor path nor empty ground, nor a yard nor a full foot where there is not a french man or a pagan. Charles calls, 'Where are you, my lovely nephew? Where is the Archbishop and Count Oliver? Where Gerin and his companion Gerer? Where is Otun and Count Berenger, Ivon and Yvoerie, whom I hold so dear?' (p. 85).

Here, as throughout, the dominant theme is that bond between the leader and his vassals, and that love between companion and companion, which is only a dim thing for us, but which is characteristic, and which, as is pointed out by C. S. Lewis in his book, *The Allegory of Love*, was the main theme of that age, just as the pain between lover and mistress was the preoccupation of the later Romance literature (and from that literature to our own has remained the chief motif in story-telling). But here it is the 'good vassal' together with the *Amis and Amiloun* association, that we are asked to consider. If we do not feel the power of that spell we shall not make much of the *Song of Roland*. To quote from the book already referred to: '. . . the mutual love of warriors who die together fighting against odds, and the affection between vassal and lord'—this is the grand passion of that time.

The primitive Welsh story *Math fab Mathonwy*, although related to another cycle (and having its roots in a remoter and more magical civilization than that which we are considering), has a passage that comes to my mind as suggestive of those two polarities: love (of women) and war, which is only felt in two passages in the *Roland*, those relating to Alde. During the battle:

And Oliver said, By my head, if I can see my sweet sister Alde, you shall never lie between her arms (p. 62).

And after the battle:

The Emperor has come back from Spain. . . . Alde has come to him, the girl that was lovely. She says to the King, Where is Roland the captain, who swore to me that he would take me for his peer? Charles is brought down with heavy grief, he weeps from his eyes and tears his white beard. Sister, dear love, you ask me of a dead man. I will give you for him the best I have; it is Lewis; I can say no better word to you; he is my son and he will hold my marches. Alde answers, Your word is strange to me. May it not please God nor his saints, nor his angels, that I should be left alive after Roland. She loses colour and falls at Charlemagne's feet. She is dead immediately. God have mercy on her soul. The French barons weep and mourn for her (pp. 130-1).

The Math story opens:

Math the son of Mathonwy was Lord over Gwynedd. . . . At that time [he] could not rest unless his feet were in the lap of a maiden, except only when he was prevented by the tumult of war.

Math's disquiet, and his salve, are familiar to us all. But here the love interest turns out to be incidental to magic herds, battle at boundary-mounds, the loves and hates of men to whom tribal ties and taboos were sacrosanct. As we have said, these and similar loyalties were the central interest until the French genius in the twelfth century began to set the course towards romance— as we use the word today.

In the *Roland* we feel all the while the earlier 'romance' and the more primitive loyalties, and throughout there is the identification of the 'good Christian' with the 'good vassal'—which the Germanic peoples largely contributed. In our Anglo-Saxon *Dream of the Rood* we have this idea serving its highest turn, for here the hero is the Eternal Word, who mounts his gibbet as a warrior—still the Lamb eternally slain—essentially 'a male of the first year without blemish', and—if one can borrow from, and pre-apply the iconography of a later period—a male with horns and carrying the emblem of his struggle.

Perhaps it is not out of place to suggest that these conceptions have, this particular stress has, more than an historical and literary interest for us. We are witnesses of a resurgence of the 'cult-hero' (in however ominous a form and with whatever violence of expression) among those peoples from whom Christendom originally, in large part, received these conceptions, and to whom She gave baptism. It is not fantastic to see in Balder's embrace of the Bough of the Cross (round which Loki's parasite cannot climb) the act which, in time, generated the particular virtues we associate with Wace's 'vassals who died at Rencevales'.

To bend inward all devotion towards a sacred consanguinity and a common soil, to perfect the mystical body of a tribal *ecclesia*, this to be seen as a last end—this, compared with those ends towards which the Christian tradition has for centuries directed the love of the Christian vassal, may well seem a crude retrogression, yet there can be seen in this reorientation an aboriginal validity, and this canalized devotion seems acquainted with a kind of urgency that lovers know about, which can only be tutored, like the wild unicorn, by a mistress with vision. It derives too much from the bowels to be amenable to ethical or legal arguments, especially should those arguments be used as wrappings for stones thrown from our own cracked house of glass. There seems something here, however difficult of expression, that we must try and understand before we can begin to find out which fits which in our tumbled European Humpty Dumpty; or if ever (for it is permitted to us to dream dreams) the North is to make again a song as basically Christian as this Franco-Germanic epic. Or (to dream deeper) if Aachen is to become again pre-eminently the place of the chapel—'*Carles serat ad Ais a sa capele*' (line 52, Text, Oxford MS.).

When the Emperor had done his vengeance he called the bishops of France and those of Bavaria and those of Germany. . . . There are great companies at the waters of Aix, and there they baptize the queen of Spain (p. 140).

Or (to dream more fantastically still), if Aix chapel should be the chapel of Carbonek—or 'the city of Sarras, in the spiritual place', or at least that there should be a visitation as at Camelot, where:

> . . . they heard cracking and crying of thunder, and them thought the place should all to drive . . . and either saw other by their seeming, fairer than ever they saw afore . . . then the Holy Vessel departed suddenly, that they wist not where it became: then had they all breath to speak.

There has, in our time, been deleted from the morning office for Good Friday (as far as public recitation is concerned) the prayer:

> *Oremus et pro Christianissimo Imperatore nostro, ut Deus et Dominus noster subditas illi faciat omnes barbaras nationes ad nostram perpetuam pacem.*

It is an unusual sensation to feel that one is suggesting that the Roman Catholic Church authorities have been too previous in coming to a decision, or that there is lacking that proper conservatism which is content to wait until an apparent anachronism becomes 'contemporary', or that there has been an abandonment of a formula which expresses a reality, but which happens to have no present embodiment. But one does rather regret the falling into dis-usage of a petition that has such interesting historical associations and such abiding metaphorical validity. It is, conceivably, for a baptized Führership that we may yet have cause to pray, if only in the sense that a sophisticated Roman of The Province would have asked heaven's prevenience for the difficult barbarian invested with The Purple; or a Celtic Christian might, just conceivably, have prayed for Edwin, with his assumed insignia of the *Dux Britanniarum*.

These contrarious and involved echoes of unity and defence beat against those equally complex elements of dissolution and attack—this from within, that from without. The thing is tangled, it is not a chess-board. This goodness for that badness—each qualified. The out-land scourge for the hucksters in the basilica, sometimes. The civic decencies for the blue savages, sometimes. Our sympathies play somersaults as we read the histories.

Of a more local unification:

> Where would you hide an Imperial crown?
> In the thorn-brake.
> Who will find the crown?
> The welsh upstart.
> What will he do with the crown?
> He will make order within its circumference.
> Will his order be good?
> That all depends.

And always:

> But thése two; wáre of a wórld where bút these
>   two tell, each off the óther, of a rack
> Where, selfwrung, selfstrung, sheathe—and shelterless,
>   thoughts, agaínst thoughts ín groans grínd

for what Hopkins here expresses (as no other man could) of the individual struggle, is true of the culture-tangle.

'From the fury of the Northmen O Lord deliver us'—this still wakes in us racial memories, and in certain moods that cry is yet potent—so long was that fear in the blood. This phobia Anglo-Celtic nurses must have utilized to quell our ancestors in childhood when they were intractable.

Those verses which have scared a few generations of children (and grown-ups too):

> Through the long long wintry nights;
> When the angry breakers roar
> As they beat on the rocky shore;
>
>   . . . . .
>
> Then through the vast and gloomy dark
> There moves what seems a fiery spark.
>
>   . . . . .
>
> Piercing the coal-black night,
>
>   . . . . .
>
> Slowly it wanders—pauses—creeps,
>
>   . . . . .

And those who watch at the midnight hour
From Hall or Terrace or lofty Tower,
Cry, as the wild thing passes along,
    The Dong! The Dong!
The wandering Dong through the forest goes!
    The Dong! The Dong!
The Dong with the luminous nose!

—those verses, however much 'nonsense rhymes' for the Victorian watercolourist who wrote them, nevertheless express that terror from without, which was more than a bogey for our ancestors in the dark age.

Our own:

> Close the door they're coming through the window
> Close the window they're coming through the door
> Close the door they're coming through the window
> My God! they're coming through the floor!

is perhaps the most contemporary expression of that in-breaking upon an established order. Indeed the words, without alteration, might be put into the mouth of a shopkeeper in the Saxon-shore Zone—as might Lear's rhyme describe what the monks in their wattled *bangors* felt, when they saw, tossing, the steer-board lights on the spume—the long ship's nose at the estuary bar. Over the *traeth mawr* the heathen men put up flares.

Always pressing upon the ordered scheme from without (miscalculated by the tired elements within—the worst enemy), the unicorns (as Penda) not to be bought off, must be reckoned with, understood, baptized, assimilated, or left to run, misjudged, 'forbidden water'—no truck with, or (which cannot be) an attempted extermination. If not the former, then the latter; if the latter, then, in the end, the Duce's 'drama':

> O Balan my brother, thou hast slain me and I thee, wherefore all the wide world shall speak of us both.

There is a point of intersection where the here-and-nowness of the Charlemagne story meets the removed, intangible theme of the Arthur Myth. There is the conception of the leader—first among equals—his peers set circularly in their fellowship about him. He, 'chosen by adventure and by grace', the giver of gifts, the bridge-builder, the war-duke, his protection co-extensive with Christendom. And this scheme ordered that that might, perhaps, be tabernacled there, from which would flow to each, 'such drinks and meats as he best loved in this world,' and in whose brightness, 'either saw other . . . fairer than ever they saw afore.'

We have seen recently, in the illustrated papers, that crown which has been removed westerly to its earlier resting-place. To see it set unexpectedly among the week's crisis-photography brought immediately back to us that dream which has been, on and off, for many centuries, with variations of time and place, the half-waking, half-sleeping preoccupation of the European mind. Naturally for us of the western fringes, the names of Arthur and Charlemagne were evoked first, and the Angevin attempt also—for, not unconnected with that attempt, the Geoffrey–Wace–Layamon sequence started the hare that became the 'questing beast' for all our generations. The twelfth-century magnates knew both the Charlemagne epic and the beginnings of the Round Table cycle. If we should say, not without reason, that the bare idea of the Christian commonwealth has little relevance, can only be a child's tale, for us who look bewildered on the European scene today—yet was the vision very remote from the actuality of idealism, legalism and gangsterism that men knew seven or eight hundred years ago.

A friend has pointed out a characteristic of the *Song of Roland* which recurrently impressed her as she read. When 'the body' or limbs of the body of the person who speaks are referred to, they seem to be thought of as a separate possession might be thought of among ourselves. It would certainly be difficult to find a more unconscious expression of the conception of 'the body' as a tool to be used, sent about its business, subject to the 'person' to whom it 'belongs'. We seem very far from this detachment.

In conclusion it shall be said that the translator has succeeded, because of his own true poetic intuition (which has enabled his use of an exact, simple, evocative word-relationship) in rendering into modern English prose an ancient French metrical work, and absolutely to convince us of the poetry of the original. He uses no archaisms, no tricks, no artificial means, to convey the metre and rhythm, yet he makes us feel the kind of composition the original is—how it belongs to that time when a poem was made essentially to be declaimed to an assembly. It is to be hoped that he will find it possible to translate other *chansons de geste*.

It should be pointed out that this edition of the *Roland* is unique in the history of such attempts—for the translator is also the printer. His work as a printer is too well known for it to be necessary to speak of the excellence of the typography of this book. If he should serve as a model to translators, he should serve equally as a model to printers. It is a book which, in every way, deserves to be widely known. Those who have any sense of the historical significance of the song, which Taillefer, '. . . *qui mult bien chantout*,' is said by the scholars, in spite of Wace, not to have sung at Hastings; and those who enjoy formal excellence in a writing, or who are capable of responding to a most moving story; those also who appreciate good, and essentially rational, typography—all these ought to possess it.

The text of the Oxford MS. is printed at the conclusion of the translation—perhaps it would have been an advantage had text and translation been printed on alternate pages. I wish also that the modest and brief note under which the translator's name appears, had been more prolonged—some sort of general introduction would be an added stimulation for most readers.

I think Catholics, anyway, ought to give this book to their friends this Christmas, for, without Charlemagne, it is conceivable that you and I might not so easily associate the winter solstice with:

> The flour sprong in heye Bedlem
> That is bothe bryght and schen.

December 1938

The Death of Harold*

Considering the many articles in periodicals, letters to the press, radio programmes, etc., which this year or more precisely this autumn have recalled what is evoked by the word 'Hastings', I am surprised that no mention has been made of the intriguing tradition which links the latter days of Harold Godwinson with the city of Chester.

One has the impression from those whose specialist studies best equip them to elucidate for us ordinary readers the tangled evidence of contemporary or near-contemporary writers, that there is no absolute certitude as to where the Saxon leader was buried. Moreover, one cannot wholly shake off a difficult-to-define feeling of uncertainty touching the story of the identification of the grievously maimed figure from among the heaped dead and dying at the fractured linden-hedge at 'the place of slaughter'. Turning from the written accounts to the visual evidence of the needlework called the Tapestry; well, here indeed we have a work which fulfils the primary and immutable rule that in the arts 'form' and 'content' must be indissolubly wed. Hence the vitality of that work and its power to convince and to deeply move us. Whether this remarkable piece of artistry offers a valid re-calling, under the accidents of needlework, of a sequence of events already actualized in flesh and blood, is another matter; if only for the reason that (according to those who should know) it was commissioned by the Conqueror's

---

* A note written originally for *The Tablet*, in 1966. David Jones withdrew it, intending to add some further material based on the *Vita Haroldi*, the manuscript in the Harleian Collection in the British Museum, but his addendum remained incomplete, and the note unpublished.

brother; and works commissioned to show forth the triumph of the victor are not usually famed for their veracity.

However, quite apart from all this, and supposing I have exaggerated the uncertainties and that, by and large, the main facts are roughly as stated in our history books, I still think this Chester tradition deserves mention.

In 1188, Sylvester Gerald de Barri found that the men of Angevin Chester believed Harold Godwinson to have survived his defeat in Sussex, to have subsequently found refuge in northern Mercia, living devoutly as an anchoret in the environs of their city of Chester, to have frequented the Mass in one of their churches, to have disclosed his identity only at the approach of death and to have been buried in a church the dedication-name of which is not given in this twelfth-century account.

Gerald, for whom the affair of Hastings was as recent as is that of the Crimea for those of us today whose great-uncles or the like served in that campaign, neither substantiates nor derides the likelihood of this tradition. He contents himself with observing that Harold sustained many wounds, suffered the loss of his *left* eye (not his right) and, as a punishment for his perjury, the loss of the battle.

Freeman, writing his history of the Conquest in the sixties and seventies of the last century, discusses, in a note, this twelfth-century Chester tradition, but Freeman did not know of a more startling piece of evidence from a fourteenth-century source, showing the persistence of this tradition. This evidence was not available to the English reader until as recently as 1952.

We are indebted to Professor Thomas Jones, of the University College of Wales, Aberystwyth, for his labours in translating and carefully annotating the medieval Welsh chronicles. It chances that one version of those chronicles (Peniarth MS. 20) continues its entries down to the year 1332. It further chances that the last entry but one records how 'after the Calends of May' in that year the body of Harold wearing leathern hose, gilt spurs and a crown was found 'in the church of John at Chester' (i.e. St. John's without the Wall). Who that regal figure may have been is, I imagine, anybody's guess. The only interest that entry has for us is that some two and a half centuries after the completion of that great needlework with its crucial superscription *Hic Harold Rex interfectus est* (words which ring in the head with a finality akin to certain very familiar words in our now fast vanishing Latin liturgy), the men of Chester not only still stuck to their received tradition but took the finding of this body as confirmation of it.

Supposing we regarded this entry as worthless hearsay, and that no one had, in fact, disinterred anything at Chester, it would still be evidence of fourteenth-century gossip.

Here certain relevant points should, I think, be emphasized. This chronicle is written in Middle Welsh but is known to be a translation (as are the other versions of *The Chronicle of the Princes*) of a lost Latin original. Further, there are very cogent reasons for supposing this continuation or addendum (one copy at least of which appears to be of the fourteenth century) covering the period from about Lady Day 1282 to about the Feast of St. Michael 1332, to have been compiled by the Cistercians of Valle Crucis or, as it is called in the Welsh chronicles, the monastery 'in the Meadow of the Ancient Cross in Iâl'. The Commote of Iâl (from which derives the name of Yale beyond Brendan's herring-pool) was a very small district of Powys Fadog within easy reach of Chester, and the Meadow-of-the-Ancient-Cross is no more than twenty miles, I suppose, south-west of Chester wall. This makes it seem a bit too close for the recording of some wholly fictitious happening in that city.

Something, I think, must have been disinterred at Chester in the spring of 1332 which the men of that city and the gossip of adjacent territories imagined to be the body of Harold Godwinson.

If such an idea was circulating in the fourth year of the reign of Edward III, it seems to me to be a matter of some interest.

29 October 1966

The Welsh Dragon*

In *The Tablet* for March 2nd, the day following the Feast of St. David, there appeared, appropriately enough, an interesting article by Mr. H. W. J. Edwards on the Dragon flag of Wales. That article caused the reader to ruminate on the dragon and what it has, in varying contexts, connoted.

But first one feels bound to express some astonishment at the cases cited by Mr. Edwards of Welsh persons objecting to their national emblem on religious grounds. One would now be hardly surprised to learn that daffodils were under suspicion owing to these being called in Welsh *cennin Pedr*, Peter's leeks.

Down the centuries the *draco* has drawn the fire of many differing foes, but it is a new thing for the *draconarius* to speak ill of the *draco* committed, by the strange chances of history, to his keeping.

The reference to the purple dragon standard of the Spanish general Magnus Maximus is certainly of great interest. It was he who in the year 383, when in supreme command in Britain, mobilized all available troops in this island (with unfortunate consequences here), crossed the Strait of Dover, disposed of what little opposition there was in Gaul, passed into Italy and made himself master of the Western Provinces of the Empire until defeated by Theodosius (another Spaniard) at Siscia, now Siskat in Jugoslavia.

Perhaps his 'British' army was fed up, it was certainly far from home. It's a long, long way to Tipperary, and in the fourth century it was a long way from Dalmatia to Rutupiae, Eboracum,

---

* More than one version exists of this unpublished essay, undated but evidently of 1966, found among David Jones's papers; the text printed here is likely to have been intended as a contribution to *The Tablet*.

Deva or Segontium or from whatever Roman stations in Britain, large or small, Maximus had scraped the bottom of the barrel for likely troops.

I was surprised to learn, from Mr. Edwards's article, that a contingent of *palatini* known as the Seguntienses derived their name from having once been stationed at Segontium, the Roman fort near Caernarvon. One would not have imagined that from among all the contingents which Maximus drew from all parts of Britain those recruited from the outpost of Segontium should alone have retained their identity. It may be that the very radical changes made, two decades previously, in the entire defence-system of the island gave Segontium a new importance, or that for some quite other reason, unknown to us, its personnel attained some special status in the army of Maximus.

However that may be, when we turn from history and recorded fact to the realm of legend, it is interesting that in the medieval Welsh tale, *Breuddwyd Macsen Wledig* (The Dream of Maximus the Ruler), the lady of Macsen's dream is sought and found in a castle at the mouth of the River Saint or Seiont in Arfon, which can only be Segontium.

The historic and factual passing from Britain of the Expeditionary Force led by Maximus passed into a Welsh triad as 'One of the Three Levied Hosts which left this island never to return'. There have been many such since then.

I observe that the authority given for the use by Maximus of the *draco* as his imperial standard is Ammianus Marcellinus. Certainly there could not be a more reliable authority, for Ammianus had himself served in the imperial armies in the East and in the West; as a soldier he knew what he was talking about. Nevertheless his statement is surprising, for the *draco* is usually said to have been the normal cognizance-flag of a cohort, and was introduced into the Roman army some time in the second century, and may have been borrowed from the Parthians. I seem to recall that the Greek-speaking Byzantine Roman emperors had as their Royal Standard a flag called, I think, the *draconteion*. But Maximus was not a Byzantine emperor, but a usurper of the Western Empire.

We know that the *draco* was constructed on the principle of a wind-sock, the open end being made of some rigid material shaped to resemble a dragon's head, and that by the intake of the air its whole length, made of some textile such as silk, undulated out in serpentine fashion.

We know also that rather as in recent centuries the term ensign, the flag, became applied to the officer who carried it, so in sub-Roman Britain, *draco* became applied not indeed to the man who carried it, but to the leader before whom it was carried. Hence, to use Modern Welsh spelling, *draig* or *dragon* meant leader and *pendragon*, chief leader. Those competent in such matters assure us that *draig* and *dragon* are doublets, that both derive from *draco* and were, like hundreds of other Latin words, adopted, during the Roman–British period, into Brittonic Celtic, of which language Welsh is an immediate derivative. So that naturally these extensive Latin loan-words passed into the Welsh language and remain in it to this day, affording a linguistic link with the Roman Britain of sixteen centuries ago.

Our English word 'dragon' has a different history, being borrowed, according to *The Shorter Oxford English Dictionary*, from French into Middle English, and is and always was used with reference to the mythological monster. In Welsh tradition this is not so. Indeed, apart from one thirteenth-century Welsh prose tale and one passage in Latin by the ninth-century Welsh monastic, Nennius, the word dragon appears to have been used exclusively as a euphemism for leader, distinguished warrior, or hero.

I am given to understand that in the whole body of that highly professional and highly conservative tradition of bardic poetry, from the earliest poems (which contain elements of early seventh-century material) to the court poets of the thirteenth-century Welsh princes, no example has been found of the use of *draig* or *dragon* other than in this euphemistic sense of leader.

It was Geoffrey of Monmouth who in his *Historia Regum*, written before 1130, either in ignorance of this traditional use or for some reason of his own, went out of his way to invent or employ a complex story of a fiery dragon seen in the heavens and a gilt effigy made in imitation of it to be carried as a standard into battle, in order to account for Uther Pendragon's sobriquet. By this fanciful and naturalistic interpretation Geoffrey obscured for future generations the authentic meaning of *dragon* as leader, thus totally obscuring its further historic connection with the *draco* standard of a Roman cohort.

I speak under correction but I do not think there is any mention of the use of the dragon as a banner by the later Welsh princes whose rule ended on that tragic December day in 1282. But curiously enough I believe there is evidence of its being used by Plantagenet armies in wars against the Welsh.

But in 1400 or shortly after, a golden dragon on a white field was adopted as his standard by Owain Glyn Dŵr. It was to serve under that golden dragon that '*les gentz de Gales deins le ville d'Oxenford*' put aside their 'bokes clad in blak or reed, of Aristotle and his philosophye' and made their several ways across the shires from Merton or from further east, from the 'Soler-halle at Canterbregge', to resume, for the last time in history, the Thousand Years' War with the Saxon.

Whatever ambiguities attach to the origin of that revolt, it quickly assumed the character of a national rising, flaming up, now here now there, rather in the fashion of a religious revival, until all Wales was involved, and for a few years the actualities corresponded with Glyn Dŵr's style and title *Owynus dei gratia princeps Wallie*.

But already, by 1406, there were signs that boded ill for the golden dragon and by 1412 the actualities are best described by lines written six centuries earlier:

> The hall of Cynddylan is dark tonight
> Without fire without candle
> The hall of Cynddylan is dark tonight
> Without fire without song.

Owain's attempt was in the authentic Celtic tradition of defeat, the dying flames of his failure outshine success. Some modern Welsh scholars by no means given to overstatement or hero-worship think that had not Owain for a few brief years united

Wales under his leadership, there might not be a Welsh nation today.

Seventy years after Owain and his golden dragon had disappeared with a mysteriousness that matches the suddenness of his rise to power and the elusiveness of his whole career, another man, of very different character, adopted for his own purposes, as one of his three banners, the dragon standard. There is nothing mysterious or elusive about Henry Richmond nor any ambiguity as to his intentions. He came to claim the Crown of England and, owing to defection and treason in King Richard's army, he made good his claim.

It was natural enough that there was jubilation among the Welsh, for they saw in Richmond's victory at Bosworth that triumph of the 'dragon of Cadwaladr' which bardic vaticination had foretold.

What those Welshmen could not possibly foresee and what was to make nonsense of the vatic pretensions of their bards, was that half a century after the apparent triumph of the dragon, Section XX of the Act of Union would totally exclude the use of their language from the courts of justice, from 'Sessions, hundreds, leets, sheriffs' courts and all other courts', and would exclude from any office whatsoever any person not using the English tongue.

Shakespeare's 'Rice ap Thomas with a valiant crew' might not have lent their native valour to Richmond and his Red Dragon had they guessed that by the time Richmond's granddaughter was dead, in 1603, *les gentz de Gales* would already be on the way to that anglicization in speech, culture and outlook which, given a few more generations, would create a dichotomy whereby an anglicized upper stratum and a lower stratum retaining its Welshness, would, by and large, be the prevailing pattern.

There is an almost touchingly frank avowal of the undeviating Tudor policy of anglicization in the bill passed by Parliament authorizing the translation of the Scriptures into Welsh, for it stipulated that an English version must be placed side by side the Welsh version in the churches so that the people, by comparing the two, might 'the sooner attain to the Knowledge of the English Tongue'. That was in 1563.

Two centuries later, we find the dichotomous pattern firmly established and taken for granted, but now we are faced with a new upsurge. In speaking of the Glyn Dŵr revolt I suggested it was, in some ways, analogous to a religious revival, flaming up here and there until the whole country was involved, and now that we come to an actual religious revival and one that was destined to mould and condition the whole outlook of many generations of Welsh people, we can perhaps reverse the analogy and see hidden within the religious upsurge something in the nature of a national revolt.

As in geological formations, so in human affairs, there is such a thing as pseudo-morphosis, and 'pseudo' in this instance does not mean false but rather that the form taken is the only form possible given the circumstances and conditions. In this sense I believe the eighteenth-century Methodist Revival, as it is commonly called, was partly pseudomorphic in character in that the release of pent-up forces took the only form possible at that date: a passionate religiousness, betraying specifically Welsh modes of expression. In retrospect one can see in it a long delayed, transmogrified and unconscious Welsh vengeance for the Act of Union and the whole policy of anglicization.

This will, I know, appear far-fetched and certainly such a suggestion would have been indignantly repudiated by those great figures who fathered the movement and whose conscious concern was solely the spiritual regeneration of their countrymen. Their itinerant preachings, prayer-meetings and meetings for sacred song were in Welsh for precisely the same reason that similar activities associated with Whitefield and the brothers Wesley were in English, that is to say the language used was the only language understood by those whom the revivalists wished to convert.

As far as the traditional life of Wales, its folk-tales, its dancing, its folk-song, its harpers and fiddlers, its remembrance of a warlike and heroic past, all that was left for others to conserve—an archaeologically-minded parson here or a squire there and the new societies springing up among various Welshmen in Wales or in London devoted to a study of the Welsh past, or at a humbler level those unregenerate tavern-going roisterers, such as the one made familiar to English readers through *The Ingoldsby Legends*, who

> Thought upon Wales and her heroes of yore
> Of Griffith ap Conon and Owen Glendore.

All of this was vanity to the dedicated men of the new religiousness. Like Girolamo Savonarola they would have had a bonfire of the vanities and almost everything was vanity other than the Welsh Bible and the books of Welsh hymns. I suspect that a great deal of the folk-tale, folk-song and dance measures was lost owing to the puritanical and Calvinistic tendencies inherent in the movement. None the less in spite of its break with the Welsh past, Welsh Dissent did create an entirely Welsh Protestant religion-culture and in so doing helped to conserve the Welsh language.

We have seen how those Welsh clergymen of the Established Church who fathered the movement were concerned only for the spiritual care of their countrymen. But there were those in authority, prelates and other dignitaries, who were hostile, partly because as upholders of the Establishment they feared that this 'enthusiasm' would result in Dissent and partly because as heirs to the Tudor policy of anglicization they sensed a resurgent Welshness under an evangelical disguise.

Time was to show how well founded were their suspicions. Within a century of 1730 Wales was fast becoming a Nonconformist country. Hence, when later in the nineteenth century other reawakenings occurred, the literary revival, the growing importance of the *eisteddfodau*, the establishment of University Colleges, the growth of nationalist movements, etc., Welshness and Nonconformity were, for the world in general, regarded as as closely knit as Irishness and Catholicism.

Well, there have been many changes, new developments, realignments of all sorts, some of little consequence, some momentous in the pattern of Welsh society since the late nineteenth century, but there has been one constant factor: the Tudor policy of anglicization is still in progress. The dichotomy created in the sixteenth and seventeenth centuries between an anglicized gentry and a non-anglicized peasantry has of course changed its pattern in the wholly changed circumstances of modern times, but that dichotomy still has its long-term schizophrenic effects on Welshmen to this day. Indeed there are two dichotomies, one created by the Tudor attempt to turn Welshmen into Englishmen and the other, by a strange irony, brought about by the reaction against that policy, but which, as we have seen, took a religious form the particular nature of which tended to cut Welsh people off from their own past. Even today there are Welshmen for whom the history of their country, to all intents and purposes, begins with the great preachers and hymnologists of the Methodist Revival, and there are many more who still think that Bosworth was a Welsh victory. But, so it seems to me, however well-meaning the Tudor intentions, their Red Dragon so far from 'arising' or 'leading the way', was taken for a ride by that dynasty.

I was interested to learn that the Somerset dragon-device was connected with the Herberts, for I had previously supposed it to be the last link with the Dragon Standard of the West-Saxon kings, and I had further supposed it to have been borrowed from the Roman *draco*, rather as Bede tells us Edwin of Northumbria adopted certain Roman insignia in token of his imperium as Bretwalda. Had Hastings gone other than it did, the Dragon of Wessex rather than the Leopards of Anjou would figure on the Royal Standard of England.

But for once in a while History allowed herself a measure of poetic justice whereby the dragon has become accepted as the flag of the Cymry. I say poetic justice because of all the peoples of this island the Welsh alone afford a direct link with that late-Roman world from within whose crumbling imperium they emerged: strangely, ironically, bizarrely un-Roman, and quickly reverting to Celticity in all respects, yet signed with the Cross from their very beginnings because the Empire was already signed with that Sign, and their dominant line of princes originated late in the fourth century from Romano-British rulers operating under Roman auspices.

For Saxon, Angle, Jute, Scot or Pict the story is different.

At High Mass the laticlaved dalmatic of the deacon, the tunicle of the sub-deacon, and at any Mass the chasuble of the celebrant, remind us that once upon a time these were the ordinary garments of any person of status in the later Roman centuries. So the Red Dragon, while reminding us of the separate identity of the Welsh nation, reminds us also that once upon a time that *draig* was the *draco* of a Roman military formation. So it is an emblem round which innumerable men have died, which alone, apart from other considerations, lends *Y Ddraig* something of a sacral character.

If those Welsh Christians of the Campaign Group, mentioned by Mr. Edwards, must insist on Scriptural references, and remind us that the dragon or serpent is used in Scripture to symbolize malignant influences, they might also recall a very crucial exception: the brazen serpent lifted up by Moses in the wilderness prefigured the lifting up, on Bryn Calfaria, of Him who is the Pendragon of the whole militia of the heavenly armies.

1966

Welsh Culture*

Sir,
  That the observations of the parish-*periglor* in your issue of September 3rd are well founded is evident from the letters from some of your other correspondents.

By the accidents of history the Catholic Church has come to have alien connotations in Wales; but, your priest-correspondent says, these are found to be more superficial than might have been supposed; and who should be a better judge of all this than a priest with long parochial experience among a Welsh-speaking population?

That the notion that some essential uncongeniality exists between the Welsh mind and the mind of the Church should be given an appearance of validity by the attitude of some Catholics themselves is deplorable, all the more so if they are Welsh Catholics. It is however fairly easy to guess the psychology behind this attitude, if one gives sufficient attention to the complex factors, social, economic, racial and political, which are, in the area called Wales, as complex, as folded and faulted as is the actual geology of that area.

To understand the reasons for the respective attitudes with regard to 'Wales' *vis-à-vis* 'Catholicism' of the Welsh-Welsh, of the anglicized Welsh and of the English resident in Wales (to use crude, inexact, shorthand classifications), one must understand something of the background—the historic past and the historic present; then one may see that the respective attitudes are not only not surprising but practically inevitable; or rather a tendency towards those attitudes is inevitable.

* A letter to the Editor of the *Catholic Herald* which seems, in view of the postscript, not to have been sent; it remained unpublished.

Tendencies can however to some extent be mitigated and it would be very ironical indeed if the Catholic Church in Wales should deserve the suspicion which in my father's day fell upon the Church of England in Wales, that of being on the whole an anglicizing agency—and that in spite of many an 'old vicar' of rooted and passionate Welshness, who knew of Dafydd ap Gwilym as well as Wordsworth and Horace.

Actually the 'nationalist intelligentsia' complained of in this correspondence has done quite a bit to break down some of that suspicion, if only by its appeal to history which involves an enquiry into roots of a Catholic nature. But the reassessment of historical data and the re-examination of causes and all such patient work of scholars takes time to bear fruit. No doubt old and rooted bigotries and, what are sometimes worse, new crude conceptions and make-shift ideas all too easily prevail in Wales; and where in the world do they not prevail?

To a large extent, again by the accidents of history and the imperatives of geography and geology, the modern Catholic missions tend to serve the industrial and built-up areas and the coastal holiday-belts and to infiltrate inward from these zones up the more open valleys, following the in some cases identical routes by which new influences have penetrated the Welsh upland zone for three thousand years or more, from Neolithic man to the men of the Industrial Revolution. The earliest Dissenting doctrines travelled by much the same course as the Bronze Age ornaments and no doubt the Bronze Age theologies.

It follows that the 'Old Religion' will tend to return in association with the new material-culture waves. So that the men in the birettas tend, on the whole, to appear along with the multiple-stores, the prefabs, the flicks and the rest, and also along with things more valuable than these. That is all right—in the sense that one cannot quarrel with the accidents of history: what Clio has sung she has sung, even though we may not always like the tune. But all the more reason that the Old Religion should be seen as a thing having had long affinity with the real past of the real Wales; seen as a returning thing, as a returned native and as something which can direct rather than frustrate the *hiraeth* of the

Cymry—which is, after all, what the Church claims to do with the *Heimweh* of any people, or with the fervent aspirations of any of us; those things of which Cicero spoke: 'the ties which hold us to our own and all that belongs to our birth'.

One of your correspondents says that priests should learn Welsh because in some parts that is the only language spoken.[1] Well, that is a good reason certainly; but what matters also is that there should be an understanding of the ethos behind that language; for it is that ethos which concerns us lest it be lost and so lost to the sum of those realities which it is, I imagine, our business to conserve if possible.

There are some who do not speak that language or who have only a partial acquaintance with it or to whom English is habitual —who 'think in English' yet who nevertheless think with a Welsh mind and who are most likely to understand the meaning of the Church if her representatives are fully cognizant of that mind. Incidentally there are, I think, in that mind, certain clues to a better understanding of some of the basic things concerning the island of Britain as a whole.

One must not take a mechanical view of this matter. It is not a question of linguistical statistics. Not: How many in this area speak no English? Not that at all; but a question of discerning the *genius loci* of this or that terrain. The whole terrain of Wales has many differing *numina* and it may well be found that in an obscure way and at a deep level the more Welsh the *numen* is, so much the more will there be found to be Catholic affinities; a view which the experience of the parish priest referred to above tends to confirm and which one's own bookish and theoretic opinions lead one to suppose.

It is further objected that such culture as Wales possessed in early times was early Roman. How could this be other? Nevertheless, just how 'Roman' and how 'Celtic' the milieu of such rulers as Cunedda or Maelgwn Gwynedd actually was, is *precisely* what scholars would give a very great deal to know.

[1] There are said to be about 300 Catholic priests in Wales, and I have been told that less than 3 per cent of these know the Welsh language. Could any of your correspondents say whether this percentage is correct?

There is so provokingly little evidence for these formative years; and although it is now more possible for scholars to say that such and such is the most probable, the almost total lack of archaeological evidence still makes it most unwise to dogmatize.

But surely one of the interesting things about the Welsh tradition is its preservation of hidden links with the Empire, so that a district-name as Welsh in feeling as Rhufoniog hides a Latin form, implying the land of Romanus, a son of Cunedda.

The collection of Welsh medieval tales translated exactly a hundred years ago this August, by Lady Charlotte Guest, and rather inaccurately called, by her, *The Mabinogion*, has been cited in this correspondence as being of mixed French and Welsh provenance. This again is totally misleading especially for the general reader, who is unacquainted with the background. Of these twelve tales, three alone might, at a pinch, be called 'French' in so much as they are native Welsh versions of three romances, similar French metrical versions of which were composed by Chrétien de Troyes. Five other stories in the collection show in various ways and in very varying degrees the general influence of the feudal world, but are saturated in native feeling and embody very ancient material; and the remaining four, which are each a *mabinogi*, properly so called, are four branches of one cycle, pertaining to pre-Christian common Celtic, and perhaps pre-Celtic, mythology, overlaid by a few post-Christian ideas and a local Welsh geography; e.g., the Celtic Otherworld is made to be situated on the borders of Pembrokeshire.

Another matter which has been raised concerns the nature or extent of Welsh influence on the cultural tradition of England.

The clue to not unimportant but not easy to define elements in the English literary deposit is discoverable in influences emanating from Welsh sources. These influences are more implicit than explicit, more undercurrents than surface be- haviours, more on the whole a matter of content than of form.

To indicate some of the more or less obvious but diverse ways, occasions and periods by which or in which these influences may be felt in English literature, one has only to recall that from Geoffrey of Monmouth and the writers and patrons of the

Anglo-Norman–Norman-Welsh world onward, these under-currents can be detected; and in such a diversity of writers as Drayton, Camden, Spenser, Milton, Shakespeare, Blake, Tenny-son, and in that very English phenomenon the Pre-Raphaelite movement and in its more recent derivatives, or collaterals. That is to say the English deposits would be recognizably different without it.

It appears in lesser or greater degree in this or that guise or rather disguise whenever the roots of the Island mythology and story are tapped. Perhaps one might say that it is more of a ground swell than a direct wind. And that is exactly what one would expect considering the factors and conditions.

To leave these traditional undercurrents and to refer to some-thing rather different; the English school of metaphysicals, Donne, Traherne, Vaughan, Herbert, Crashaw and Cowley. It is not without interest that so high a percentage as four of these six should have names with Welsh or Welsh-border affinities.

These then are a few of the ways in which a Welshness has had influence in England, an influence somewhat pseudomorphic in character.

Finally it would be unseemly not to refer to an influence in again a different category; this time an influence to do with form. To Gerard Manley Hopkins, S.J., goes this palm, in that he, being intrigued by the old Welsh metrical forms (*cynganeddion*) and experimenting with them to some extent, profited by that acquaintance, so that they influenced his particular and uniquely important contribution to the common tradition of English poetry. The compressed meanings in the words, the subtle correspondences and consonance of the exactly chosen vocabu-lary, the interweaving and the compounds. . . . We do not know how much of this may be derived from his, unhappily curtailed, study of the Welsh prosody; but those who are most competent to speak of that very strict prosody agree that all of these qualities are especially characteristic of it.

So here again Welsh influence is to be detected as an under-current, and in this case *not* an undercurrent of traditions but one of technique and inward feeling, that has made its contribution, through the genius of this totally Victorian Oxford Jesuit, towards the poetry of the Island as a whole—indeed towards a re-vivification of that poetry. For most certainly the appearance of Hopkins's verse in the 1920s was a red-letter day for all who love the Muses of Britain.

9 September 1948   DAVID JONES

P.S. Since writing this letter your issue of September 17th has appeared, containing Walter Dowding's admirable summary, which really makes this letter of mine unnecessary.

                                                            D.J.

Art in Relation to War*

Enough has been written in recent years on the subject of Art in almost every possible relationship to make one chary of adding more, nevertheless, the heightened sense of the nature of our age which the war has occasioned, brings a new necessity to examine some of those relationships. The time of writing is 1942–3 and what is written is, to some extent, and for the writer, a conversation with himself, in which problems long since discussed (during the last twenty years with various friends) with no very positive conclusions, are again turned over to see if they look much the same. It is written with reference to man as artist as distinct in category from man as moral being. As all men share the quality of being artists it may re-echo some of the thoughts which twist and turn and seek to gain some sort of equilibrium in the minds of all of us at this time. The reader is asked to consider it as a tentative attempt to give expression to some of the questions rather than as offering answers or solutions. It may be found to wander from the objective to the subjective, but the nature of the thing discussed and its interrogatory attitude make this perhaps excusable. Because the Land is Waste (or seems so to the writer) it seeks to do what the hero in the myth was rebuked for not doing, i.e. it seeks to 'ask the Question'. Although, alas, unlike the myth, it does not suppose that in asking the question the land can be 'restored'. Although if all the world asked the question perhaps there might be some fructification—or some 'sea-change'.

Considered historically 'war' is one of the most noticeable

* In the original typescript, revised and corrected by David Jones but unpublished, the title is 'Art in Relation to War and Our Present Situation'.

activities of man, and 'art' certainly the chief means by which we know man from the rest of travailing creation. Man is the only maker, neither beast nor angel share this dignity with him. It is customary to speak of the 'Art of War', and as man's warfare must at least involve his qualities as artist it would seem that this common and universal description of war as an art, is, to this extent, valid.

But there is more to it than that, for on top of the evident existence of some kind of art in war, there is the enormous influence, direct and oblique, of war upon the other arts of man. The world's literature alone makes this evident, both as to form and content. Thus far in historic times war has exerted, along with human love and the mysteries of religion, incalculable influence upon every kind of 'poet' in whatever material he prosecuted his making.

But this should not lead us to suppose that, if we could conceive of a society with no war (in any of its historical significances), no human love (in any of its 'romance' connotations), no religion (in any of its recognizable forms), the arts would suffer cessation, though they might seem to be deprived of much that has hitherto informed them.

It is important, in this connection, to remember what some recent scholarship has indicated, concerning the more pacific nature of archaic societies. Mankind has become more, not less, warlike—that is not perhaps the best way to express it, but rather man's cultures have become more and not less determined by wars, war has become more an 'instrument of policy'. The contention is that the warrior-cultures succeeded to the more pacific archaic cultures, and that even today some of the few surviving primitive peoples are essentially pacific. The prevailing notion on which one was brought up that man had shown a fairly steady progression from the 'ape and tiger' stage, towards a more pacific state, can perhaps be accounted for in two ways: both from the fact of our receiving part of our tradition from those very warrior-cultures which in pre-history began to dominate the world, and also from the fact that ideas of progress and enlightenment, both religious and secular, and dreams of restoring some 'golden age' of primitive peace *may* reflect some dim remembrance in the race-consciousness of an actual pre-power-politic state, when Mars was still the god of agriculture and not yet the god of war, when 'our Arthur' was hardly the Bear, still less the *Dux*, was not yet a Celtic battle-deity, let alone a Roman cavalry leader, was not even a male, but as yet, perhaps, some female goddess of fruition—not the warrior, but the creatrix.[1]

Mr. Christopher Dawson says in his *The Age of the Gods*: 'History as a rule gives an account only of the warrior peoples and the conquering aristocracies, but their achievements were only rendered possible by the existence of a subject peasant population of which we seldom hear', and in a later chapter: 'The earlier changes of culture in Europe had been predominently peaceful. There is no sign that the transition from the palaeolithic to the neolithic age or the expansion of peasant culture in Eastern or Central Europe, or even the beginnings of the age of metal in the Mediterranean were due to any degree to warlike invasions. In fact from their open settlements and the lack of weapons, war can have played little part in the life of the neolithic peasant peoples.' And again of the earlier states of the Nile valley, 'society was not organised for war as in later times' and citing Professor Breasted, 'the Egyptians of the Old Kingdom were essentially unwarlike.' All this against the sweeping assertion that 'man is a beast of prey' and that primitive society was one 'in which the weaker were constantly killed off and possibly eaten by the stronger—*Homo homini lupus*, as the Romans said—regardless of the fact that even beasts of prey do not usually prey upon each other'.

And again of Troy he says, 'Unlike the peaceful unwalled cities of Crete, Troy was a powerful fortress with walls and gateways and bastions.' I think there is a great 'poetic' significance in this. For when one thinks of the enormous importance to us of the whole Trojan story, how it is woven in all our legend and

[1] According to some scholars the legend of Arthur contains all these ingredients, starting with the Gaulish female deity Artio associated with a bear-symbolism.

literature, how it is the symbol of 'love and war' for us Europeans and especially for us of this island,[2] it is illuminating to find proper scholarship and research pointing to it as one, at all events, of the *first* strongly fortified places. It is always pleasing to find symbol and thing signified having a factual relationship, whatever the sign, and whatever the thing signified, good or bad. To take an example from a writing of fiction: Mr. John Cowper Powys, in his recent novel *Owen Glendower*, in introducing the figure of Broch o' Meiford (perhaps the most interesting and convincing figure in the book), hints at this same 'primitive pacifism'—by means of this figure of prodigious physical strength, inheriting the racial memories of the megalithic age, before the bronze-using Celtic aristocracies had made all things depend on war and the hero-drama. It is worth remembering that while it is customary to think of the 'Celts' as the 'poets' and the 'seers', they were in fact proto-typic of, and pre-eminent as, warrior-aristocracies, imposed on an earlier and quite different complex of races (i.e. the 'Peasant Cultures')—this conflict of strains is particularly observable in most so-called 'Celts' even to this day and perhaps accounts for some mysterious contradictions in people of the modern world and particularly perhaps of this island, and most of all in Wales.[3]

All our tradition is of war, and the hero at his tasks, either to gain or defend a land or to gain the 'giant's daughter', but behind this we are half-conscious of traditions more 'cosmic'—less wholly warlike, more magical, from the archaic peoples, compared with whom Celt and Teuton are chiefly to be distinguished in that the first was anterior in establishing a warrior-rule and seems always to have been the better artist, as the Hallstatt and

[2] Because of the Troy–Brute–Britain myth-cycle which from the twelfth century onwards plays its part in our Romances and chronicles and even got in our politics, as for instance, the letter sent by Edward I to Boniface VIII with regard to the English claim to the dominion of Scotland.

[3] How often does one hear it said that Mr. So-and-so is a 'typical Welsh Celt, dark and small and introspective, etc.'. Whereas it appears that the 'Celts' of antiquity were large, grey-eyed, ginger or blond, and although something approximating to this type is to be found among Welshmen, it seems that the older non-Celtic elements, at all events physiognomically, predominate.

La Tène cultures show. And later, in historic times, the Celtic poetry that survives, though, like the pure Northern sagas, it is concerned so largely with battle, treats of that subject with a difference and that difference *may* not be wholly undue to the Celtic absorption of the pre-Celtic 'wisdom'? It is an interesting speculation. However that may be, as far as historic times are concerned, for us in the West the arts and the art of war have been in a rather special relationship. We have thought very much in terms of war, and the arts have in various ways reflected that thought, because the artist does not determine the nature of his society, he accepts whatever is to hand from his environment and conditions, he 'illustrates' in the strict meaning of that word, and keeping in mind its origin, what his particular culture and time makes available to him. It is of course true that a state of war is harmful to the practice of certain arts, a certain degree of stability and tranquillity is necessary. In the continually warring unstable societies of the Highland Zone in Britain (in medieval Wales, for instance), a highly intricate and sophisticated poetic tradition could flourish, but not the arts of painting and sculpture.

But here and now we are considering more the effect of large-scale war upon city-civilizations in the later stages of their development, and here we can speak with intimacy and understanding, and not without feeling. Many of us have had direct participation in one large-scale war inflicted on just such a civilization, and now all of us, in varying intensity, are experiencing the infliction of another and larger war upon that same civilization grown a little more complex, far more disillusioned, more highly organized, more megalopolitan, more neurotic. We need not speak theoretically, but experientially, not as students of history or exponents of past cultures, but as persons who have seen with our own eyes and felt with our own bowels. We need no longer compare theoretically the panoply and the bravery with the sordidity and grief, or speak any more of 'old unhappy things'. The 'battles' are not 'long ago'—they are today and also tomorrow. We have a fairly good hang of the whole proceedings and the mixed reactions. It is not in the nature of a boast but a modest statement of fact, for this generation to declare that it has some understanding of these things.

We can guess, better than our immediate forebears, something of what a paid foot-soldier at Crécy *felt* about a damp bow-string and the heavy Picardy mud, and the relationship between these immediate, intimate, bodily-known things and the Plantagenet pretensions, the rising will of the French monarchy towards supremacy on French soil, and the credits of the Florentine banking houses, without which, they say, no English transport could have weighed anchor, or any *bombarde* discharged those shots which presaged the 'scream of the twelve-inch shrapnel', and the coming world of material-as-power, and the end of the medieval dream, for dream it was, even if a 'vision'.[4]

Because of our immediate contact with warfare we know that the lines in Michael Drayton's *Agincourt*,

> Down the French peasants went
> Our men were hardy

mean about as much to us as, are as nauseating as:

> Jerry can't take it.

Whether we trust our personal, intimate, truly known, valid experiences or not is another matter, for all of us tend to deny or forget what we have experienced in deference to some 'general line' or out of respect for some other necessity—and the necessity may be real enough. But this can have serious artistic consequences. I am in no position to speak of the prudential ones.

There have been, one way and another, during the last century a number of voices asking us to consider the relationship between the arts and our society, and most recently and more explicitly Mr. Eric Gill has contributed his diagnosis. All that was true in what such men said with regard to our age in peace is seen to be more clearly true now that our age has been compelled, as all

---

[4] We may note that the development of banking and the development of artillery were contemporaneous. Explosions are grand things but they cost money, and the bigger they are the more they cost and now they cost all there is, and that is one of the meanings of 'total' war.

ages are compelled, to implement its particular technique as a technique of war.

When Spengler, with a kind of satisfaction at the grimness of our destiny, advised young men, if they would excel, to abandon the muses for technics—'the sea instead of the paint-brush, politics instead of epistemology', he too was showing a prophetic astuteness, even if we think it was the astuteness of an evil genius. He, so to say, bid the devils believe, but not tremble; for he believed it to be the devils' hour. The hour of the daemons of power that take possession of the Waste Land when true cultural life is at its lowest ebb and the 'young hero' has not yet restored 'the maimed king' and the time of resuscitation is not yet. When all is 'doing' and there is no 'making'. When the end is all, and the means nothing. When there is no organic growth, but only organization and extension of dead forms.

The artist, however, in whatever age, and whatever the determined destiny, has both to believe and to tremble and somehow or other, to affirm delight.[5]

'The goal of painting is delight,' said Poussin. No one ever said a truer word. Where there is no delight there is no art. Bishop Andrewes said, as far as I can quote from memory: 'Even militar persons, who come with fire in one hand and a sword in the other, seek peace, as seek it we must all, in the end.' He might have said, not 'peace', but 'delight', with equal truth. He was of course referring to the end to which war proceeds, that is, to peace; but he might, with equal accuracy, have been referring to the actual *art* of war, which being an art, must seek delight— the delight of the 'splendour of form', without which delight man is a beast.

The most convinced and clear-sighted pacifist, whether Christian or not, or the person suffering and outraged by one of the many contingencies of war, who takes up and reads a description of brilliant strategy, or an account of a well-executed tactical movement, is compelled to experience a measure of delight whether he would or no. Nelson, writing to Lady

[5] Remember William Blake's question to another artist, which ran something like: 'Do you, sir, paint in fear and trembling?'

Hamilton before Trafalgar of the feelings shown by the senior officers of the fleet when he disclosed to them his dispositions of battle, says: 'Some shed tears, all approved—it was new—it was singular—it was simple.' Is this the *splendor formae*[6] of St. Thomas 'shining in the proportioned parts' of the art of naval attack? Is it a clear example of the famous definition of beauty:[7] 'That which being seen' (to the eyes of the mind by practised sailors) 'pleases' (to the extent of tears)?

'It was new, it was unique, it was simple, I could have wept.' These might be the words of any one of us describing our reactions to the sudden realization of form in a great work of art; and though not often in a lifetime are we privileged with an impact of that intensity, all of us have at least once or twice experienced similar emotion.

But there is another side to all this, or rather many other considerations. When we contemplate the art of war, two lines, reiterated, are apt to echo in our heads: ''Tis some poor fellow's skull, said he', and 'But 'twas a famous victory'. Or that line from the earliest of all 'war-poetry' that this island has produced, the line from Aneirin's *Gododdin* which turns for a moment from praising the swordsmanship of the heroes to reflect that: 'His sword rang in mothers' heads'. (Horace's 'war, detested of mothers' means the same, but does not lift up an objective image, as the Welsh poet does, and which the best poetry must.) We share the conflicting and unresolved emotions of old Kaspar, Wilhelmine and Peterkin, and of those of Southey himself, and of the Welshman, Aneirin: for the sixth century no less than the eighteenth shared our dilemma. And it is the business of a poet in the sixth, or eighteenth, or any century, to express the dilemma, not to comment upon it, or pretend to a solution.

[6] In some instances which occur later, it may be complained by some that I fail to distinguish between 'form' in the philosophical sense and 'form' as we use it vulgarly of a relationship of shapes. But the 'form' of which we speak as artists is only the visible expression of the *forma* that the philosophers speak about. The 'informing principle' determines the relationship of shapes (of whatever sort) that we commonly call 'form'.

[7] *Id quod visum placet* (That which being seen, pleases).

But with regard to the art of painting *qua* painting, we have no grisly relics 'so large and smooth and round' to disturb our play, to haunt our delight, and no outraged sisters to cry: 'Why, 'twas a very wicked thing', but only, for the artist: 'Great praise the Duke of Marlboro' won', and, for the work itself: the putting to rout of formlessness, the 'famous victory' of design, and leading captive of delight.

So it may seem, to the onlooker, to the person who appreciates the picture, but for the practitioner, the splendour of form, even in so innocent an art as painting, is only achieved by something analogous to, though vastly different in kind and degree from, the stress that accompanies war. That the analogy should seem so far-fetched and forced as to be wilfully obscurantist is only because all the conditions, the forms, modes and accidents, of the two arts are so much at variance. But in so far, and only in so far, as they can both be called arts, they both proceed towards 'splendour of form', and, as arts can be practised only by men, it becomes a truism to say that they both share, in some way or other, the stress and storm, the contradictions of the 'body of this death' and that both seek to be delivered from it.

We have heard of the German theorist of the eighteenth century who said that in ideal war, the campaign would be won without the loss of a single soldier, without, in fact, a shot being fired, by reason of the skill in the disposition of units and materiel —here is the human mind, attempting to conceive strategy and tactic on an angelic plane, here is the irrational lion that war lets loose, and the rational lamb of genius that war demands, led by the young child who sees all things with an 'innocent eye'—in fact led by the artist as strategist. We can smile indulgently at that dream of that most civilized of centuries, or be merely enraged, because of the actuality that we know so well, yet it would be appropriate in us not to smile too broadly, for we ourselves have indulged, on a bigger scale, and with less refinement, in illusions not less absurd. All of us have done so, except perhaps those remaining inarticulate, 'unlettered' men and women who still retain a native and shrewd understanding of the nature of this world, who may, along with their labouring lives, have inherited a realist tradition stretching back to the age of 'the pitiless bronze' and beyond. Who know that there can be no garnished fowl on the dressed dish, with all the arts and furnitures of the feast, without the practice of another art, on a neck, in the yard; no matter what the sensibilities, or the uncarnivorous aspirations or the humane talk of those at table, who are 'about to receive from Thy bounty'. These are less evasive as to this duality between splendour of form and the necessary means, by way of immolation and destruction, to achieve it. Artists, also, as such, are acquainted with this duality.

It is 'the business of the moral theologian to speak and of the prince to act' when arts are practised which, from a moral point of view, outweigh in their immolation and destruction any splendour of form they are likely to achieve. But as all are 'moral theologians' and all 'princes' as far as an ultimate decision of conscience is concerned, some may and do have to speak and act in disagreement with both the prince and his moral supporters, and bear the consequences of this disagreement in various ways and degrees. That men, animate creatures, capable of delicately balanced individual perfection, should be used by the masters of war as the masters of other arts use their inanimate material (mere stuff which is dead till man shapes it), introduces an element with regard to the art of war absent from most other arts, and is sufficient cause for moralists to hold their heads in thought, for men of affairs to tremble at the exigencies of their art of rule, and provides some excuse for us common men to tend to say to each other: 'Damn them all, all who rule and all who counsel', or: 'Let us curse God', according to how, in our heat and indignation, we simplify the issue, or in what direction we seek our scapegoat.

In spite of all this, as artists, we cannot deny, in as far as any art still resides in war, that the art of war is capable, at all events, of a form-creating quality.

No wonder in such times as these, when the art most practised is that of war, and practised in such a manner as to retain its ancient and irrational concomitants in almost every respect, and indeed in some respects is made more grievous by the extremely rational techniques and applications of those same irrationalities, when it is now not only a 'war hated of mothers' but a war upon mothers scarcely less than upon sons, by the necessities inherent in a 'war of peoples',[8] no wonder at such a time, if other arts than war should be looked to by some merely by way of 'alleviation'—for it is native to us to find delight in form somehow or other.

In such an age, there may well be the paradox of an appreciation of the arts, an interest in them, because this age at war, even more than at peace, accelerates those deprivations which in any case characterize it. Its technical and utilitarian demands become more all-embracing, affect far larger numbers and classes of the population, are more difficult to evade, are more exacting. And it must be said, more degrading, at least for many, though doubtless for some there are compensations, real compensations both 'bodily and ghostly'—it would be inaccurate to deny this, so let's not deny it, or the denial will return like a boomerang sooner or later.[9]

In our civilization one stratum after another is reduced to formlessness, or the form is so vast and at such a remove, and its shaping in the hands of so few and the general inhumanization so against our natures, that many people consciously or unconsciously tend to cast their eyes to those remaining arts which in as far as they can be practised are still outside the new leviathan. Hence most of the 'artiness', the collecting of 'art-works', the joy in 'antiques' and the other attempts to find delight where delight still appears to reside.

I take it as true that any hunger for any art-form is a good in

[8] It would seem that codes and rules of warfare can sometimes be observed when the issue is between groups whose war-aims are limited and within a common structure—but when it comes to really serious trials of total strength, then necessity will stop at nothing. This has been more and more clear as the present contest develops. Neither the enemy nor ourselves have shown any regard for any limitations of method that might seriously endanger the end in view—total victory. This is now taken for granted, though still covered by aspirational phrases and platitudes.

[9] Ruling out all romantic illusions, it is undeniable that 'the trenches' are objectively a 'better' life than that to which vast numbers are condemned by their avocations in the 'peace-time' world of today.

itself. The *'panem et circenses'* of late civilizations, the means used by authority to meet the demands of delight-hungry men, to alleviate, to palliate the lot of the city proletarians, whether rich or poor, low-brow or high-brow (for all[10] are 'proletarians' now in essential culture, none are rooted or integrated), may and does include a variety of the arts, from 'the pics' to exhibitions of pictures. Although painting under these conditions may be considered a palliative, a 'cloak' against our cultural December, yet it need not be, and cannot be and is not, only a cloak, for the creation of form and the delight it occasions to the eye of the mind, is, to use loosely a theological analogy, a 'good' in itself, and not like Luther's 'righteousness' imputed, but rather like the 'sanctity' of accurate theology, actual and native. For there is nothing more native to man than this good which comes from form.

Man as a moral being hungers and thirsts after justice and man as artist hungers and thirsts after form, and although these are ultimately one, because of the truth of that best of sayings that 'the Beauty of God is the cause of the being of all that is', nevertheless for us they are not one, not yet, not by any means. Although in the processes and tragic developments of successive civilizations, in the world of 'fact' as opposed to the dreams of 'progress', man may be denied both those desires of his soul, yet those hungers cannot be eradicated, and in those thirsts he knows the chief proof of his being a 'stranger and a sojourner'. For even in the arts, which of all things require material and a material world for their existence, he is foxed and betrayed and humbled in culture after culture. Not only the Preface for Christmas, not only Norman vaulting, not only Piero della Francesca's *Nativity*, but Rommel's desert tactic and Nelson's Nile touch, are empty of all significance—'they need not have bothered', unless form is good in itself. And for a thing to be good in itself it must be part of the whole good and that good is clearly not 'of this world'.

---

[10] It is a continual cause of surprise that even cultivated, comfortably off, relatively leisured people now appear to require the dope and vulgarity of the cinema and all the rest of it just as much as the masses, though they have not the same excuse.

For here 'goods' do not fulfil each other, they cancel out as often as not. In view of the fact that so much is talked of the 'development' of one art-form from another, it is necessary to state that there is a sense in which this notion of development and evolution and fulfilment is altogether misleading. Only in a crude material sense, in the sense of sequence, is it strictly true to speak of the fulfilment or development of one 'period' of art, in or from another. Baroque may be a flowering and rioting from Gothic and classical forms, but in the hour of its triumph it was the death of both.

There is not so much a fulfilment as a struggle, in which these forms go down before those forms, and their splendours and refinements can only be set side by side without mutual antagonism and destruction, 'in heaven'. Here and now they can no more blossom in the same garden at the same time, than can a March daffodil and an August gillyflower. Certainly there are under many forms the 'second springs', and the 'later religiousnesses', the revivals and 'neo-primitive' activities of all kinds, but these, however glorious and compelling, are ephemeral, and though no less genuine and valuable for that, are outside the main cultural trend, and are, as it were, of the greenhouse rather than the garden or the hedgerow—are rather specialist productions and *tours de force*.

Certainly men never more needed to contemplate form, they need all there is to remind them that all evidence to the contrary, the end of man is happiness. The 'parts that are united in one' in an art-work may be, for some, the most convincing analogy which they can get in this world of the 'proportioned parts' of the heavenly city, to delight in which, religion says, is part of our redeemed destiny.

There is the thorny question of the effect of particular wars on particular arts. We may speak very briefly of the apparent effect on English painting of the last war and of this. As far as I can see the last war stimulated, in some artists at all events, the creative ability—provided some element that might otherwise have been lacking. It is too complicated a subject to pursue at length here. I will quote what I wrote, five years ago, in another place: 'I think the day by day in the Waste Land, the sudden violences and the long stillnesses, the sharp contours and unformed voids of that mysterious existence, profoundly affected the imaginations of those who suffered it.'[11]

There is evidence, from the series of exhibitions of war pictures organized by the National Gallery, that, at least in some of its aspects, this war has already been not unproductive of some interesting painting—and it is early days yet. The saying of Wordsworth about 'emotion recollected in tranquillity' is most important with regard to the artist's reaction to war, and his subsequent expression in form of those reactions.

We are faced with the hard-to-express question of 'symbol'. Our age, the age of technical perfections, of function, of material efficiently directed towards a material end, is of its nature un-symbolic, or anti-symbolic, or rather its 'technics' are its 'symbols'. Now the artist, one way or another, deals in symbols, as far as his content is concerned, he deals, obscurely it may be, obliquely, in however hidden a fashion, with things that are lifted up, carried about, adored. He is, at bottom and always, an inveterate believer in 'transubstantiations' of some sort. The sign must *be* the thing signified under forms of his particular art.

The *Materialismus* that our present enemy talks about is real enough and has surprising implications. The modern world would have to substitute for each Mass an actual crucifixion if it would make the Mass integrated with itself in the sense in which I speak. It is alien to the whole conception of 'sacrament', and the artist is concerned all the time with something akin, or rather analogous, to 'sacrament', he seeks always an efficacious sign. Now the artist is at once on the side of the beasts and of the angels, his *Gemeinschaft* must include the beast 'whose hide is covered with hair' and the nine choirs, 'the nine bright shiners', who sing: *Pleni sunt coeli et terra gloria tua*—the *et terra* is important. Now it will matter to the artist what kind of 'bread' is available to him when he presumes to 'show again under other forms' the eternal things, and art is nothing if it fails in this. He is not always convinced that the 'bread' available today is 'valid matter',

[11] *In Parenthesis*, Preface (1937).

because it has itself been emptied of creatureliness on the one hand and is alien to 'sign' (or is patient only of being a sign of itself, that is of material-as-power) on the other.

I am not capable of expressing logically and convincingly exactly what I intend, but perhaps this conveys some hint of the delicate problems involved.

It should be noted that all this has immediate bearing on that turning towards 'still-life', 'landscape', and the shying away from 'content', the search for expression in 'the abstract', or again the search for it, at the other extreme, in the neo-romantic, all of which opposing tendencies characterize the work of many of the better artists of today. Not any one of them can be said fully to 'illustrate' the age in the sense, let us say, that Paolo Uccello's battle pieces illustrate the later 'chivalry', or the animal paintings on the rock-walls of the Dordogne or at Altamira, illustrate the Magdalenian culture. I mean here by 'illustrates', what I mean by it in an earlier paragraph (page 127), that is, as 'making illumined', 'bringing light to bear upon'. It is a word, like so many other of our best words, which has got somewhat worn and devitalized in its current use. So that today 'an illustration' is almost a derogatory term. The present world-feeling is rather to be looked for, is better 'illustrated', in a bomber plane, or an electric elevator, than in painting, and certainly rather than in a 'painting of' either.[12] But this is far from saying that painting now is 'unimportant', of no consequence, better not bothered with

[12] A realization of this is shown in certain schools of painting where a conscious or well-intentioned attempt has been made to adjust the sensitivities of artists to the forms and feeling of the contemporary scientific inventions and gadgets. This seems on the face of it reasonable enough, and is at least a realistic attitude. It has produced a few interesting and many exceedingly boring works. As a theory it does not take into account the complex nature of man, and it is inevitably intellectualized, forced, and undigested. Poetry, and painting is poetry, is essentially arrived at by the long digestion of certain conceptions, you can never say 'ought' to it. It is useless to say that Keats 'ought' to have sung of the primitive wonders of locomotion which his age was witnessing. 'Puffing Billy' is only now beginning to have some poetic significance. And an almost reverse thing is sometimes true. Some of Picasso's paintings of many years ago indicate forms and a disposal of shapes now seen by everyone in aerial photography.

(Spengler's error, which seriously mars his observations on the position of the arts in the West).

The truth is that a considerable degree of genuine and valid expression has accompanied the practice of painting in our days, in works which could not have been created in any days other than ours, so that obliquely and almost, in a fashion, by antithesis, they do reflect the present world-feeling—or rather they reflect, by their extreme sensitivity and other qualities, a kind of reaction against the functionalism, the *Materialismus*, the utility, the technics. If they are typical of the age they are so more in the sense that the hermits of the *Thebaid* could be said to be typical of the later Empire. That is to say they are freaks, if interesting, sought-for, honoured freaks with a scarcity value, and recognized as witnesses to values elsewhere neglected.[13]

This very turning from the 'content' of the world-scene, from the play on the world-stage, to withdraw to the wings, to seek form quietly in a juxtaposition of small objects between the 'flats', or even behind the back-cloth, is of great significance. It throws more light on our culture and its effect upon men than many pages of Charlie Marx. The truth is that the practice of such an art as painting is, today, a somewhat different kind of activity from what it was in the preceding epochs. Its perfections are largely a different kind of perfection. It is in the hands of somewhat different kinds of people. It is now essentially a highly conscious aesthetic activity. It has almost ceased to be a 'craft', a 'trade' in the old sense, and this 'release' has had within its own limits many interesting effects—once more loss and gain. From being a trade practised after apprenticeship and in a closed tradition and with fixed standards, it has become the vehicle of individual sensitivity. The attitude of the representative modern artist towards his work is undeniably somewhat different from that of even his immediate predecessors. The gulf between professional and amateur has been, in some ways, lessened, while

[13] A similar paradox is pointed out by Henri Pirenne in his *History of Europe* when he writes: 'They were filled with enthusiasm for the ideal of poverty but they sought riches.' He is speaking of the thirteenth-century city commercial class, who, he says, were devoted to the mendicant friars.

it has become a more esoteric activity in other respects. A high
state of professionalism and technical ability is still found and still
of great importance, but speaking broadly, the *intention* and
aesthetic of the artist is what interests both other artists and their
clientele more than before.

There *is* a sense in which much modern painting is 'amateur'.
There is also a sense in which it is still 'impressionistic', it leans
towards 'expressionism' and 'feeling' and away from the concrete, and that *in spite* of the intellectual and theoretic revolution
which the movement called 'post-impressionism' brought about
in the direction of emphasizing that a painting must be itself
a concrete 'thing' with a life of its own rather than the repre-
sentation of some other thing. That is now well understood—
even the general public have some inkling of this. At my first art
school, before the 1914–18 war, practically *no* one knew it. The
whole subject of aesthetics and the function of the arts has been
well aired during the last decades, and a more intelligent attitude
is apparent. All of which is satisfactory and has borne fruit in all
kinds of directions both in practice and appreciation. The
standards are in some respects higher, but put it as high as you
like, it remains that for reasons outside the scope of all this
practice and appreciation, and owing to causes deep in the nature
of the age, and affecting acutely all the arts and crafts and work
of our society from top to bottom, this promising improvement
as to theory and practice and appreciation has not been able to
restore to the art of painting those qualities which it once
possessed when it was a trade like any other, with a tradition of
technique and workmanship, apprenticeship and all the rest
of it.

It is *somewhat* analogous to the art of farming. All intelligent
people now know how important is the 'land' and many have
tried to 'return' to it. The life of the country is genuinely
appreciated and thought about, and people make conscious
efforts to practise theories with regard to it, and many have
'considered a field and bought it', but none of all this genuine
appreciation and practice can restore, or be the same thing as, the
tradition and technique and the unconscious craft of the growling

farmers with their wretched labourers carrying on the unbroken tradition of husbandry: literally *making* the landscape and forcing nature herself to have 'form' and to take on those very forms that we now call 'nature'! It is sometimes said that 'Architecture is the mother of the Arts'—but husbandry better deserves this title, though that is also wide of the mark as the 'hunting peoples' of pre-history show.

But to forget for a moment 'artists', art-works and specialist activities, and glance at 'applied art'—where symbol or decoration, or both, meet utility. The matter is even more obvious. When we see even the shoddier sort of tommy-gun, we recognize some sort of functional form, some sort of valid expression, and in consequence experience some measure and some kind of 'delight'. But when we see the average newly designed badge or motto or a *signum* of some sort we recognize nothing in particular but a somewhat dead tradition of design, or even worse, occasionally an inept, commercialized attempt at the 'abstract'. The *signa* in general are no patch on the field-kit, the technical devices, the forms wholly determined by mechanics, trajectory power, convenience, use. All the weapons and equipment have form in marked contrast to the *signa* and trappings. There is no more inevitability or conviction in these latter things than there is in contemporary 'church art', or for that matter, civil art at the same level, as a thousand shop windows declare.

Let us return for a moment to the effects of war experience, as we know it, upon some kinds of artist. A trench lived in in 1915 might easily 'get into' a picture of a back garden in 1925 and by one of those hidden processes, transmogrify it—impart, somehow or other, a vitality which otherwise it might not possess. Even a picture in the gayest possible mood may achieve that very gaiety by a mode not at all gay—by some acid twist, hidden may be in the bowels of the artist. Ruskin, writing of Turner's treatment of the sea, says that however calm the sea he painted he always remembered that same sea heavy and full of discontent under storm. That is half the secret, more than half, of good painting, of good art. Great painting triumphs over mediocre painting because it has every sort of undertone and overtone, both of form and content, it *is* both peace *and* war; it must make the lion lie by the lamb *without anyone noticing*,[14] it must hint at December snow, when summer's heat is the text. In painting a persistent 'desire and pursuit of the whole' is needed.

These things are possible of being achieved in both the most 'visual' and the most 'abstract' painting. There are as many 'ways' of doing it as there are kinds of artist and kinds of culture. Sometimes it may seemingly be resident in the 'subject' of the picture, and sometimes the 'subject' seems far removed from the all-inclusiveness, the universality achieved. There are all sorts of ways, but 'splendour of form' there must be. In Fouquet's *Agnes Sorel as Our Lady*, which is a very visual, 'illustrational' (in the vulgar sense) picture, he does somehow manage to make of the French king's mistress a *theotokos*. And certainly not by muting the superficial attractiveness of the physical and bodily, that is there, candid enough and almost overpowering, but more powerful still, he gets the solemnity and nobility of the 'subject' in its more profound sense, and all in terms of the painter's art and unified by splendour of form.

This may seem to be a far cry from the modern artist, attempting, if any do attempt, to 'interpret', to 'illustrate', to find a way of 'saying again under other forms', modern war in terms of modern art. But perhaps to an angelic intelligence they may not be all that dissimilar. He too would be faced with the profoundest contradictions and he must resolve them all, not losing one, and still create delight. It is this business of gathering all things in that torments the artist.

Though the dealer's clumsy title is: *Still Life with Desert*, yet, if the forms are so contrived, it *may* be that some of the 'content'

[14] That is the point: the old tag about art disguising art is true. It must look 'natural'—as 'natural', that is, as the sword coming out of the mouth of the 'one like to the son of man' in the Apocalypse, as 'natural' as the shifting points of vision in 'pre-perspective' painting, and again in 'post-impressionist' painting. Its 'fidelity to nature' consists in its being fidele to 'super-nature' in some way. Both the surrealist and the 'pure abstraction' schools do, in quite opposing directions, assert this truth, rather as some heresies assert, while they isolate, some particular truth. I expect we all are in material heresy by now.

of the Tellus[15] on the *Ara Pacis Augustae*, the fruits and grain stalks, the gifts of the Augustan Peace depicted on that monument to concluded war in the West, will get into that apple on the dish, and into the bunch of flowers—if the artist is a sufficently subtle master of whatever is meant by *recta ratio facti-bilium*—and all which that may imply with regard to the art of painting, and if, further, he has Tellus for his mother, or at least has sucked a little at her breast, and has not altogether disowned her. For remember, what is signified must be always much the same, whatever the diversity of means. It is always Leda and always the Swan. It is always this 'admirable commerce' which is the 'subject' of art.

The artist is anthropomorphic to the core; so that unless his *anthropos* is also the Unbegotten, he must be an idolater. There is no other way. I wonder what the final implications of this are with regard to some of the things we have been discussing?

Cézanne, who as has been well said, 'knew what he was talking about', and was one of the first and one of the most persevering of the 'desert fathers' in art, said we must 'do Poussin again after nature'. Perhaps we might almost say that we must do Cézanne's apples again, after the nature of Julian of Norwich's little nut, which 'endureth and ever shall for God loveth it'. It is still Leda and still the Swan. 'That which the whole world cannot contain, is contained.' It is some such free rendering of that sacred text which drums in the head of the artist, and causes him something of Blake's 'fear and trembling', even though he is painting only a still-life, a portrait of a cat, or designing an 'abstraction' or is sent by authority to depict some war scene.

It is still the same question: Will the twins be heavenly twins, or, like the fruit of Leda's other loves, be wholly earthly, be just material-as-power?

It is round about these deep questionings that artists contend when they work. All artists, whether of war or of peace, in peace or in war, and against such a background that the virtue of their several arts is to be considered. Do they, in short, 'fill up' in their

[15] *Tellus Mater*, the deity of Mother-Earth; honoured, together with Ceres, as the goddess of fruitfulness, she was both womb and grave.

arts 'what is lacking' to the continuing processes of conjoining heaven and earth, or do they not? That is the question.

The question is not so highfalutin as it may sound, it is of common application, to the commonest work of art and of all art, and no doubt, by it, the successive cultures are to be 'judged'. When Michael shouts his own name: 'Who is like to God?' as a challenge to man as a moral being, we may perhaps be allowed, by analogy, to indulge the fancy of transferring that challenge from the moral order to the domain of art, and render the question: 'What is like to God, in all this straw?'[16] Not till a 'pure intelligence' gives us the answer can we truly know how Chartres stands to the Parthenon, the *Primavera* to Picasso's best, the light-fitting of 1942 to the chandelier of 1882, or how the strategy and tactic of Cannae stands to *Blitzkrieg*, that of Zama to Valmy, considered solely and absolutely as expressions of that 'virtue of the practical intelligence' which belongs to art, considered exclusively as being 'things made' and only in so far as 'making' adheres at all to each of the ten examples cited.

In view of the immeasurable discrepancies of every sort and kind between the various arts, distinctions have been drawn, by very able minds, between arts which do and arts which (it is said) do not, have beauty as an end. It seems to me that if art is making then it can only make one thing, that is: a 'shape'. It can, and constantly does, make a mess, but that is only a bad shape. If then all art of its nature tends to make a shape it tends towards a relationship of shapes which we ordinarily call form,[17] and if it tends towards form then it must reach towards splendour of form in some sense or other, no matter how it is designated or what are its erratic processes. I believe it can be said that all art, as such, has beauty for its end, without qualification, both the art of war and the arts of peace.

That in the 'fine arts' a deliberate and conscious, determined, sustained, frontal assault is made to take beauty, as it were, by violence, cannot be denied. The practitioners of those special

[16] I was of course thinking of the story of St. Thomas, how he said on his death-bed of his finished *Summa*, that it was 'all straw'.

[17] See note 6 above, on the two uses of this word 'form'.

arts *think* in terms of beauty, and indeed, as we know, talk their hind legs off about how to achieve it; what sudden deployment or crafty infiltration can best secure the Goddess. Everything from the metaphysical to the dung heap is ransacked in the effort. They lie in wait like cats and pounce on 'splendour of form' wherever they think they see it shining, and carry what they can to their dens, as raw material to contrive more, and other, splendours of form, by this transmutation and that, this violence and that gentle persuasion, this frenzy or that patience.

But they do nothing of all this by virtue of practising art, as such, for all arts without exception tend to make a shape, and so, in this respect, are equal in having beauty as an end, but, and it is a most important 'but', there the equality begins to fade, for the fine arts differ from the other arts in their whole attitude towards that end. But again, in fact, no strict dividing line separates these distinctions. So we shall speak of 'fine-artness' as well as Fine Art. We shall break up the academic categories for the dear truth's sake. Fine-artness discovers itself in arts not commonly called Fine. We are clearly in the presence of a qualitative thing and the quantities are disseminated.

This quality not only causes those arts in which it asserts itself to proceed at a different tempo but in a different manner. It puts off the old Adam of utility. It becomes a fool for Beauty's sake, it begins to play. It no longer pretends to any other end, it proceeds as it were shouting its intentions. It induces in Martha something of Mary's indifference to the price of spikenard, indeed it makes those works in which it operates tend more and more to Mary's part. But, being bound always to material expression, it must continue to labour like Martha (as has been pointed out by Jacques Maritain), no matter how high in the category of 'fine' the particular work is.

Further the elements used to create the shapes are altogether more complex and subtle the more fine art predominates. The matter germane to the multiplicity of shapes affecting the whole form is infinitely more wide and deep, and *can* (e.g. in a great poem or a great painting) include spoils and gleanings from the whole gamut of man's emotions and aspirations, his spirituality and materiality. It is somewhere in this region, in this part of the frontier zone between the fine and other arts, that we detect a change of emphasis and behaviour, and are confronted with an assertion.

Englishmen and Welshmen equally desire beer, but walking in the Marches the traveller may suddenly find beer referred to, not as *cwrw*, 'beer', but as *cwrw da*, 'good beer'. There has entered into the Welsh speech the affirmation that beer is, in itself, 'a good'. It is somewhat in this affirmative way that fine-artness bids art in general remember, rather than forget, the end of art, that other good, which is beauty. The degree and intensity of this tendency towards beauty is as variable as are the arts by which it operates, but when it becomes dominant and plainly the ruling principle throughout the whole work, then we know ourselves to be faced with the phenomenon of Fine Art in its fullness.

It would not be easy for a cobbler, however great an artist in shoe-making, or however filled with that brooding spirit traditionally associated with his trade, to inform the shape on his last, no matter if bespoke by Martial's Erotion, who trod lightly, or Olwen,[18] whose tread made flowers grow, or even Mercury himself, with quite the significance of one line from the word-last: 'having your feet shod with the preparation of the Gospel of Peace'. Nevertheless there have been shoes made in all the cultures that nearly do it—I mean achieve under the accidents of leather, under the forms of line and mass, and strictly conforming to utile requirements, great subtlety and distinction and a 'content' altogether extra-utile. But no matter whether from the prose-last or the shoe-last, from the sonnet's strict mould, or from the matrix of the foundry, whether bursting with content and full of deliberate aesthetic intention, or with the minimum of content, to the highest degree utile and preoccupied with materiality, in all cases the shapes proceed towards some kind of beauty. The procession towards beauty in the shapes of a poem, a pair of shoes, a strategy obvious and all-determining in the first, capable

[18] 'Four white trefoils sprung up wherever she trod, therefore was she called Olwen.'

of gaining ascendancy in the second, most difficult to position in the third, is yet inevitably present, in some fashion, in all.

In the domain of 'doing', in the moral order, the end of War is Peace, yet historically (in the historic-present and the historic-past), in the world of observed fact, war proceeds to further war, rather than peace, as in mythology the God of Agriculture becomes the God of War, never, I think, the reverse. War, as we say, 'sows dragon's teeth'—and this the party politicians did not hesitate to instil into us when Army Estimates were as yet an election issue. But dragon's teeth or no, we are now heavily engaged in that sowing, and it is well to remember that conceptually at all events the end of war is peace (a good). Similarly, it is well to remember that the end of the art of war is beauty (another kind of good), even though that beauty is of so abstract, difficult to posit, remote and removed a nature, as to be perceived only by a process of induction, and calling for little more than a nodding intellectual assent. We are necessarily very very far from the Angelic vendors offering the strategic plans, in their abstract splendour, in the streets of that city 'whose parts are united in one', to the old street cry: 'Buy a song, only an ha'penny a piece, a New Love Song, only an ha'penny a piece.' For in so far as strategy consists of the unifying of parts to an end, it is, in its redeemed and glorified aspect, no less a love song than are the other arts of man.

We know how, in any struggle between individuals or groups, a great burden lifts when either side in that struggle, by gesture or utterance, admit some abstract excellence in the enemy whom it is their duty to oppose. And the war-leader of any group or nation, wishing to implement the Divine command 'love your enemies' strictly within the difficult terms of his position as prosecutor of a war, and his complex responsibilities in the world of fact, can only do so by making some such gesture of admittance of some such excellence, 'which, being seen, has pleased'.[19]

---

[19] Mr. Churchill only recently displayed a salutary example of this when he paid tribute to General Rommel's African strategy—even so his gesture was resented, by ignoble minds in this country.

This proper use of the intelligence in separating the contingent and concomitant things to be hated, from those things which must be loved wheresoever they appear, is the ground of charity as it is of art. It is the only ice-cutter in 'this world' and the operative principle of the 'next'.

It is noticed how both kinds of pacifists and kinds of killers-by-proxy are sometimes at one in being oblivious to the virtues of the arts of war, in their common moral indignation directed to opposing ends. It is, as often as not, left to the soldier, to the practitioner, to keep his charity and to practise his art. This is not to be wondered at, because both art and charity behave themselves in an analogous manner: they tend, both of them, to nose out the abstract 'goods' and 'beauties' behind the detestable accidents: that is why, in operation, both art and charity seem to be misunderstood by 'pure moralists'. Perhaps, in a cryptic sort of way, the Welsh proverb:

> Here is a mystery which never shall cease
> The priest promotes war and the soldier, peace

hints at something of this meaning.

We are living in an age when assent to what is abstractly true is increasingly necessary; such assents provide, as it were, the vitamins we most need, the hidden honey-food which no contemporary rations supply, indeed which are carefully abstracted from those rations. Or again, such assents may be seen as the narrow planks to raft us across the inundation, partly subjective and partly objective, that we know today, across the fast torrent of 'what's best at the moment', 'what works', against the half-truth propagandas that buffet us with the word 'obscurantist', if we seriously seek to make true distinctions.[20]

This period is sometimes imagined as having, in general, a resemblance to the beginnings of the Dark Ages—that may be a completely invalid imagining, yet in one respect we think we see a like attitude, whatever the general inaccuracy of the comparison, in that physical courage and moral courage are in ready demand and are as readily supplied, whereas intellectual courage,

[20] 'The truth shall make you free' and the object of propaganda is to bind.

that other desideratum, is far more hard to come by. Like Boethius, who they call 'the bridge', we in our distress and bewilderment must clutch at what true definitions we can find to bridge over our intolerable waters, for as the physical, in the end, depends on *morale*, so in the end do *morale* and the moral depend on what is true, though they may bluff successfully for two millennia. Thus even the consideration of so abstract a question as we have been concerned with here is not of no consequence, even in this 'midnight hour'—or is it only late evening? We don't know. But no matter if early or late, the definitions are instruments we need if only to help us read the hour, and sound the shallows, and detect the false dawns and in general get our bearings.

Now it may seem at first sight that this attempt to vindicate what we believe to be true, viz., that all art proceeds to beauty, although perhaps interesting as a rumination, is so remote from, and contradicted by, the world of fact, as to be altogether beside the point in its obtuseness and also that the whole thesis is an intellectual escape from 'reality' by way of a spuriously other-worldly pre-supposition. Of course it must be admitted that to minds which rule out any reference to 'absolute values' let alone any notion which implies 'God', all of this is unrewarding. But to those who believe that the Word makes the Flesh and not the Flesh the Word, then perhaps it may seem not so unrewarding, even if still open to objections. But even those most hostile may admit that this much can be said for our argument: that it has the common support of the attitude and phrase of man as a whole. That is to say men speak as though this thesis were true; they do so by a kind of 'unity of indirect reference', which I take to mean that the by-ways, the meanders, even the culs-de-sac, *all* roads, lead to the omphalos. It is precisely in the ubiquitous, indirect signs and indications which ordinary men display that we find our chief support.

We must be impartial and submit to a plebiscite of all the workers, from 'all Estates', from 'the champion in the stour', from 'makeris among the leave' (Dunbar's *Lament*). We must include past as well as present in our 'mass observation', because we are concerned with 'man' and not with one generation of men living under the peculiar conditions of a particular civilization, and that a very unique one. What can be gathered from the attitude of man as a whole, how do men behave and how speak with regard to their 'work'?

It was said of Helen of the Hosts, in the *Breuddwyd Macsen Wledig*, that 'the men of the Island would not have builded these roads save for her'. The 'roads' in hard historic fact were the 'army paths', slaves' work, and dedicated to ruthless material ends, worse, to conquerors' ends, but in the myth it was for Helen (read Beauty) that they were builded. And who shall deny the myth its validity?

It will be found that it is with reference to this Helen, Beauty, that men speak when they are describing their activities. All use the language of the artist, of the aesthete. The instances are so numerous, obvious and familiar to all of us, that it seems unnecessary to quote from them; however, to refresh the memory: it is 'beautifully clean' for the housewife, it is 'very pretty sir' for the cricket fan, it 'looks ugly' to the reader of the communiqué, 'she runs beautifully' for the mechanic, 'she's a beautiful build' for the shipwright, it was a 'beautiful case' for the physician, it promises to be a 'beautifully synchronized attack' for the staff, it turns out to be '*the* most beautiful balls-up' for the 'P.B.I.' This last instance is somewhat crucial, because it shows how a 'mess' can, by 'being seen' in certain relationships, 'please'. This is the foundation of all that kind of beauty which has 'humour' as its mode. There could be no laughter of any sort without the unconscious acceptance of objective values. As Mr. Chesterton said somewhere of the man imprisoned for saying that George IV was fat, how he must have laughed in prison when he remembered how fat George really was. When we are moved by objective values, we choose the 'better part' that no one can take from us.

That is why the theologians say that charity is the first of the three theological virtues, because it is the only one that remains with any meaning 'outside time'. And what charity is to man with regard to his last end, so is art with regard to man in relation to his work—to any and all of his works. To speak now strictly subjectively, and only with regard to man's subjective reactions, if the situation is such that men can no longer regard what they do as though it possessed this quality of 'art'—then indeed he is of all creatures most miserable, for he is deprived of the one and only balm available to him, as a worker. 'Good man' he can still be, and heroic may be, but a complete man he cannot be. And that is the kind of deprivation which the conditions of our kind of age seem to impose upon great numbers of people, upon most people. This deprivation is, in the sphere of art, analogous to a sterilization or a castration in the physical sphere.

In the sphere of art, conditions can arise where the men of a whole culture are made eunuchs, owing to the particular demands that utility and materiality, profit and power may make within that culture. This indignity leaves man with 'nothing to live for' outside the consolations of the body, the consolations of the speculative intellect, and the 'Consolations of Religion'. That is to say it leaves man with his ordinary physical appetites, and his obligations and intuitions as a moral being, *but* it deprives him, with regard to his 'daily work' (which means, in the end, his play as well), of the one thing that is his explicitly and peculiarly, to the exclusion of brute and angel, his one birthright that he has by nature, and through which, moreover, as the history of the cultures show, 'religion' is also served, and which 'grace' itself by no means despises as a channel. If our or any civilization can effect this deprivation in large masses of men, then that alone is a conclusion which must modify any considerations affecting our attitude towards that civilization. We must keep this well in view. We must understand the intractability of our material, which is man—the whole man, man the one creative animal. That's the way up it must be. Man must first of all be considered as a creative beast, and a creative beast he will be, one way or another.

It is sometimes complained that the policy of the Reformers left the Establishment with the legacy of a Canon Law of a sort but with little moral theology which could make that law sweet and tractable. I am not concerned with the truth or untruth of this complaint, but use it as a kind of parable for our domain of art: To expect a man to practise 'the moral virtues' and bid him hope, either 'for heaven' or, far more irritatingly, for some future 'wellbeing of mankind' (for here moralist and 'saint', materialist and vitalist, Communist and National Socialist all make the same demands—demands on heroic virtue), and yet to deny him both his chief and natural consolation in this world and the chief and normal 'sign' of the existence of absolute values, of 'heaven', is unreasonable, and turns man into some sort of implicit Manichee: Either he will say 'Body is all' or 'Spirit is all', either 'Let us eat, drink etc.' or 'Let's be strong and heroic' or simply 'Let's be other-worldly'. Now it is the artist in man which is the chief safeguard against this surrender—he knows that the tension between matter and spirit is both permanent and normal and in his work he knows that they are 'both real and both good'. But what a long long process of induction most men in the world today have to make when they arrive 'on the job' to *feel* that much about the work of their hands. It is obviously ridiculous to ask it. This is where so much of the talk of the 'nobility of labour' breaks down and fades into sentimentalism. Ruskin came perilously near it in his confusion between 'art' and 'morals', but it should be remembered that there was more excuse for him, because the full sub-humanizations of Industry, the total claims and implications, were not so obvious as they now are.

It has been one of the purposes of this writing to establish that outside his 'feeling' and though altogether unbeknown to him, the shapes which any man makes or helps towards making, inevitably have beauty as an end, and further that his common speech with regard to his work or recreation *still*, even now, bears witness to that fact, but we do not claim anything over and above that. We do not expect men to know the 'artists' joy' (as they call it) when engaged in these servile tasks.

When an 'operative' uses the terms of the artist with regard to a mass-produced 'part' we are very moved, as if an invalid spoke of the beauty of physical exertion. We do not expect to find so great faith in the victims of the particular system under which we, by an historical development, must needs live. It is important to realize that it is a long historical development, and not to place the 'blame' on some one turn of events, still less on some historic individuals. It is however our business to note, and not to gloss over the disadvantages as well as the advantages, the deprivations as well as the fulfilments which accompany each turn in material and possibly in spiritual progress. There is a constant tendency for people to drag a red-herring across any objective understanding of this subject by saying: 'I wonder how *you* would like to live in the pre-industrial age, how would *you* like to have been a medieval serf; think of the conditions of the majority even as recently as the last century—don't you believe in any sort of progress . . .?' All such questions are irrelevant and misconstrue the objective difficulty, which is that in spite of all possible progression in a civilization, in this or that direction, the position of man as artist can nevertheless deteriorate. It must be admitted that many of those with a strong appreciation of this deterioration as to art, have asked for misunderstanding in that they have themselves tended to confuse the issue by trying to find a moral or ethical basis for their otherwise true observations and have sadly idealized the past and have placed 'blame' on movements and persons which were in fact symptomatic, rather than causal, the causes being of the utmost complexity and amounting to trends and situations outside man's volition.

It is irritating when an observation of fact is called 'pessimism', if it does not appear to be in line with some contemporary progression towards some other 'good'. It is also irritating when it is supposed by those who are rightly and accurately pessimistic over some particular and observable trend, seek to deny the excellences of all the trends, and look backward to a largely imaginary past. We suffer from both these irritations, and largely because, even if we try hard not to, we confuse the domains of art and morals in their very widest sense. We seem almost incapable of taking in that every big turn in human history brings with it a 'swing and roundabout' situation—there can be loss and gain, *real* loss and *real* gain.

It is argued here that during the present phase of world history there are symptoms of real loss to man as artist, whatever the gain may be, or whatever the losses in other spheres. That is, I think, a modest statement, but the issues are so complex that a modest statement is best. It is further argued here that it is of some use to probe and examine this loss, if it exists, even on 'practical' grounds, that we may understand our age better and assess its achievements and likely developments more clearly. What we ask is that any loss shall not be glossed over, but faced. It is indeed no use crying over spilt milk, especially if the milk is spilled by agencies altogether outside our own volition, but it is equally no use, and worse than no use, to refuse to look at the empty milk jug, the wet stains on the table-cloth, and the expression of contentment on the cat's face, and worse still to pretend that we have no use for milk anyhow, that we always did think it useless stuff—those techniques of the 'optimist' that we know so well: those who refuse to call death by its terrible and exact name, but employ any euphemism which will disguise the reality of loss.

There is nearly always an attempt made in the minds of most of us to pretend that the loss of some admitted 'good' in any epoch is 'worth it' because of some quite other 'good' in the following epoch, and thus a legend of general progress is maintained, to the detriment of a true understanding of the situation. This is particularly noticeable where excellences of art and morals are confused and set off against each other—like a sort of profit and loss account. Again the people who 'believe in progress' and the people who look back wistfully are almost equally unreal, for both tend to 'pool' the perfections which all men desire, and both tend to hide the skeletons in their respective dream-cupboards. And when I say this, I mean we *all* do it to a large degree. I think we must make a conscious effort towards refusing to be fobbed off by talk of sublimation. We must call deaths, deaths, and admit a real loss. If we inherit advantages from such deaths—that's all to the good, but the gain makes the loss no less real. This sounds trite enough, but there is in this matter of art and morals and the development of civilization a pretty rooted conviction that this transference of values can be effected and that there is a sort of accumulating credit to which we are heirs. I do not think this is true, although no doubt it contains a half-truth, or a truth on another plane. World history is more of a rake's progress than the conservation of 'goods'. It is a criminal dissipation of noble things.

When, to take one example from so very many, any civilized imperium is extended over a savage culture, it is the worst sort of delusion to suppose that a real death has not been inflicted and all the subsequent 'goods' accruing to the 'civilizing' of the people of that culture do not alter by one iota the reality of the thing done and no future development, development 'in time', can compensate. Incidentally that is why the word 'justice' in any profound sense has *no* meaning unless we pre-suppose a 'divine order', a supernatural economy, by which such words as 'compensation', 'fulfilment', 'sublime-ation' can have meaning—but that is another matter, we are speaking here of this world.

In our world, the loss of a thing as artistically formidable as say the culture of the Incas to two dozen Renaissance fire-locks and a few cavaliers is something which strikes a note of questioning and of despair in our hearts, which the comfortable arguments do no more than aggravate. We have no conception of the arithmetic by which such accounts are audited. It is 'of faith' that they *are* audited. That is the most we can say. I chose this outstanding and tragic example, not because it is unique, but because on the contrary it is a glaring example of something which is ubiquitous and universal and which is happening all the time in many millions of lesser ways—to lesser perfections of all kinds; it is in fact, history, your history and my history no less than world history.

It is a kind of cowardice to look on history and not to despair if we confine ourselves to the natural order. Strictly within that order, 'optimism' is all right as an indulgent aid to a certain kind of *morale*, it can be objectively 'all right' only if we pre-suppose an 'other-world' order—'call it what you like', as the Cheshire cat said. Conceive it in what terms you like, it has to be conceded. Even if Utopia began tomorrow, even if the state was visibly 'withering away' (instead of which 'So Jupiter me succour, it flourisheth more and more'), even if that quarrelsome pair, Liberty and Equality, could be finally got to set up house and Fraternity be brought forth, the New Man would be a Sub-Man if he forgot to weep for the past: there is no decent escape from the *lacrimarum vale*, the lament for the makers is a world lament, like the weeping for Thamuz.

That is where all forms of secular 'millenniumism' display a shallowness of conception—they leave the past utterly un-rectified, behind the advance of the banners of progress the 'back areas' are full of ghost-guerrillas, eternally defiant and having no part in the new perfection. The whole state of Man-militant here on earth has no meaning, warrants and demands despair, unless we can allow a state of Man-Triumphant—not some 'Future-Man' triumphant, but you and I and great-grand-uncle Ned whom they shot at Peterloo, and Adam and Eve and Pinchme—all men. It is no longer a question of being a 'religious' person: those of us who most suspect the 'supernatural', those who have least use for metaphysical postulates, who are by temperament 'agnostic', if we open all the cupboards and bring out all the skeletons and consider the frustration which history past and present offers as a 'pattern', are compelled, if we presume to a shadow of optimism, to posit the necessity of other-world values.

There is one alternative: defiance towards the tragedy which is presented to us and in which we are compelled to act, and to find 'optimism' in the 'heroic'. But even that uncovers our guard against an admission of other-world values, because courage is one of the Four Cardinal Moral Virtues and those who evoke it cannot logically do so without an admission of the other three. And behind those again stand the three theological ones (Faith, Hope, and Charity), ready to ask the question. We see how among our present enemies and among our temporary allies and among ourselves, there are those who are supported by 'materialist' and 'vitalist' conceptions of reality—who boast a fidelity to the world of fact, but who, in fact, have to posit an optimism which only other-world values can warrant. This optimism is an absolute necessity for the attainment of blatantly this-world objectives. Both this 'materialism' and this 'vitalism' are inexplicable along with the determined heroism called forth, unless there are extra-phenomenal values. I do not mean that an indifference to or a denial of these values detracts from the efficacy of these heroisms, it clearly does not. I mean, simply, that the virtues practised have ends and explanations, which may be, and often are, repudiated by the men who practise them most.[21]

But to return from this digression: We must admit in our own age the possibility of serious and possibly uncorrectable deprivations, and the clearer we see where they reside the more we shall be alive to our achievements in other directions, or even if we don't like the look of things at all, at least we shall be less easily deceived by this false scent and that, which is something, when there is so much to deceive us.

This 'intransitive activity' called art seeks of its nature to evade the consequences of the 'fall', and, needless to say, in its operations in the world of fact only makes the 'fall' more obvious. But it does succeed (if we can speak of its 'contribution' to the moral order) in 'reminding' man, in keeping before his eyes, that perfection which is unity (beauty is a kind of unity as, I believe, Augustine said).

Even in the most servile arts, even under the most slavish conditions it does succeed in saying: 'You are not altogether under Martha's star—there is such a thing as objectivity, even you can have music some of the way.' But whether some part of the way or 'wherever she goes', hardly perceived, or denied, or consciously revelled in and paraded, it is the quality of art which has been a kind of music accompanying the labours of man even under the most appalling physical and moral circumstances. The idealizers of the past have, no doubt, absurdly over-estimated the subjective aspect of this and imagined a fictitious world of 'happy craftsmen'—almost a new version of the 'noble savage' of the eighteenth-century dream, but it can quite soberly be said without any idealization, that past shapes of society did permit more chance of the 'artists' attitude' to life being more widely spread. I think it would be difficult to deny this altogether, and

[21] Note, 1946: This was written four years ago; now, in the post-Nuremberg world, it gains fresh support.

even if so denied, it would remain objectively true that whatever the feelings or conscious attitude of the workmen, the work itself belongs to the world of the 'artist'—it shows signs of 'play'. This is not due to any 'good will' on the part of those past epochs or cultures—it means only that the accidents which evolved our sort of world had not come into operation.[22] But if it is true that our age has lessened for most men the chance of any normal creativity in this work, if the silencing of this 'music' is to be taken for granted in a civilization of our type in its present phase, then we may as well understand that fully, and note the implications. I think that no one could very well deny that such is the case, that a new chilliness is in the air and that the temperature is falling.

This deprivation must, of course, if it is integral to our time, affect all and include all. It is in *some* respects a 'new thing under the sun'. Not new, in all respects, by any means, all the great civilizations in their development have experienced something of it, and in any known culture there must have been more of it than is admitted by various types of idealizers of those past cultures, but new in kind and in degree and far wider spread in the separate societies, and for the first time in history, global. Even the deep and terrible issues of this present war do no more than begin to touch this particular characteristic of our epoch, it is something common to all, like certain characteristics of the stone age which produced a common technique of life. Though whether we, or our present or future enemies, handle those techniques is of overwhelming importance to us—and to them. For it is a struggle to decide *what* men among twentieth-century men shall control twentieth-century Man and his techniques, and to what 'cultural', economic, political and religious ends that control shall proceed.

In the machine-culture, man-as-machine-user will be the common material employed by the twentieth-century magnates,

[22] Some say that the whole of our mechanic development was implicit in Greek theory and that the practical and inventive genius of Western man put those principles into practice as soon as conditions developed which favoured this possibility.

by Man, that is, as World-planner. Those men will indeed be 'Directors of Toil', as the *Gereint* fragment calls Arthur. But they will not, as in this Welsh triplet,[23] direct only 'brave men hewing with steel'—the direction of the toil will be to shape 'the merchandise of gold . . . and iron and oil and wheat . . . and the souls of men' to some sort of rational plan, to which there may be no alternative. It is conceivable that it will be in these frigid, uninviting regions that the most creative geniuses of the twentieth or the twenty-first centuries will find their medium. Just as already, lower down the scale, it is noticeable how children during the last decades have almost a connaturality with mechanism, they seem to imbibe an understanding of the machine with their mother's milk. As we know, parents often say that their male children, at least, show little interest in the world of 'nature', but are, at a surprisingly early age, avid for anything remotely mechanistic, and it seems probable that already many boys who would, even ten years ago, have found openings for their creative genius in one or other of the many 'arts', are in fact becoming 'technicians', 'experts', or organizers of whatever sort.

Against this, however, we must remember what Spengler noticed with disapproval, and which he regarded as ratting from the task of the age (for it is surprising how 'determinist' theories leave room in practice for moral indignation). He calls this tendency which he observed, 'treason to technics', and he says, with his nose well down on the scent of the débâcle: 'The Faustian thought begins to be sick of machines' . . . 'it is precisely the strong and creative talents that are turning away from practical problems and sciences and towards pure speculation.' He sees in this a most dangerous weakness which must be overcome if Western man is to continue to dominate.

But what concerns us here is that he was right in noting this duality: on the one hand the machine, ubiquitous and controlling all, and on the other hand the rebellion of the *best* of human

[23] The fragment from an early Welsh poem called *Gereint filius Erbin* reads in free translation: 'At Llongborth I saw the brave men of Arthur hewing with steel, men of the commander, the director of toil.'

nature against it. And when he gives one of the general reasons for this rebelliousness, he is again on the spot: 'The tension between work of leadership and work of execution has reached a level of catastrophe. The importance of the former, the economic value of every real personality in it has become so great that it is invisible and incomprehensible to the majority of the underlings. In the latter, the work of the hands, the individual is now entirely without significance. Only numbers matter.' Here, it seems to me, we have the actual character of the situation, stated with brutal frankness, and the fact that his intention was to steel the wills of his German readers to resist this quite inevitable and proper rebellion of human nature against the monstrous regiment of the power-age, should not prejudice for us the truth in the analysis. It is indeed 'human nature' that is rebelling—it is man-as-artist that is in rebellion, and it is men-as-artists who are casualties in the struggle.

Had Spengler had a different metaphysic, his analysis, at least of this particular subject, might have remained unaltered—but his inferences from the evidence might have been different. His realism as to the this-world facts is here most salutary. His 'pessimism', as far as this subject is concerned, can be attacked only on other grounds, and those are metaphysical ones, that is to say, in the last resort, by the 'optimism' of the Saints, which optimism, human nature in all men recognizes as valid, and which is notably *reflected* for man in his 'intransitive activity' called art, for to 'make anything' pre-supposes that such activity is 'worth-while'.

The new orders will demand the disposal of genius where it can best be utilized as material-as-power, and the new totalisms, as we already are witnessing, can set no limit to their demands. We speak of the 'unfathomable maw of concupiscence', it is just such a maw that 'stateism' has. But just because it is a 'work of art', it must gather in all things. All must be 'integrated', all are 'necessary to the completion of the whole' as the dictionary defines it, but what *is* that whole? That is the question which concerns us as men, as creative animals, midway between angel and beast, but which the controllers of the world-orders will not be able to answer any better than the historic rulers of any of the kingdoms of this world, and for the same reasons. At this juncture man the artist and man the contemplative can afford to wink at each other from their separate hide-outs, a wink of recognition, for they both know a thing or two, by way of their respective trades, that enables them to get a common line on this new world-shaping. But it's rather a sad wink, none the less, for they both know and love the 'two cities' more than all men and would rather 'muck in' than 'muck out'.

Some who are aware of these 'deprivations' have spoken of a 'leisure state'. It is said there is no way of meeting, what they recognize to be a necessity to man in our kind of age, except by relegating the artist in man to 'off-time' occupations. Let him be an efficient automaton at his work, and reserve his creative faculty for his leisure hours, which it is said, under proper organization, could be a great deal longer than they are. I have no doubt that in a purely 'practical' way this claim is not absurd. That given some sort of 'peace' some such 'state' is within the bounds of the possible. As an idea it is singularly unsatisfactory but there is such a thing as a choice between two evils, even in idea. It is obviously, at a deeper level of thought, and apart from what necessity drives us to, a most undesirable solution, indeed no solution at all at that level, deeper still, where considerations of what man really *is* begin to knock and question. Then we see this 'solution' as no better if no worse, than that 'solution' which makes of the Mountains of Snowdon, that place saturated with historical meaning, into a 'National Park', a scenery museum, rather than give it over to the speculative builder. Or that humane 'solution' which provides a 'territory' for the remnants of a culture which once made a pattern of fear against all intruders, and allows them a familiar habitat, where they can harmlessly charade their great tradition with bows and feathers, like a psychotic who is prescribed 'occupational therapy'.

These 'solutions', even when the only possible ones, are debilitating to contemplate, as is any emasculation sad to see. Blake says

The robin redbreast in a cage
Puts all heaven in a rage.

Yes, but for us men, perfection in the cage of mediocrity, and
the vulgarization of what once had the vitality of refinement, the
disintegration of what was a unity, the emptying of being of
what once was proudly full of being, the 'signs' inadequate to
what they signify, is most cause for 'rage'—for perturbation.
And it is for this cause that we are perplexed when we see no
other way but these kinds of 'solutions'. And it is precisely these
kinds of perplexities which neither men of action or affairs, as
such, nor planners as such, nor moralists, as such, nor indeed men
of piety, as such, except at certain levels and in certain relationships, know, but man as creator knows this perplexity all the
time. So that what is essentially man in us knows it all the time
and is troubled, but can find no easy answer. How, we ask ourselves, given on the one hand the nature of man, and on the other
hand the conditions of the age, and the rapid intensification of
those conditions in the future, can man fulfil himself with
respect to what Eric Gill, with his genius for precision, termed
'the one intransitive activity' of which man is capable?

The process by which he does assist this, his essential character,
and the means by which he is enabled or compelled to do so, are
hidden from us. Those things which we have hitherto accepted
with regard to man's nature, from our own intuitions, from the
reasoning of the ancients, and from the definitions of the
Christian Church, are either true or, in that order, subjective
delusions, rational conceits and metaphysical fictions—all equally
'fond things vainly imagined'. But if true, then objective
measuring rods with which to measure the degree to which
different cultures and epochs permit man to behave in most
accord with his nature as a creative creature.

But even if we reject all traditional and objective criteria and
say that nothing can be postulated of the 'nature of man', that all
abstract ideas are invalid, nevertheless our instinctual judgements,
because we are men who make those judgements, will still tend
to appraise the worth of cultures according to the true demands

of our natures. So there is no escape however much our moods vary. We either attempt to measure with rods that we regard as having some sort of reliability or with rods that we suppose to be quite unreliable, but which in fact have correspondence with our deep human instincts, and these instincts must correspond somewhere with the 'traditional' criteria. However stoic we are and however prepared to face whatever is to be, with detachment, however much we think it 'an interesting age', even if we are like those:

> . . . that lend their ears
> To those budge doctors of the Stoic fur
> And fetch their precepts from the Cynic tub

nevertheless our deeper instincts will register some disquiet, and the very character of our stoicism and the texture of our cynicism will be tell-tale of the nature of that instinctual disquiet.

What then are our instinctual apprehensions or misgivings with regard to our time and more particularly with regard to the further developments? What is it for which, seemingly, 'the bell tolls', when we consider the main shape of our age of technics? Not for the 'moral virtues' in man, for in spite of the limitless horrors, some of the moral virtues are noticeably alive. We are killing and torturing each other by the million with the stoicism of Red Indians to assert different interpretations or emphases of those virtues and so are displaying them to an extraordinary degree, to a fanatical degree.

Certainly not the speculative faculties; never was science, whether 'pure' or 'applied', more devotedly served—served with an admirable zeal and concentration—so what is it the bell tolls for? You may be sure it tolls for you, otherwise you wouldn't hear it, for something deep in your nature. Does it then toll for man-as-artist, as hitherto understood? That I think is what we *feel* when we hear this knell, even if our reasons for saying that we hear it do not convince those in whom the noise of the achievements and the concentration on 'much serving' has induced varying degrees of deafness.

Now deafness, I believe the theologians say, can set up a kind of spiritual deprivation. Darwin is said to have complained that he could no longer 'enjoy poetry' because of his heroic concentration in the domain of natural science—that was a terrible penalty which he had to suffer in this world; it seems to us a sad one, we might say an 'unfair' one, for the author of the *Voyage of the Beagle* was obviously an artist—it is a very 'poetic' book, because it presents with affection all its matter. But however that may be, that was his confession of the price paid—something of the 'whole man' and that a very essential part, suffered deprivation. It is in that same region that we, creative animals as we are, living in the post-post-Darwinian age, the age of technics, world-planning, rival ethics, warring moralities, in the paradise of the natural sciences and displaying in a notable degree many of the speculative and moral virtues under the most severe and heart-breaking conditions, begin to wonder if or how we can in peace or war avoid that deprivation for which the bell seems to be tolling. 'The one intransitive activity of man': if that is true then, you will say, the bell is tolling in vain or those who think they hear it are suffering delusion. In the long run—however long the run, there is some truth here—man will find a way. But civilizations can cause man to suffer deprivations in various directions and we think that it is in this direction that the character of our civilization is mainly defective.

It is obvious that, supposing there is truth in our beliefs as to man's nature, then the bell *cannot* toll for man as artist unless it tolls for man as man—but it can and does toll in a civilization when this 'intransitive activity' is, for whatever cause, deprived of meaning for most people, and when the general trend obscures from our sight man's inalienable character, and weakens in him the solace which is most natural to him.

Since writing the above I have been shown the words of a worker in a war-factory of today: 'From the opening of the gates until the evening, the factory is as real and vital a life as that of the field, there is no difference in value but only in the nature and the uses of the material things with which God shapes our way to His Will.' It is expressive of the heroic attempt on the part of a religious mind to see work of the factory as part of the creative activity of man, but it will be noticed that it is an act of faith which has to be implemented and a religious motive has to be posited. It is, so to say, magnificent, but it is still not the attitude of the artist. It is by a pious intention that this work is seen as 'a good' and it leans towards the moral order, and asks to be justified on that account.

What then is the complaint? That is all to the good? Here is the regeneration and sanctification of one aspect of the working of the modern world? The tolling bell has been silenced by the faith of this factory hand? No. That is not the point. We are still in the domain of morals, though using the terms of the art. '. . . The material things with which God shapes our way to His will': most true, no doubt, in the prudential order, and towards our Last End, but the domain of art is concerned only obliquely with that theological 'last end'. It has no end but its own perfection.

Like most heretics, the men of the '90s were proclaiming a truth in isolation when they asserted that 'art is for art's sake'. An act of art is essentially a gratuitous act. It does not have to be justified by metaphysical argument. It is essentially 'play'. It can indeed be justified as an activity by metaphysicians, because metaphysics support the contention that play is an activity most native to us—the only thing we 'want to do', just as in the other order, the only thing men 'want to do' is to contemplate—another kind of play, to play always, as is said of Wisdom (Book of Wisdom, VIII). It must be understood that 'art' *as such* is 'heaven', it has outflanked 'the fall'—it is analogous not to faith but to charity.

One more point from this most heroic utterance of the factory worker. 'The factory is as real and vital a life as that of the field.' That is not true. It is wholly untrue. But it is untrue not because of our affinity with angels, but because of our affinity with beasts. It must never be forgotten, at least the 'artist' in us must never forget, that we are beasts. If Uranus is our father, Gea is still our mother.

And at least this much the civilizations of antiquity, even when 'totalitarian' and 'mechanized' and in many respects similar to our own, were, for various reasons, not so able to forget as are we ourselves. This forgetfulness of our affinities with fur and foliage, with 'the life of the field', may not matter to man as far as his speculative, scientific, or even his moral aspirations are concerned, but it is, once more, an impossible strain, a great deprivation to man as artist, because, as has been already suggested, one of his operational flanks rests on the strong-point of animality and the other is 'fluid', not, we hope, as when soldiers say 'in the air'—but is 'mobile' where it contacts the celestial allies. Somewhere in the middle sector of this line are posted those regulars, those all-round troops, those most representative of normal man, well dug-in, with medium weapons, whose techniques and *esprit de corps* alike proclaim their recruitment from that median category, not animals, nor angels, but makers— the human 'infantry of the line'. Without which the human species loses its rightful *imperium*, its native *Raum*, its double homeland along all the frontiers and uncertain borders of matter and spirit. Man, like King Hurlame, is Lord of the Two Marches, and must keep the difficult dignity of his dual role. In this epoch the whole March is in revolt and the March-wardens are at their wits' ends. There will be, doubtless, a 'pacification of the March' —history inclines us to believe that also, but we don't know and can't imagine what form it will take.

It is remarkable, to say the least, that man should have preserved his optimism and his dream of a pacific order in spite of the long historic necessities which have made him essentially the 'warrior' and more and more caught in the double encirclement of the power of 'money' (call it what you like) and the power of the 'sword'—these two traditional foes which seem to have become his Scylla and Charybdis, his destroyers. The traditional virtue of the one and the traditional baseness of the other have now become so interlocked and confused as to be both now seen only as material-as-power—both implying domination and neither stopping at any degradation to both man as artist and man as moral being. Yet in spite of all this, or perhaps because of it, he still clings, in one form or other, to the story in his race-consciousness of 'once upon a time'—that once upon a time the god of war was the god of agriculture and the cities had no walls, and that Arthur might reverse his roles, and that even before the Heroes there was Man and always man the Artist, practising his 'intransitive activity'.

1942–3, 1946

A Christmas Message 1960*

In contrast with some beliefs the belief of the Catholic Church commits its adherents, in a most inescapable manner, to the body and the embodied; hence to history, to locality, to epoch and site, to sense-perception, to the contactual, the known, the felt, the seen, the handled, the cared for, the tended, the conserved; to the qualitative and to the intimate.

All of which, and more especially the two last, precludes the ersatz, and tends to a certain mistrust of the unembodied concept.

It commits its adherents also to the belief that things of all sorts can, are, and should be given special significances, set aside, made other, raised above the utile to the status of *signa* and revered with corporeal, manual acts. It commits them to the 'creaturely'.

Now the retention of any such belief must depend upon what sort of creatures we reckon we are. It appears that for tens of millenniums one of our 'creaturely' characteristics has been to make *signa*, that is to make things, artefacts, having an extra-utile intention.

The great cave-paintings of the Palaeolithic epoch are, aesthetically, neither better nor worse than the embroidery known as the Bayeux Tapestry or paintings by Tintoretto or Bonnard, and all four are equally extra-utile and all are *signa* in that all 'show forth under other forms' the beliefs, mind, requirements and aspirations of widely separated phases in the chequered story of one order of primates, that is of ourselves. When we look at the Lascaux animal frescoes as when we read, in Gospel or

* Published in somewhat shorter form in *The Catholic Herald*, 2 December 1960, under the title 'Nor Fire nor Candle Light: Symbol and Sacrament under Technology'. Material from the manuscript drafts found among David Jones's papers has been added to make up the version printed here.

Epistle, of the Institution of the Eucharist or when we are present at Mass we recognize a connaturality of behaviour and intention with ourselves.

Jack Smith may be convinced that there is nothing beyond the utile and the functional, he may call poetry 'bunk', he may think that religion has been or is being explained away and that the whole concept of sign or sacrament is a delusion. Nevertheless that conviction will not inhibit Jack from sending by 'Interflora' roses to Jill. This he does without a suspicion that such an act, at whatever remove and in however devious a fashion, links him with the Palaeolithic sign-makers and also with a sign-making in a supper-room in the Roman procuratorship of Judaea.

We all of us, seeing that we are of the same civilizational phase as Jack Smith, are subject to like conditionings. We may not share Mr. Smith's convictions, we may hold, with some intensity, quite other views, but we cannot be free of the dichotomy we observe in him: Being on the same stove we pots observe how calcined is the kettle.

As a 'desire and pursuit of the whole' is native to us we find nothing so frustrating as unresolved contradictions of whatever sort. In our personal relationships most of our pain comes from a feeling that a pattern is unresolved, that, as we say, 'it doesn't make sense', that sign and what we took to be signified appear to be at odds, in short that the *signa* are invalid.

In the making of things an analogous distress is even more marked and is much more patient of analysis and more to the point here.

The artist, no matter what his medium, may work with technical ease or he may find the going hard—such differences are of little consequence—what matters to him is whether or no the forms he makes resolve themselves in such a way as to show forth, re-present, embody or make corporeal the incorporeal reality envisaged in the eye of his mind. Or, to put it another way, though art 'abides on the side of the mind' its products are of the body, are always and inescapably a sort of 'word made flesh'.

The individual artist does not judge his works by his intentions but by the resultant forms. Should these not show forth his intention he must, necessarily, suffer distress because he has failed not in some peripheral matter but in a matter which touches his central function as *homo faber*: remembering that man is not only man-the-maker but man the maker, user and apprehender of signs.

Here we are confronted with something of very great complexity and something which requires qualifications of all sorts, but by which we seem forced to one conclusion, viz.: that a sign-making element however minimal, obscure and hard to define does adhere to all human artefactures; so, presumably, to television contraptions as well as to paintings, to door-mats as well as to crucifixes, to space-ships as well as to velvet frocks.

As with the artefactures of individuals (painters and the like), so with the artefactures of a whole civilizational phase. Should these appear to be wanting in, for example, the creaturely (hence defective as human *signa*), we cannot avoid wondering how this can be.

In spite of our astonishing technological advance and the evident benefits (leaving aside the horrors) which have accrued from this intense application of human intelligence and exploratory genius, a deprivation of some sort must also be noted. Of what sort is it?

We are not 'pure intelligences' as our theologians define the angels, nor are we intelligences informing bodies whose sole function is the ordering of those bodies to material ends. We are mammals of sense and sensibility with apperceptions which (however they may be accounted for) place us in a very peculiar, difficult and, it would seem, unique position.

While quite a large part of our artefacture would appear to be as much ordered to the merely utile as is the artefacture of other creatures of our animalic world (birds' nests and beavers' dams are but two of the innumerable examples), we have from our first recognizable beginnings been concerned with the extra-utile, with something I have termed a sign-making or a showing-forth.

Should we chance to be Catholic or of Catholic inclination we know that what is proposed for our acceptance presupposes this sign-making proclivity in man and that without it our religion is not only meaningless but could not have arisen.

Here I am not thinking of our extensive use of ceremonial, for were this cut to the barest minimum (as in some non-Catholic cults) there would remain, owing to the Incarnation, this same explicit commitment to creaturely signs.

When we put up a candle before an image we first kiss the wax (or whatever substitute now does service for wax) and lighting our candle from the light of another we fix it on to its iron spike or fit it into a socket on the iron hearse and drop a coin into the box to defray the cost. All these manual acts are congruent with our natures. We are accustomed to kiss what we love or what betokens that love, and, in everything, we have to defray a cost.

We also make fast or position in some way tokens of our regard, that is: we set up, set aside, make over, dedicate or make anathemata of, a diversity of things. It may be anything from a bowl of flowers to an oar which with seven other oars won or lost a race years ago; whereby recalling, along with much besides, companions now long separated from us, perhaps by death.

In lighting our votive lights from those of others who lighted theirs from others again there is a continuity back to the New Fire of the previous Easter Saturday, thus there is a communal significance—'no man is an island'.

I may be inaccurately informed, but I'm told that in some places instead of this sequence of significant manual acts a quite simple, utile substitute has been devised which is indeed far more congruent with our present workaday world but which is less congruent with our natures: A coin is dropped into a slot and for that coin's worth of time, it is, as Belloc wrote:

> . . . patent to the meanest sight
> The carbon filament is very bright.

Supposing such a practice to exist, it can be said that, as it is the intention that matters, all is well. But it is evident that though the intention may be unimpaired there is an impoverishment of the manual signs by which that intention is shown forth.

And there, to quote from that source of so many English quotations, is the rub.

It is that rub, considered in numberless contexts of every conceivable kind, which brought to my mind the words of my 'text', from an English folk-song:

> Neither fire-light nor candle-light
> Can ease my heart's despair.

When that poem was made the poet's mind went instinctively to two, everyday, familiar and necessary utilities, fire-flame and candle-flame, as images which ought to offer some consolation, not to the body, but to a heart in despair. That is to say the technics of the then contemporary world, and the sense and sensibility of the men of that world, were in easy alignment.

It is as though we, with equal spontaneity and naturalness, were able to say in expressing our griefs something of this sort:

> Neither neon light nor radiant heat
> Can ease my heart's despair.

In so far as we don't seem able to do this, it looks as though an estrangement must have occurred between our characteristic artefactures and ourselves. A defect of some sort must have accompanied our tremendous and fascinating, if also horrific, technological advance. Until that estrangement is somehow or other overcome the dichotomy which I have tried to indicate would seem to me to remain.

A further, and especially seasonable, consideration: the Incarnation and the Eucharist cannot be separated; the one thing being analogous to the other. If one binds us to the animalic the other binds us to artefacture and both bind us to *signa*, for both are a showing forth of the invisible under visible signs.

The mewling babe in the ox-stall, the quasi-artefacts of bread and wine (products of tillage, of the oven, the vat) are to be regarded, so our religion demands, not as signs only but signs which are also the Thing signified, namely the Eternally Begotten Word, the Logos which gave *poiesis* to the expanding or contracting (whichever it should turn out to be) cosmos.

In the case of the Eucharist the reformers objected to this Catholic identification on the grounds that it overthrows the nature of a sign. Why did they not extend this objection to cover the Incarnation? For though the two cases are not identical, they nevertheless involve an identical principle; in that both are creaturely signs and both are what the signs signify, hence both or neither are open to the same objection.

But we are here not so much concerned with deviations of opinion touching a specific sacrament but rather with the fact that all Christians are explicitly involved in sign and sacrament and that all men are implicitly so involved owing to their natures.

This in turn has led us to a tentative consideration of the nagging and ever-present awareness (which we all feel in varying degrees) of a difficult-to-express disparity between our technological civilization in which sacrament with a small 's' has been to a large degree occluded, and our religion with its absolute insistence on Sacraments with a capital 'S'.

It is evident that such a religion must confide that the sacramental continues to be man's normal mode of apperception. Indeed were it possible to eliminate from man every vestige of the sacramental then we should have sub-men, no matter what their technological, intellectual, or, for that matter, moral or even spiritual achievements.

Jack could still (after a fashion) love Jill but he could not send her roses, for that would be a significant or sacramental act and therefore logically impossible in a wholly utile order of society. And what sort of life is it if you can't send roses to your beloved?

Browning made his intrepid bishop say that even 'if this life's all, who wins the game?' That is what I am inclined to say, though with much trepidation and for reasons other than those of Browning's Bloughram.

These then are some of the thoughts with which the present writer approaches the Feast of the Nativity, 1960.

It is significant that the Roman Church uses the same Preface for the Mass of Corpus Christi as the one She uses during the Christmas season. In it we are reminded that by the love of a thing seen we may be drawn to love what is unseen.

Thus, in the first and most moving of the Prefaces, the compact and concise words show forth 'in little space' (as is said elsewhere in a reference to God's Mother) the wide implications of a religion which is explicitly dependent upon small, intimate, enclosed, known and dear creaturely signs.

Like the majority of English-speaking children of my generation one of the first bits of versification to which I was introduced was that of Macaulay's *Lays*. One of those easily remembered rhymes runs:

> Pomona loves the orchard
> And Liber loves the vine
> And Pales loves the straw-built shed
> Warm with the breath of kine.

No difficulty about that: the corporeal, the earthy, the earthly, the artefacted, the creaturely, all have here their celestial correspondences and implications. All here is congruent with the Incarnation and the Mass. It images and incants a world very other than the world which you and I enjoy or suffer today and of which we are, willy-nilly, an integral part.

We cannot here consider the interplay of innumerable causes which have led to our present set-up. In any case it is impossible to indict a technological development, no matter what we may think, on balance, of the resultant advantages and disadvantages; and there is plenty of evidence of both. But whatever we may think of the advantages it is imperceptive not to recognize that our technics tend to erode the creaturely and to alienate us from the sacramental. It is not, as I see it, a question of blame, but simply that such appears to be the case.

Were our religion concerned purely and simply with the conceptual, with a state of mind, with a system of ethics, with a condition of the soul, etc., then we might I suppose be unaware of or able to outflank this dichotomy. But with a religion which so emphatically insists on Sacraments this is not possible. Hence the tendency is to departmentalize the sacramental principle, to accept it on authority only and as applicable only to certain rites and formulae of a traditional faith and usage.

The Sacraments of the Church are sometimes referred to as 'the normal channels of Grace' (that is Grace in a strictly theological sense), but along with this, our material world (especially when, as in our artefactures, it has received the imprint of Man) should, in some analogous sense, channel graces; and for this there is plenty of evidence. But we must remember the internal combustion engine that gets us to the Mass as well as the antique and gracious paraphernalia, the chant, the carried lights, the ritual movements of the Mass itself; for all these things belong to a material artefacture which we have inherited from a past culture; but which, because they are consonant with our natures, we take for granted as appropriate to worship, though they are now far removed from our everyday lives.

In the wide diversity of human artefacture a not inconsiderable gulf separates the carburettor from the chalice. It is a separation about which our ancestors, whether of a few hundred or a few thousand years ago, knew nothing whatever. For them the horse-cloth and the cloths of an altar were all of a piece. They had no inkling of the sharp and growing division between the strictly 'utile' and the strictly 'significant'. But we are men of today: beneficiaries of a now world-wide technological civilization which is in process of revolutionizing our mode of living and of making and of thinking in every conceivable context.

It is possible that the apperceptions of the French Jesuit, Teilhard de Chardin, may help us to see our situation in a wider perspective. But even he for all his stimulating and majestic thought and in spite of his essentially poetic mode of expression, does not (unless I am too stupid or too differently conditioned to perceive it) resolve this dilemma of Technological Man, with his alienation from the creaturely and from the thought-modes of Man-the-Artist, with which a sacramental religion is necessarily bound up. If it is not so bound up what are we to make of the Liturgy? Is it a picturesque survival belonging to a 'fading oracle' as so many of our friends either say or think? One would think with them, were it not for certain considerations which I hope I may have made moderately plain or at least have to some degree suggested.

In the meantime, and especially at this present time of the Liturgical Year, we are asked, irrespective of our feelings, to be glad, 'For', in the Lallans tongue of the Scot, Dunbar,

> he that ye mycht nocht cum to
> To yow is cumin full humly

under the sign of actual, visible flesh at an actual, identifiable site, at a very late date in the history of us sign-making and sign-comprehending mammalia.

In the eighteenth century the hymn-writer, Charles Wesley, could say 'Late in time behold him come'; but he had no idea how late. That we today have a more accurate idea of that lateness is due, in part, to the test known as 'Carbon 14': a good example of the marvel of our technics put to great use—if 'The Greatest Muse is Truth', which I take it may be granted. There is then an immense time-space between the earliest known human artefactures and that Divine Artefacture which we call the Incarnation; which in turn made possible the employment of our artefactures as the central *Signum* of all, in the Upper Room on the first Maundy Thursday and at every Mass since.

Well, a Happy Christmas, and as some of your readers belong to Wales where at one time the few remaining Catholics were known to their Protestant fellow patriots as *meibion Mair*, 'the children of Mary', I would like to recall a very ancient fragment written in a kind of proto-Welsh, which has been translated into modern Welsh and means: 'It is not too much work (or, it is not redundant) to praise Mary's Son.'

Finally don't let us forget the words of the Christmas carol:

> Animals all as it befell
> Who were the first to cry: Noel.

A piece of charming medieval fancy, may be, but if we forget the animals we are halfway to forgetting the creaturely in ourselves, and that in turn will impoverish the sacramental in us, for though the beasts know nothing of sacrament we could know nothing of it either did we not share the bodily with them. No wonder the theologian most associated with the angelic hierarchies should have declared that our having bodies is an advantage.

1960

Use and Sign[*]

W hen it was put to me that I might have something to
say about the possible relationship between poetry and
religion, I felt very disinclined towards the proposal.
The main reasons for this disinclination being, firstly, the many
ambiguities attaching to the two terms, and secondly, the feeling
that in a short talk I should be unable to convey what I have
found overwhelmingly difficult to convey at far greater length
in occasional writings.

At all events it must be made plain that we are not here concerned with what are sometimes called the 'Truths of Religion'.
We are concerned only with the addiction of man to certain
practices which are commonly called 'religious', but to which he
is in fact equally addicted in secular or non-sacral contexts.
Secondly, with regard to poetry, the word is not used here with
reference to versification or metric, but with reference to a far
wider field. This field I have, for convenience, termed the
'extra-utile'. A rather ungainly term, but I think it serves our
purpose.

At the outset we are concerned to note that the animal we call
man is a creature which, from its earliest known beginnings, has
consistently shown a duality of behaviour. On the one hand it
has occupied itself, as have innumerable other creatures, with
astonishing ingenuities directed towards quite obvious and
practical ends. On the other hand, unlike other creatures, it has
been equally occupied with activities which are far from having

* A talk broadcast under the title 'Poetry and Religion' on the BBC Third
Programme on 26 April 1962; published in *The Listener* 24 May 1962, as 'Use
and Sign'. The version printed here is based on a fuller manuscript draft of the
broadcast talk, found among David Jones's papers.

an obvious end. But all acts must be directed towards some end. And the only end that suggests itself is that these activities are done for a sign. They are significant of something other. We feel justified in calling this creature man not only the supreme utilist but the only extra-utilist, or sacramentalist. The 'legion's ordered line', a thing of total practicality and devastating utility, ordained towards an end as obvious as are the tactics of any beast of prey, confronts us in history along with the ordered line of the hexameter, a thing wholly extra-utile and explicable only as a sign.

But this occasions in us no surprise because we take it for granted that man, whether in his most primitive stages or in a high civilizational development, is a creature whose psycho-somatic make-up demands and produces perfections of these two kinds. For the same reason we are not surprised, in looking at the highly practical weapons of Celtic barbarian war-chiefs of the La Tène culture, to note the extreme refinement in metal and enamel of the abstract forms that embellish those weapons, displaying a sensitive aesthetic of such subtlety and vigour as to make the work of civilized artists not only less vigorous but immeasurably less refined.

In the technological and the scientific, the graph of man's progress is relatively simple and the advances incontrovertible. The 'arts', *poiesis*, offer no comparison whatever, for what we gain on the swings we lose on the roundabouts. Michelangelo is no 'better' than but only different from, the Palaeolithic masters, as the caves at Lascaux show. Even that astonishing and most perceptive man, Père Teilhard de Chardin, appears not to have been perceptive over this crucial distinction between the enormously increased apperceptions of man as a scientist and his static condition, not to say his declension, as an artist.

When I was a little tiny boy, my mother, almost any time between Christmas and the Ides of March, was apt to say: As the light lengthens, so the cold strengthens. As the lengthening light of our technocracy illumines and conditions us all, so the strengthening chill of the utile shrivels roots in us all, the shoots of which have helped us to tolerate our mortal state and to yield blossoms in our most lachrymal valley—the only terrain we know—for many millenniums.

We have spoken of a duality in man; perhaps we had better spoken of a nuptials. For thus far, over the whole of man's existence, a mutual intermingling of the utile and the inutile has characterized his cultures. Indeed that marriage is what we mean by a human culture. True, it's been a kind of marriage of convenience, but of astonishing and very varied fruitfulness. And, every now and again, the progeny of that union has caused later generations to wonder with a great admiration. Hence some have spoken of the 'miracle that was Greece' and others of 'that dear middle-age these noodles praise'.

The latter example is of interest in that the men of that particular noodledom (all Peter's chains about their necks) were immersed in the technological. They were in love with the mechanistic. Gadgets had for them a special fascination. Revolving lecterns and the like appealed to their childish minds. Yet the Cathedral of Chartres alone is sufficient evidence that with them the utile and the extra-utile were indissolubly wed: there was no diriment impediment to that union. The men who assiduously applied themselves to the technics without which the stone could not have climbed so high to canopy the Sacrament were the same men who, by the same addiction to the technological, figured out the weight behind the pull of the arbalest: a gadget of formidable utility indeed, which the ban-the-bomb clerics of that day considered too utile by half.

Concentration upon technics has brought us a long way from the ratchet-drawn arbalest which, as I say, disturbed the nicer consciences of that backward age, to the extermination-devices of our forward-looking century of the common man, which very soon will extend its dominion to the journeying moon and then to Venus and beyond again, taking with it this duality.

The enthusiasms of the fathers are, they say, visited upon the children, and certainly this is true as to technics. 'Let me see the wheels go round', says the child in *Helen's Babies*, a book that was read to me when I was very young. But we now see that an innocent obsession with the turning wheel can become a bit too obsessive, so that things other may tend to go by the board.

'I must say,' said the drunk in the opera-hat to the railway-ticket puncher in the old *Punch* joke, 'you punch 'em most extraordinarily well'. Practice makes perfect, and the whole human race, taught by the precepts of the declining West, can compliment itself on the perfections it has acquired in the domain of technics: it is doing most extraordinarily well, superlatively well, and it will do still better.

But how's it getting on in the domain of the sacramental?

> The Devil is sick, the Devil a monk would be,
> The Devil is well, the Devil a monk, not he!

now takes on a kind of inverted meaning. For it is more particularly when we are ailing that the majority of us look to the strictly utile for aid. We don't want magic formulas or old wives' remedies, but what the best demonstrated theories in the realm of the psychosomatic and the most advanced techniques in therapy have made available. These would not be available except for man's fanatical concentration on science and technology. For us, 'King Bomba's *lazzaroni*' may 'foster yet the sacred flame', but what we demand is that 'the wheels go round' not 'significantly', not as *signa* of something other, but with maximum utilitarian effectiveness.

At first sight, then, it would appear that man-the-utilist is in, and that man-the-sacramentalist is out. Some say: Good riddance, but they are saying more than they bargain for. We must not be like the collater of a Situation Report who notes the massive concentration in depth of an advance but who offers no data as to the still unliquidated resistance groups behind, and intermingled with, that advance, and which, indeed are recruited from the disaffected personnel of that advance. Or, rather, more confusing still, are the *alter ego* of *all* that personnel. No wonder the Situation Report fails to assess the actual situation.

Perhaps a more concrete instance might better illustrate the point I am laboriously trying to make. Let us take the names of Picasso and Joyce as world-famous practitioners of the extra-utile within our ever-accelerating utility-putsch. The one something of a magician and a superlatively able artist in various disparate media, from painting to ceramics, the other a master of the metamorphic who, in one medium alone, commands the incantational power of a number of media. Whereby the aural and the ocular senses of us are confronted with a new art-form of unparalleled complexity, of signification piled on signification, thus producing a work of exceptional sacramentality. Whether we like it or not is totally irrelevant.

It may not unreasonably be asked: If such works can be accomplished within our age, what's all the fuss about? Is not all well? Does not man remain just as good, if not better than before, on his extra-utile side? What does all this talk about dilemmas amount to? Wherein resides this paralysing and inhibitive factor for the *poeta* of today?

'I answer that', as they say in formal syllogistic debate, 'the difficulty remains', and I will attempt to indicate why.

For one thing the potency of both the artists named resides to a great extent (to a crucial and overwhelming extent with Joyce) on the continued validity of a whole unbroken past, as particoloured as Joseph's coat, as seamless as the *tunica* 'wove from the top throughout' for which the soldiers cast lots. Incidentally, that seamless vesture is an apt figure of art. For either you have it all or (in the long run) you won't have it at all. You can't dissever it.

Almost all the motifs employed depend upon some apperception of that continuous sign-making which is an entailed inheritance, coming to us from our remote forebears. In that sense, neither of these two artists, although wholly of our time, is typical of the main trend of our time, which is one of a cutting-off from the past.

Nothing, it is said, succeeds like success, and no one can deny the successes following upon man's intense concentration upon the utile, upon what, in fact, works here and now. It has already carried man to outer space, it has already demonstrated to the savage that aspirin is effective whereas the witch-doctor's signs or sacraments may or may not be effective.

Hence the people we today call 'artists' or 'poets', being men whose excuse for their existence is that they serve the extra-utile, are anachronistic, scarcely less anachronistic than the priest. Civilizational changes make unexpected bed-fellows.

Of course, as we all know, the artist, the poet, and for that matter the priest are regarded as most desirable, in that each serves a very real 'psychological' need. The adage that man cannot live by bread alone is fully appreciated, and is indeed, and with absolute sincerity, the main theme of all culture-wallahs. It is also successfully exploited, not to say prostituted, by various entertainment-wallahs. These latter 'know the time of day' with regard to human nature better than do many of 'the children of light'.

But all this lands us back to our original contention, that the nature of man demands the sacramental. If he's denied the deep and the real, he'll fall for the trivial, even for the ersatz; but have it, he will. But we must assert with the greatest emphasis that this demand for the sacramental is not like the demand for a health-giving medicine. It is not because it affords him some consolation. Still less is his addiction to the extra-utile that of the drug or drink addict. His incurable thirst is best expressed by the Psalmist: 'Like as the hart desireth the water-brook' without which, as the English carol says, there could be no 'running of the deer' nor 'playing of the merry organ' nor 'singing in the choir', concelebrating with angels and archangels and the whole war-band of heaven.

But let's suppose that we take the other line, and follow to its logical conclusion the proposition that, after all, the utile is all. What then of Johnny, who has 'gone to the fair' to buy Angharad or Sally or Jill 'a bunch of blue ribbon to tie up my bonny brown hair'? 'Oh dear! what can the matter be?', says the song, that my Johnny should be so long at the fair?

Well, perhaps he was converted to the strictly utile *en route, in via*, and being an honest Johnny and of a logical mind, had decided that to give his beloved a sign or sacrament of his devotion to her was unworthy, indeed impossible, for one who consistently had tried to convince his mates that 'poetry', 'art', and especially 'religion' were illusory comforts—'opiates to tolerate our state'.

But poor Angharad or Sally or Jill: 'No bow or brooch or braid or brace, lace, latch or catch' for her. She were better affianced to a baboon, for even those primates have, according to certain observers, an elementary apperception of some otherness in that they are said ceremonially to mourn their dead. Which report, if true, betrays an extra-utile tendency. But this makes matters only worse, though it may, possibly, have a bearing on the apostle's word that the 'whole of creation groaneth'. It can but groan for the extra-utile.

When Mary Maudlen fractured the alabaster of nard over the feet of the hero of the Christian cult, the Sir Mordred at the dinner-party asked: To what purpose is this waste? But the cult-hero himself said: Let her alone. What she does is for a pre-signification of my death, and wherever my saga is sung in the whole universal world, this sign-making of hers shall be sung also, for a memorial of her. A totally inutile act, but a two-fold anamnesis (that is, a double and effectual re-calling). First of the hero Himself and then of the mistress of all contemplatives and the tutelary figure of all that belongs to *poiesis*. The woman from Magdala in her golden hair, wasting her own time and the party funds: an embarrassment if not a scandal. But an act which is of the very essence of *all* poetry and, by the same token, of any religion worth consideration.

But supposing, which is by no means impossible, we are driven to the last extreme, and, within our own selves, feel forced to the incredible conclusion that, in spite of all this, the utile *is* all. What then?

Well, it is something of a facer. It would then be a matter of *Ite Missa est* with a vengeance: and not only for the vested man at God's board, nor yet only for all poets, all artists at their boards, but for all lovers of whatever condition, and indeed for all sorts and conditions of men in every conceivable conjunction of their lives. Say it with flowers? Crosses for kisses? Take off your hat, dear, to Auntie Mary? Stand to attention in addressing a superior officer? Won't you, please, take my seat? Put out the second-best china? Put out more flags? Take away that bauble? Put on your prettiest frock? Let all things be done decently?

If the 'significatory' were wholly eliminated in every detail of our daily lives, if we can imagine a world where this was ruthlessly and without discrimination applied to all our actions (irrespective of and excluding what we call 'religion' and 'art'), the result would, I think, astonish us. Indeed, there would *be* no 'us'. We should appear as some genus other, if not of some other species.

Mere fantasy, you may say, a *reductio ad absurdum*. Nevertheless such a fantasy helps us to envisage how much is involved in a total, root and branch rejection of the sacramental. 'Hang out our banners on the outward walls', commands the defiant Scot, Macbeth. What a criminal waste of time and energy at the moment of truth, supposing the utile to be all. And what reprehensible fudge to make a recalling of this imagined act, in an art-form calculated to drug the centuries by means of something called the 'language of Shakespeare'.

The story of the broken alabaster could still be told, but as a cautionary tale only, and as a classical instance of the ridiculously inutile practices of our species in what, by then, would be a kind of pre-history, before Man-the-Technocrat had fully evolved and had put away childish things.

The lecturer could not, of course, expect any plaudits at the termination of his address, for that would mean that the implications of his cautionary tale had failed to sink in. For the clapping of hands would here involve at least a measure of the sacramental.

So we are back again within the old orbit of the extra-utile, in all its multifarious manifestations, within the pull of which orbit we would appear to have been caught up a very long time ago. Indisputably we were well within that orbit tens of thousands of years ago and, possibly, for hundreds of thousands of years before that. The dating, though fascinating, hardly affects our question. And what little I have said is meant as a kind of question. A question to which I do not know the answer and which perturbs me all the day long.

But you will recall how the hero in the ancient tale (Peredur, better known as Percival) was blamed, not only for not 'asking the question' concerning the Waste Land, but for actually causing the land to be waste by failing to ask the question. Which seems a bit hard, but hardly more so than the traditional belief, which is now a commonplace among psychologists, that the obsessions of the fathers condition the children.

Well, these are but a few tentative considerations touching the subject of our talk: Poetry and Religion.

24 March 1962

An Introduction to
*The Rime of the Ancient Mariner**

In 1928 or late in 1927 I was asked to make some copper-plate engravings as illustrations to Coleridge's *Rime of the Ancient Mariner* which Mr. Douglas Cleverdon was proposing to publish. I agreed to attempt the task and in due course the work was completed and published from Bristol sometime in 1929.

It is not altogether without interest that Mr. Cleverdon lived in and published the work from Bristol, for it was from that city that *Lyrical Ballads*, containing poems by Wordsworth and Coleridge, including *The Ancient Mariner*, was published in 1798.

Now, in 1964, Mr. Louis Cowan of New York in collaboration with Mr. Cleverdon in London has issued this new edition to be available in the United States and in Great Britain, using the plates engraved by myself thirty-four years ago, and I have been asked to contribute a `foreword of sorts, relating to my intentions and feelings when making the illustrations to this great poem.

It is difficult to recall with any exactitude one's feelings concerning work done three decades back. One thing, however, I can vividly recall, and that is an ambivalence; pleasure in being given the chance to illustrate a work very congenial to me and which, like most people, I had enjoyed from childhood, but also a painful awareness of inadequacy in carrying out the job. For,

---

* First published in 1972, as a book in itself, by Clover Hill Editions, London. Written originally as an introduction for the 1964 Clover Hill Edition of Coleridge's poem, in which David Jones's engravings of 1928 are reproduced, in the end its length could not be accommodated, and only the opening section appears there.

after all, *The Rime of the Ancient Mariner* is one of the great achievements of English poetry, and not only great but unique.

There was a further problem of a purely technical sort, and altogether independent of the particular nature of the work to be illustrated.

While, by 1928, I had become fairly efficient as an engraver on wood, I was a novice in the very different craft of engraving on metal. The differences between the two media are not differences of degree but of kind. Hence, given my relative lack of experience in copper-engraving, it was obvious that nothing elaborate should be attempted.

I decided that simple incised lines reinforced here and there and as sparingly as possible by cross-hatched areas (e.g. the hull, masts, yards and spars of the stricken ship in the third full-page illustration), was the only way open to me. I decided also that these essentially linear designs should have an undertone over the whole area of the plate, partly as an aid to unification. This is easily and naturally achieved in copper-plate printing by not wiping the plate totally clean of ink before putting it in the press. I think this a legitimate practice. In any case, legitimate or not, that is what I decided upon and the designs were made with that in view, and fall to pieces if printed without it.

Engraving in metal is a somewhat arduous process, there is a certain intractability and resistance, a thing altogether absent in engraving on wood; wood-engraving has its own and different problems. On the other hand, once one has mastered the initial difficulty of making the tool used (the burin) incise the recalcitrant metal in the direction required, the result is one of linear freedom and firmness hardly obtainable in any other material. At first one tends to skid all over the place, like an unpractised skater.

A line in an earlier version of this poem subsequently changed by Coleridge (and changed, incidentally, for reasons of exact fidelity to observed fact worthy of Joyce) runs

The furrow follow'd free

—words which might be applied to the particular felicity of the furrow made by the sharp steel burin in the resistant copper.

As in so many other contexts, the more exacting the *disciplina* the more free and flowing the ultimate result.

But no artist can pat himself on the back for this particular beauty, for it is innate in the character of the line the engraver makes in that particular material. All he can do is to make the most or the least of what the medium offers. In my own case it may well have been an advantage rather than a handicap that I was a novice in the craft of metal-engraving when asked to engrave these plates, for at least that precluded cleverness and any attempt at complexity.

Although the great masters and superbly skilled craftsmen have performed miracles of accomplished ingenuity in this medium (and one has to have made one's own attempts, however amateur, to appreciate the extent of their skill), yet I am of the opinion that the most specific beauty, that which belongs to copper-engraving, *sui generis*, is a lyricism inherent in the clean, furrowed free, fluent engraved line, as quintessentially linear as the painted lines on one type of Greek vase, or in Botticelli's (strangely neglected) illustrations to the *Divina Commedia* or the purely linear designs in Anglo-Saxon illustrated MSS.

As far as I can recall I made between 150 and 200 pencil drawings for these 10 engravings. That may seem disproportionate, but it is advisable to get the exact dispositions of the lines composing a design before one transfers it to the copper-plate and commences to engrave. It is possible to make corrections and alterations after one has commenced to engrave but the process is tedious and troublesome and takes time. Hence I designed and redesigned, eliminated and eliminated until I got the kind of drawing sufficiently simple for me to tackle on copper. Even so it was necessary in most of the plates to make minor alterations and modifications during the process of actual engraving.

Of the ten plates, four had to be redesigned and entirely new plates engraved; these were the head-piece, the first and last of the full-page illustrations and the tail-piece.

I destroyed the pencil sketches or 'working-drawings' other than ten, one of which was included in each of the ten copies of a special edition issued at the same time as the ordinary numbered edition in 1929.

I have already referred to my reactions when asked to illustrate this great poem. On the one hand the poem was one which I greatly loved and which is eminently illustratable, on the other there was the quite reasonable and justifiable feeling of misgiving as to my ability to carry out the task.

Like all the great creative works of man this poem operates at a number of levels, there is layer upon layer of meaning.

But unlike most works of comparable depth, it has a deceptive surface ease and facility and a simplicity of artistry, so that the rapid and easy flow of its versification makes it read as though it were written without effort. In fact *The Rime of the Ancient Mariner* has the sort of *rhyme* that almost anybody can enjoy, from the most sophisticated and critical to the least.

This is not just a matter of art disguising art, for most works of any worth conceal, under an apparent artlessness and spontaneity, great labour and stress behind the scenes.

It is something far deeper than that which characterizes this poem. It is that behind the fluent artistry and the popular ballad-form, sustained without a lapse through the many stanzas of its seven parts, it conceals or discloses deeps and strata of meaning where, in the words of the Psalmist, *Abyssus abyssum invocat.*

In a figurative sense deep calls to deep in all great works, but here, owing to the subject-matter of the poem, the remaining words of the verse of the psalm, *in voce cataractarum tuarum,*[1] are equally applicable.

So for this reason too it has a connatural appeal to the people of an island, for whom the troughing ocean was once upon a time called the 'keel's lair'.

If the voice of the water-floods and the cataracted foam resounds throughout this poem the same resounds throughout so much of our heritage-store.

I suppose one of the commonest echoes of our childhood is the remembrance of hearing enclosed in little space the sea-shell's muffled echo of the limitless ocean's ceaseless surf-break.

[1] Ps. 41:8, Vulgate; Ps. 42:7, A.V.

A childish illusion, yes, but it is no illusion that resounds throughout a millennium of history echoed in recorded verse. From the tenth-century entry in the *English Chronicle*, 'over the gannet's bath, across the teeming waters, over the whale's domain' to the 'inboard seas' and the 'sloggering brine' and 'Sydney Fletcher, Bristol bred/(Low lie his mates now on watery bed)' of nineteenth-century Hopkins.

I have referred to the elusive quality of this poem and also to its deep allusions. These allusions are themselves elusively presented, for its imagery has a metamorphic quality. With swift artistry, with something akin to the conjuror's sleight of hand, the images seem now this, now that, a little like the shape-shifting figures in Celtic mythology.

There is something of this element in *The Mariner*. The Welsh 'have a word for it': *hud a lledrith*, meaning 'magic and illusion' or 'magic and fantasy'. There *is* fantasy in this poem so long as we exclude altogether from fantasy anything in the nature of whimsy.

The Rime of the Ancient Mariner is as free from whimsy as Shakespeare's *Lear* or Homer's *Odyssey*, but it has its own *hud a lledrith*, that is to say it spellbinds. It is not only the Wedding-Guest who 'cannot chuse but hear', but you and I.

In that it has a bearing on my approach to *The Mariner* and hence on something in my illustrations, I would like to quote in shortened form a note to a passage in my book *The Anathémata* in which seafarers in peril use the suffrage 'Count us among his argonauts whose argosy you plead'. To this passage I appended a note somewhat to the following effect: What is pleaded in the Mass is precisely the argosy or voyage of the Redeemer, his entire sufferings, death, resurrection and ascension. It is this that is offered on behalf of us argonauts and the whole argosy of mankind and indeed in some sense of all earthly creation, which, as Paul says, suffers a common travail.

This was written about 1950, but a couple of decades previously when working on the *Mariner* engravings associations of a like nature were already an influence, though less explicit.

Apart from the journeyings and ordeals of classical antiquity and from those remoter far, from the proto-voyagings of Mesopotamian epic, or the sacral sailings from Upper Egypt to the land of Punt, there are those from nearer far, from our own Celtic West.

Everybody knows about St. Brendan's voyage to the islands of the Blessed, but behind that stand a succession of Irish wonder-voyages, such as that of Bran son of Febal and that of Maeldúin with its innumerable fantasies and strange varieties of experience as involved and intricate as the interlacings on a page from Kells, which, as we know, influenced the writing of Joyce, and certainly Maeldúin's saga out-Swifts Swift and what Joyce calls 'your gullible's travels' and also 'Gollovar's Troubles'.[2]

There is also the Welsh early and obscure narrative of the thalassic expedition of Arthur and his men in his ship Prydwen, reflecting of course various features of the Irish tales. But by and large the Irish voyagings seem to fetch up in places of various delights and seem to be (or have become thought of as being) in a longitudinal and westerly direction whereas Arthur's odyssey gives the impression of a latitudinal and northward raid of severe ordeal and heavy casualties: Three full cargoes of Prydwen, sea-borne we set out; seven alone returned.

I must emphasize that what I say is entirely the subjective impression of a layman. My intention here (as throughout this foreword) is to record my personal impressions, and largely those of some decades back. A couple of notes to *In Parenthesis*, which book I began writing in the same year (1928) as that in which I made these engravings for *The Mariner*, are evidence of my association of Arthur's voyage with northern waters. It was with the Sea Fret or dawn mist, and the Sea Fire, that phosphorescence called by the Shetlanders 'mareel', that I imagined the warrior-navigators of Prydwen to have encountered, and I thought also of Thorshavn (perhaps only because of the significance of the name) 62° lat. N., or beyond again, of the fog-walls and ramparts of ice.

[2] See *Finnegans Wake*, p. 173: 'Did you anywhere, kennel, on your gullible's travels or during your rural troubadouring...', and ibid., p. 294: 'like your Bigdud dadder in the boudeville song, *Gorotsky Gollovar's Troubles*'.

If the voyage was associated with the terrestrial polar north then of course it was associated with the celestial constellation of Arctophylax, the Bear Watcher, and Arcturus, the Bear Warden. A pretty obvious association considering the name of the cult-voyager and leader of the raid, Arthur; the Celtic for bear being *artos*.

So far, I have been giving my impressions of, mainly, some years back, but latterly I have been reading some of the writings of that veteran geographer Professor E. G. R. Taylor, who can contribute highly technical articles to *The Journal of the Institute of Navigation*, but who, unlike so many specialists in scientific matters, is within the tradition of Humane Letters and is conversant with the mythologies and cosmologies of man. And I note that in her book *The Haven-Finding Art* (London, 1954), in referring to the Latin account of the legend of St. Brendan, she makes it clear that behind the miraculous element common to such hagiographical writings, the physical phenomena described, such as the heavy sea-mist that makes invisible the men in one end of the Irish sea-going curragh from those in the other end, the concerted cries of the colony of sea-birds, the sea itself, *quasi coagulatum*, and other sights, sounds and general conditions are all indicative of North Atlantic latitudes.

So perhaps my early impression of the Welsh cult-hero voyaging north for trouble had a mythological validity; and this did not conflict with the far more copious Irish accounts of the Celtic wonder-voyagings[3] in that they too may have been descriptive of northerly rather than westerly odysseys, the essentially western concept coming later.

However that may be, the reader may well ask: What has any of this to do with the matter in hand, the voyage and ordeals of the Ancient Mariner?

[3] In any case it is now more and more realized by Celtic scholars that the Welsh mythological deposits have parallels in the Irish deposits. The names of the heroes may be totally metamorphosed and the events may occur in a very exactly defined locality but the motifs again and again are found to be indicative of a common heritage. Tangled accretions and differing influences of all sorts over centuries of time camouflage the resemblances and identities.

Well, having tended to locate these strange ordeals in latitudes towards our own Arctic Pole, they have become associated in my mind with the northerly gale which drove the Mariner's vessel into the domain of the numen of the Antarctic Pole. And these two mysterious zones mark the two extremities of the axial line of our own dear earth's diurnal rotation. If deep calls to deep, pole calls to pole, and . . . *Stat Crux dum volvitur orbis.*

If there is in this poem that which evokes themes of basic myth, it is, none the less, of its own particular epoch and precise date in history. It could not have been written either before or since. It belongs, if ever a work did, to the Romantic Revival of the eighteenth century, and is, I suppose, the most successful single English literary contribution to and product of that many-faceted movement.

I am far from forgetting William Blake or Christopher Smart, but *The Rime of the Ancient Mariner*, taken by itself, as a literary work of some length, neither too long nor too short, whole, self-contained and sustained in its artistry throughout, seems to me to stand apart and unique.

Its achievement is all the more astonishing in that while it evokes these deeps of meaning to which I have referred, it manages to do so with ease and grace and lightness of touch, without a suspicion of ponderousness or of the heavy burden with which it is cargoed-up.

There is the voyaging, the terrible and mysterious hazards, the offence that must be purged, the loosening of the spell by an interior act of love when the Mariner, observing the iridescent beauty of the water-snakes, 'blessed them unaware'.

That act of praise is, I suppose, the crux of the poem. Here Coleridge's theology is faultless, for all are agreed that the prayer of praise far excels that of petition.

Immediately the burden of the dead bird slips from his neck and there is a brief interim of untroubled slumber.

> 'To Mary Queen the praise be given!
> She sent the gentle sleep from Heaven'.

But the ordeal is by no means over, for the tutelary spirit who presides over the antarctic water-sphere and atmosphere and all its denizens 'both great and small' demands, and rightly, a kind of wergeld in satisfaction for the wrong committed against a creature whose tutelar and guardian this numen is, hence

> ' "He loved the bird that loved the man
> Who shot him with his bow" '

and he loved him because the bird was his by a kind of kinship and the tribal codes demanding 'vengeance for the insult' echo somewhere in our minds as we read. I have no idea whether Coleridge intended any such unvoiced allusion. As we have noted the whole poem is full of elusive evocations, half-suggestions of this or that, but whatever the poet's intentions, our sympathies, before we are scarce aware, are now wholly with the outraged tutelar of the place.

Nevertheless there is an hierarchy of being, and the numen of the Antarctic Zone holds his power vicariously and within a complex celestial-terrestrial economy. The principalities and powers are not equal, so although the tutelar of the 'land of mist and snow' has, within defined limits, inalienable rights and obligations, the banded seraphim, far above him in majesty and potency and as it were legates of the heavenly Curia, now begin to intervene and to assume control.

But not wholly nor abruptly, for they act with courtesy towards the numen in allowing his agency. This I find one of the most moving passages, and again what is moving is unvoiced and perhaps not meant.

This 'lonesome Spirit', from 'under the keel nine fathom deep', now alone propels the helpless, stricken vessel. Her shrunken timbers, her canvas, shrouds and all her cordage are a sad spectacle, her ship's complement, the 'many men so beautiful', strewn open-eyed upon her deck.

There is a passage in an early Welsh poem which, without mention of the word death, says of the slain after a battle 'the English sleep . . . with light in their eyes', and I always think of this verse of sixth-century origin in reading this eighteenth-century use of the same image, which was so important an element in the Mariner's torment.

Now the seraphic admiralty orders the numen, who still from the under-deeps alone keeps the vessel in motion, to head her on a northward course and to Keep Her So.

This course is to be held to far, far beyond the numen's domain of ice, to the torrid and equatorial waters, as far as the Line and not a fraction of a nautical mile further. The reader may say that this goes beyond what the text or the poet's marginal notes or rubrics affirm, for all that is said is that the vessel is brought as far as the Line.[4] But if unsullied light and therefore infinite agility are part of our image of celestial beings, a seraphic exactitude would seem to me to be part of that image too.

With this celestial command the numen complies, but not without ceasing to demand what he can no longer enforce: full requital for the thoughtless bolt-shot from the Mariner's arbalest (nor must we forget the Mariner's fine-weather mess-mates, very like ourselves: ''Twas right, said they, such birds to slay'); which shot had transfixed the innocent and wholly beneficent victim of whom this numen was guardian.

Seemingly assured by the seraphs that justice would be done, he turns back from his deep-fathomed pilotage, or propulsion rather, back to latitude 70 South and beyond to 'where he abideth by himself'.

As it was this numen 'that made the ship to go', with his sudden but ordained departure

> 'The sails at noon left off their tune,
> And the ship stood still also.'

We now reach another junctional point in the poem. Just as the slipping off from the Mariner's neck of the immolated bird is pivotal and central to the whole theme of the poem, now the abrupt bringing of the vessel flat aback, as though by a dead wind of great suddenness and force, marks the beginnings of a new phase in the feel of the poem which will develop into deeper and conflicting strangenesses.

[4] But see remarks on pages 206 to 210.

At first the new agency is natural, or at least natural phenomena are agential.

> 'The Sun, right up above the mast,
> Had fixed her to the ocean'.

I am far from certain what this implies, but the fixedness is of short duration and now the behaviour of the craft seems very odd indeed.

> 'Backwards and forwards half her length
> With a short uneasy motion.'

Throughout the poem what is natural and within the range of our five senses and consonant with the phenomena of our workaday world and patient of being described in nautical or other mundane terminology is closely intermeshed with the supramundane, very often with the unearthly in the sense of the eerie, the macabre, the disturbing, sometimes with fantasy of a delectable nature, sometimes with celestial vision, but always with total artistry.

Perhaps in this passage of the poem the mysterious and unearthly tend to be more pervasive. While the actual poetry may rise to greater heights of magical beauty the logic behind the elusive imagery may be harder to trace. But soon we shall pass into yet another phase when the feel again changes.

There are still contended powers, but as far as the vessel carrying the Mariner is concerned, though we are no longer in a world of natural phenomena, the supernatural in its beneficent sense has wholly taken over.

But before we are sped homeward by angelic agencies there are a number of matters upon which I should like to comment. This will I fear occupy a good many pages, may necessitate a reconsideration of some matters already touched upon, and may meander into byways seemingly remote from the poem in itself, but which, in my view, the underlying nature of the work inevitably causes our thoughts to explore.

Early in the poem, after the bolt-shot whereby all was 'turned to grete dole, tray and teen' (though I presume that infelicitous

act is not unsymbolic of the *Felix Culpa*),[5] but before the real
load of trouble is upon us, we are told that the vessel has escaped
from the perils of the Antarctic Zone (whence she had been
driven by a severe northerly gale) and that 'a good south wind'
enabled her to reverse her course. That 'fair breeze continues'
and she enters the Pacific Ocean and so proceeds north until she
reaches the Line, at which latitude she is suddenly, instantly and
totally becalmed:

> 'Down dropt the breeze, the sails dropt down,
> Twas sad as sad could be'

and it transpires that the Polar numen had pursued the ship all
the way:

> 'Nine fathom deep he had followed us
> From the land of mist and snow'

and it is here, on the Equator, under 'a hot and copper sky' that
the real ordeals begin and continue.

We have noted how the loosening of the spell began when the
Mariner blessed the creatures that surfaced round the becalmed
vessel; the creatures towards which he had previously felt a
special loathing. The essentially tropic beauty of these water-
snakes thus became the material cause, and more, of the Mariner's
blessing them.

I like to think that Coleridge may have got his water-snakes,
'their rich attire:/Blue, glossy green, and velvet black' from the
first century A.D. Greek writer Arrian of Nicomedia among
whose works was included one on navigation (since known to
have been wrongly attributed) in which surfacing water-snakes
of various hues are reported as being observed in great numbers
by sailors voyaging from the Gulf of Aden towards India, so
within the Tropic of Cancer.

[5] The 'Happy Fault'. This expression, owing to its own happy conciseness,
has for many centuries been used as a kind of code-phrase for the whole dogma
of the Fall and the Redemption. It is used with its fullest poetic effect during the
Blessing of the Paschal Candle on Holy Saturday: '. . . O truly necessary sin of
Adam . . . O happy fault, that merited such and so great a redemption.'

From the moment the Mariner's vessel is 'stuck' and utterly motionless it is likened by Coleridge to a 'painted ship/Upon a painted ocean', an unfortunate analogy from the view-point of a visual artist for whom the supposed words of Galileo *Eppur si muove!* apply to any decent painting, however static the content—but no matter.

From this sudden becalming at the Line right on to the latter part of the poem we remain in the Torrid Zone. Every detail suggests this: in Part 3, the text reads 'At one stride comes the dark' and a marginal gloss reads 'No twilight within the courts of the Sun'.

In the final stanzas of Part 4 the Mariner makes his act of love by blessing the water-snakes and is freed from the load about his neck and (Part 5) the Mother of God lulls him for a while in slumber, as in a kind of Pietà, and while he slumbers she invokes the heavens to refresh him with gentle rain.

In his sleep-dream the ship's buckets, their coopered staves and hoops shrunken or gapped—more colanders than containers—seem, to the dreaming slumberer, watertight and full to the brim with heavenly dew, and, when he awakes, a gentle rain is falling and his whole being drinks.

The Crux-cry, 'I thirst', that for 'Seven days, seven nights' had been his unvoiced cry and for long days before that had been the unvoiced cry of his now dead mess-mates (unuttered because every tongue was 'withered at the root'), was now, for him alone, given effectual response.

Earlier, the pulchral, gilt-tressed, white-limbed Life-in-Death (almost a kind of *fin de siècle* version of a Celtic *bean-sídhe* of the quasi-valkyrian sort), had by a diced chance won the Mariner alone, of all that ship's company, from skeletal Death.

You will remember how she cries out '. . . I've won! I've won!' and 'whistles thrice'. With extraordinary skill and a touch of humour Coleridge conveys that slight whiff of idiotic, but very human, excitement that games of chance seem to engender.

For half a second she reminds us of a delighted winner of the final rubber on a pleasure cruise.

But hers is no such frivolous triumph. I have just said that there is something valkyrian about her. Owing to the compound, chooser-of-the-slain, coming to us from the Old Norse, all of us think of anything valkyrian as belonging exclusively to Nordic mythology, and, on top of that, there's Wagner.

Only the other day in conversation with a young woman I suddenly perceived that, for her, Drystan ap Tallwch and his Irish love, Esyllt Fairneck, wife of March ap Meirchyawn, of immemorial Welsh tradition, were Wagnerian operatic inventions.

Well, it's nothing like as bad as that with regard to the choosers-of-the-slain, for their main provenance is most certainly Teutonic, but there are, I understand, in Celtic mythology, not altogether dissimilar figures. Joyce's 'Washers at the Ford' in *Finnegans Wake* have been said somewhere to be not unconnected with Irish-Celtic[6] 'banshees' of a quasi-valkyrian sort, and in Wales too there lingered on, certainly as late as my father's lifetime (born 1860), a special kind of *gwrach*, hag or female goblin, mainly connected, in rustic superstition, with the demise of some person, but it is possible that once upon a time these unlovely hags *may* have been fair enchantresses, akin to choosers-of-the-slain. We all deteriorate, we all lose our looks, and of nothing is this more true than the figures of a discredited cult.

Coleridge's Life-in-Death might be said to be a chooser-of-the-living, but the one she chose was reserved for a living death 'Alone . . . all, all alone . . . on a wide wide sea'.

But however we may choose to interpret this belle whose lips were red, whose looks were free, this siren *sans merci*, the impression is that she had not reckoned on the *Vergine Bella* of Dufay's *canzone*, the 'hodiern, modern, sempitern, angelicall regyne' of the Scot, Dunbar, the *Eia, Mater, Fons Amoris* of the Mass Sequence, Villon's imperatrix of the infernal marshes,

[6] I cannot, unfortunately, recall where I read this suggestion touching Joyce's Washers at the Ford, nor indeed can I trace a reference to the more general idea that figures partly akin to the Teutonic valkyrie can be detected in some Celtic mythological sources. *A priori* the idea seems not unlikely, in that both mythologies, though so different in feeling, have certain remote common Indo-European origins; and, in historic times, there were the various close contacts between the Scandinavian and the Celtic peoples. But these are matters for specialists to discuss.

Mater Amabilis (the Welshmen's *Mam Hawddgar*),[7] Mother of Mercy and Queen of Peace, yet *Virgo Potens* and imaged in the Roman liturgy as the delectable bride of the Canticle 'terrible as an army', and not just an army in column of route, but *acies ordinata*, an army deployed in Order of Battle. I don't know whether Jerome in his Vulgate translation had here in mind the *triplex acies*, the three-fold battle-line, once favoured of the Legions. But certainly we can say of the activities of the Mother of God that she moves from within a triune formation, still gladius-pierced and juxta the stauros to which yarded tree now is bent the imperial purple, the *arbor decora et fulgida*, the 'tree beautiful and shining' that in the hymn *Vexilla Regis* wins back life from death.

Granted her powers to enthral, what chance had the insubstantial valkyrian gamer against such might? She too had won back from Death a life, that of the Mariner, at least to a life of sorts, a life subject to the caprice of a truly 'monstrous regiment of woman'.

But even if she had not counted on any intervention from powers immeasurably more potent than her own we are in no position to blame her. For how many of us do the celestial formations seem other than very remote? For large numbers of us the seraphic linden-hedge or shield-wall appears splintered, gapped, out-flanked, if not *aufgerollt*, long since.

The apparent realness and effectual triumph of what is inimical (and to that extent deficient of reality), obscures for

---

[7] This bracketed translation of *Mater Amabilis* is inserted for a special reason. In English prayer-books 'Mother most amiable' is the accepted form, but appears to please no one because of its unidiomatic English. The Welsh happen to be more lucky for their word *hawddgar* chances to correspond with *amabilis* and is, I'm told, perfect, idiomatically. But there are further reasons which make *hawddgar* perfect as qualifying *mam*, mother. *Hawdd* (pronounced 'howthe') means fluent, rid of any intractable hardness, and *hawddgar* (howthe-garr', *g* hard, accent on first syllable) means loving or worthy of love, but is equated with half a dozen other words meaning genial, gladsome, gentle, tender, dear. It also evokes cognates meaning welcoming, Welcome!, ease, tranquillity, serenity. So *Mam Hawddgar* could hardly be bettered in any language as one of the titles of the Mother of God.

most of us, most of the time, for some of us all the time, that Reality upon which fixed lode philosophers *cyn Cred*[8] and Christian theologians alike would have us take our bearings.

What has the majority of us ever made of a Reality in which it is said that the good and the real are interchangeable terms? If the enchantress aboard 'the spectre-bark' that had no boards took little heed of that *realitas*, it is not for us to throw stones, and her glass house at least was magical, whereas ours is merely glass.

A consideration which may give some satisfaction to the many Dr. Cairds who by now must pack the Shades as closely as they pack our present world, where so many of us 'take particular facts for no more than they are',[9] where the natural acceptance of type, sign, sacrament becomes less and less congruous with our mode of thought and practice. Where a spade is simply a spade, not even a 'bloody shovel'. For in that old Cockney chestnut one can detect an oblique reflection of something of the haecceity of 'thisness' of a shovel, the instrument whereby the concept 'to shovel' becomes incarnate.

Anyway, she, Life-in-Death, had checkmated Death her mate, and so, by the rules and ethics of the game, the Mariner was hers. Her gambit had snatched him from the fate of his mess-mates,

[8] *Cyn Cred* (pronounced approximately 'kin kraid'), literally 'before the Creed'. In Welsh *cyn Crist* equates with English B.C., but *cyn Cred* is also used. Coming upon it suddenly it evokes a great deal and makes our 'B.C.' seem perfunctory. No doubt familiarity has taken the edge off 'B.C.'. But there is, I think, more to it than that, for *Cred* does not only signify 'Creed', 'belief', 'formula assented to', but can mean our entire religion-culture and indeed is sometimes used to mean 'Christendom'. Even *ante Christum Natum* is, in a sense, less incantative than *cyn Cred*, which in such little space encloses and discloses so much. For we feel in it those many tens of millenniums of the argosy of mankind before the Christian *ecclesia* brought to the argonauts her charts and manuals, before the ship's master had stepped for mainmast the Dreaming Wood.

[9] The words quoted are those of Edward Caird, the Scots Hegelian philosopher, Master of Balliol College, Oxford, from 1893 to 1906. With serene assurance he envisaged a world in which the notion of the sacral would not exist, where the whole idea of this or that material thing being the sign and figure of something other than itself would be excluded, except by artists and the like.

and for so long as the voyage-ordeal endured so too must endure the effect of her winning dice-toss. Fair's fair, and endure it did.

But there was in the 'Queensberry Rules' of that spectral dicing-bout nothing that the spectre-quean could implement in order totally to preclude any amelioration of that ordeal.

The poem, in the opening stanzas of Part 5, and in an accompanying gloss indicates to what extent the celestial powers chose to grant a measure of amelioration.

On one day only in the whole cycle of the year, 'Bytuene Mershe and Averil' when

> 'The little fowl hath her will,
> In her language, to sing'

the Man in the Planeta, standing at the Epistle corner of the altar, has also, in his language, to sing, these suffrages: '. . . . *aperiat carceres: vincula dissolvat . . . navigantibus portum salutis indulgeat*'.[10]

Well, the Mariner could not, any more than countless others in like case in man's long argosy, be vouchsafed the immediate and plenary effects of those general liturgical petitions. But the *Virgo Potens* accepted the conditions as they stood and acted as Consolatrix.

She did not deprive the enchantress of her diced-for man-gain nor sweep aside the spell-wove fetters.

All she did, as Comforter of the Afflicted, was to visit the Mariner *ad Vincula* (eighteenth-century Newgate would have allowed that Corporal Work of Mercy), she did not break his chains nor free him from his ordained ordeal.

But she did bring him the gift of brief slumber. That too, no doubt, was often brought by those many and very various sorts of comforters of the afflicted to those confined within the many Newgates throughout the long torment of the ages.

So far what the Consolatrix had done was, in kind, similar to what consolers of all sorts might do for others in like need.

---

[10] These three petitions, 'open prisons: break chains: grant secure haven to mariners' are taken (with omissions) from the ninth of sixteen Collects or Suffrages chanted consecutively as part of the intercessory prayers of the Roman liturgy for Good Friday. They are used on no other day and are very ancient.

But now comes a change. It is while the Mariner sleeps like a babe that we sense the change. In order to allay the agony of his thirst something more was needed. We might say that at this juncture, though she may draw close about her the duffle wrap to cloak her, we get at least a glimpse of the golden tissue of the Colobium Sindonis,[11] that gleaming tunica of an imperatrix.

Clement, loving, *O dulcis*,[12] yes indeed, but here we catch the accent of her imperative 'Hevins, distil your balmy schouris'.

In a marginal gloss Coleridge says 'By grace of the holy Mother, the ancient Mariner is refreshed with rain.' Yet the blessed respite is brief indeed, for all too soon upon the Mariner's awakening the very moisture of the refreshing shower seems now no blessing, but rather furthers his adversity. For now he is sensible of nothing but chill and dankness.

Then, almost immediately, new astonishments are suddenly upon us.

> 'And soon I heard a roaring wind:
> It did not come anear'.

The vibrating air, as from the erratic and all but spent blast of some far-off heavy detonation, stirred a little the limp and threadbare sails still bent to their rotting yards.

Four stanzas later we read

> 'The loud wind never reached the ship,
> Yet now the ship moved on!'

---

[11] I use this figure of speech because the garment called the Colobium Sindonis has for a millennium and a half or more been especially associated with sacral and regnant figures. The *colobium* itself was a tunica worn by both men and women in antiquity and the dalmatic and tunicle worn today at Mass by deacon and sub-deacon are descended from it. The word *sindonis* refers only to the soft fabric used for special sorts of tunicas and appears eventually to have been used only of the tunica of gold tissue worn by Byzantine rulers. At some early date it became part of the vestments worn by English monarchs and so was worn and seen by many in 1954 at the Coronation of our present Queen.

[12] See antiphon *Salve, Regina*, the concluding words '. . . *O clemens, O pia, O dulcis Virgo Maria*'.

and a gloss tells us that 'The bodies of the ship's crew are inspired, and the ship moves on'; and four stanzas after that the gloss is continued and explains that the ship did *not* move by the action of the dead men 'inspired' and handling her cordage and steering-gear but by the agency of 'angelic spirits'.

The agitation in the upper atmosphere, the sheen of the hundred darting 'fire-flags', the pallid star-dance, all this convulsion in the elements is now accompanied by these most macabre stirrings aboard ship, and then by mysterious but happier, one might say blissful, fantasies.

Mingled with those happier fantasies, and by means of two or three lyrical stanzas, we have a sort of mirage of great delicacy, as English as a miniature by Nicholas Hillyarde and as evocative of England as surely as the fleeting dog-rose, or the abiding words

> Ac on a May mornynge, on Maluerne hulles
> Me befel a ferly of fairy me thoughte.

Coming just where it does in the poem, after the prolonged ordeals, the heavenly alleviations, the renewed miseries, the terrifying storm, and its accompanying strangenesses, but before the events which were ultimately to bring the Mariner back to haven from those far-off seas, this mirage-like image of leafy June is surely perfect in its timing or placing within the narrative.

But to return to the situation we were discussing: the hurricane-like wind, the blackout by the great cloud, the blinding lightnings, like a 'river steep and wide', the drench of cataracted rain, all faithfully indicate tropic storm-conditions.

It is with these natural phenomena, characteristic of but one area that belts the terrestrial globe, that the marvels and fantasies are mingled.

We have noted that our early monastic hagiographers, our pre- and post-Christian tale-tellers and poets meddled the miraculous and the magical very closely in the weave of their wonder-tales of the voyagers. Yet, none the less, the phenomena described are tell-tale and are indicative of the latitudes in which the marvels are said to have occurred.

What is accidentally tell-tale of the sea-going curragh of

Brendan or of the gleaming hull of Arthur's ship, Prydwen, is tell-tale too of the Mariner's troubled barque.

As we have seen, the vessel, in Part 2, is suddenly becalmed at the Line, there she remains fixed until, during the great storm and its strange and awesome happenings (Part 5), we are told the ship moved on 'Yet never a breeze up-blew' and eight stanzas later we read

> 'Till noon we quietly sailed on,
> Yet never a breeze did breathe'.

We are told neither the direction nor the extent of these movements, which were due not to wind or current but to the direct action of the Polar numen in obedience to the seraphic command. But we are not told whether or no or at what point this tutelary spirit had put the ship about so as to bring her back from equatorial waters towards the waters of his 'land of mist and snow'.

'. . . and sudeynli there was made with the aungel a multitude of heuenli knyghthod',[13] or as Coleridge puts it, a 'seraph-band' or an 'angelic troop' now intervenes and while allowing the agency of this feudatory power, commands him to follow a course directed by themselves.

This is our first intimation that the numen-propelled vessel is now, perhaps, many leagues to the south.

A marginal gloss tells us that the numen is ordered to carry on the ship as far as the Line and the text says of the numen

> 'Under the keel nine fathom deep,
> From the land of mist and snow,
> The spirit slid . . .'

So that our immediate assumption is that we are again somewhere near, or at least making towards, the numen's own domain even though the last meteorological indications give no hint of

---

[13] Wyclif, Luke 2:13, translating *Et subito facta est cum angelo multitudo militiae coelestis.*

renewed cold, nor indeed is there any indication of change of any sort—other than that the vessel is no longer stationary.

But the ship having 'moved on' must have moved in *some* direction. A circular movement, such as persons lost in the Australian bush and elsewhere are said to make, or Pavlov's unfortunate dogs, or any of us when in confusion and mental distress, would have had a most appropriate significance, but there's no hint of that either.

At all events, owing to the lines above quoted, I myself have for long imagined that the numen had (until the seraphic intervention) propelled the vessel, wholly at his mercy, far to the south. But now, on closer reading, I am altogether uncertain. An almost identical formula was used of the numen when, in Part 2, the vessel was actually brought to a standstill on the Equator, the only difference being that then the numen had followed, whereas now he propels.

When he followed her she was as yet undamaged, wholly seaworthy, proceeding under sail before a good southerly breeze, her crew unharmed and complete. But now, in Part 5, she moves by the numen's agency, but on a course dictated by the seraphs. Her sails, significantly enough, not unlike the 'restless gossameres' of the 'spectre-bark' which, in Part 3, had fallen in with her—that similarity was no accident. Her timbers now are rotted, her complement of two hundred and one, all dead, bar one, the Mariner: he who alone returned.

Again we catch an unconscious echo of our own Arthurian north-west: Of full complement, sea-borne we set out, seven alone of us returned.[14]

So I suppose we can presume nothing of the ship's position between her being becalmed on the Equator in Part 2, stanza 6, and her movements following the tropical storm and its attendant mysteries in Part 5, stanza 9. Hence we know nothing of her

---

[14] Cf. *The Spoils of Annwfn* from the Book of Taliesin.

> *Tri lloneit prytwen yd aetham ni ar vor*
> Three freights of Prydwen went we on sea
> *namyn seith ny dyrreith o gaer rigor*
> Except seven none returned from Caer Rigor

position until, in a gloss to stanza 20 of Part 5, it is plainly stated
that the Polar numen, in obedience to the angelic troop, has
propelled her, from beneath, to the Line.

But propelled her from where? Even numina can't move a
vessel from nowhere, nor needless to say, would the seraph-band
have bid the numen bring the vessel north to the Line were she
there already. Hence my sense of ambiguity.

Had the numen to grease his elbow for nearly 4,000 nautical
miles, over the 60 to 70 degrees of latitude that separate his
'land of mist and snow' from the waters of the Line, or for
a league or two, a mere few minutes of latitude?

You may say: But what does any of this matter? Of what
consequence are such questions, seeing that we are dealing, not
with a log-book, a manual, a Periplus of the Antipodean Seas, or
even with a work of considerable artistry which chances to
demand the accurate narration of certain mundane facts, but with
a work of very great imaginative poetic genius?

It is precisely because of the greatness of the poetry and the
imagination which informs it that these things do matter. In
poetry everything matters, and the greater the poetry so much the
more is this true.

The more imaginative the genius the more we probe for
possible significances, hints, allusions, clues, in every line and
every word.

Moreover this particular poem, by its not infrequent references,
in both text and glosses, to positions, the ship's direction and the
like, invites us to take note of such matters.

To take one very simple example, a line such as 'The Sun now
rose upon the right', the opening words of Part 2, emphasize that
the vessel was now on a northward course. The poet was Devon-
born, and resided for a while in Bristol, in his day still the second
most important port in England and no doubt full of ancient
mariners with whom he could converse. But leaving aside his
native feeling for the sea and nautical matters, it is clear that, in
this poem at all events, he had an awareness that in poetry
everything matters.

Irrefutable evidence of his almost over-scrupulous and most

meticulous care is to be found in the footnote (referred to early in this foreword) where he explains that the words 'the furrow follow'd free' were changed, in a subsequent edition, to 'the furrow stream'd off free' because the white wake of a moving vessel as seen by a person in that vessel 'appears like a brook flowing off from the stern'. Whereas it appears to follow only to an observer on shore or in another ship.

When such comparatively unimportant details, not affecting any crucial happening in the poem's structure, receive such attention, we may be forgiven for being concerned with what appears to be an ambiguity as to the vessel's position at the extremely crucial moment when the seraph-band orders the numen to propel her back to the Line. We are entitled to ask, back from where?

It may be, of course, that there is no ambiguity and that some failure of perception on my part has caused me to miss the clue, that is indeed likely.

I am reluctant to believe that Coleridge was himself vague as to where in that thalassic inferno the paradisal intervention occurred.

For Dante to be found uncertain of his bearings at some crucial point in the complex meander of his *Comedy* would, I imagine, be unthinkable.

We can't, for various reasons, presume the same for Coleridge's *Mariner*, but none the less the poem is constructed with great care and its words are chosen to convey exact situations relevant to the theme. It has little truck with generalizations.

In, I think, *Romany Rye* the 'man in black' observes 'there's nothing like a good bodily image', and *The Mariner*, as in all incantative poetry, lifts up bodily images, no matter how mysterious, ethereal, metamorphic some of those images may be, or how conceptual the matter of which they are the *signa*.

But much as we may hold that the imagination takes-off best from the flight-deck of the known, from the experiential and the contactual (I suppose the English proverb 'Fact is stranger than fiction' has somewhere behind it something of this notion), the doubt raised above concerning the position of the vessel in no way interferes with what I take to be the main import of this

Death and Life-in-Death

Copper engraving by David Jones, from the set for
The Rime of the Ancient Mariner

poem, an import not unconnected with a passage somewhere in the Rig Vedic scriptures about the soul of us being sea-borne as in a vessel by him in whom is comprehended all that is.

I chance to be writing this on the Feast of Corpus Christi, 1963, a day with which one has long associated, and once looked forward to hearing sung, the words *nova mentis nostrae oculis lux tuae claritatis infulsit*.[15] They are part of the Preface of the Canon of the Mass for Christmas, which was used with poetic and doctrinal appropriateness for Corpus Christi too, until some years back when the authorities precluded it from the latter Feast.[16]

But at this juncture of *The Mariner* when the celestial powers

[15] Usually translated in English Missals as 'The light of thy glory has shone anew upon the eyes of our mind'.

[16] One had always supposed the use of the Christmas Preface on the Feast of Corpus Christi to be of special significance. By this Preface the correspondence of what is present under the *signa* of bread and wine with what is present under the *signum* of actual substantial, mortal flesh, of the flesh of the *puella*, the Fiat Giver, was given liturgic expression.

What is paid latria by the Church in the Sacrament of the Altar is identified with that to which, according to the Lucan narrative, the herdsmen, after they had heard the words 'And this shall be a *sign* unto you', came to pay their latria in Liknites' cave in the House of Bread.

'He placed himself in the order of signs' and what those rustics saw along with the beasts in byre—we must not forget the patient animals if only because they evoked that untranslatable Respond in the 2nd Nocturn of Matins for Christmas: *O magnum mysterium, et admirabile sacramentum*, ut animalia viderent Dominum natum, *jacentem in praesepio*—was neither less nor more of that 'order of signs' than is that sign indicated in the Sequence

Dogma datur Christianis
Quod in carnem transit panis.

To the author of that poem was entrusted the job of piecing together the Proper of the Mass of Corpus Christi, so I presume the choice of Preface was his. However that may be, the choice linked the two central Mysteries.

Hence it is difficult to understand why the Congregation of Rites, in 1960, made general a disusage already noted in 1956. So that now the Nativity Preface is disallowed on Corpus Christi and in all votive masses of the Blessed Sacrament. One would have thought that at this moment in history, what is required is a stressing of the identity of what is signified under differing *signa*.

take over direct control, I am reminded of those words, for a clarity does seem to shine anew into the eyes of our mind.

From remotest antiquity, an oculus was painted on either outboard side of a vessel's bows and even today the extreme forward end of a vessel is called the Eyes of Her, and certainly of this seraph-sped ship we feel that the eyes of her shine with a new light as she homes north over the waters north of the Line.

We have already suggested that as quintessential light, hence limitless agility, are predicated in our image of seraphs, then a supernal exactitude must be theirs also.

We can but speak by analogy, we are anthropomorphic creatures, and the exactitude we suppose in seraphs is deduced from the exactitude we know to be essential to man-the-artist. No matter what the media, all the arts depend for their perfection on exactitude. Sensitivity, that first and absolute requirement without which nothing whatever can be accomplished, is in itself a kind of exactitude, little as this is appreciated, and even when appreciated, liable to misunderstanding and misinterpretation.

But let us recall the position of the vessel immediately before she was homeward bound under seraphic control. We know the exact latitude, though nothing of the longitude, of her position. We know that she stands in equatorial waters.

If we suppose her forefoot to be dead on the Line, then her bow-flare, the foreward and upward sweep of her stem-post and certainly the reaching steeve of her bowsprit incline already above the waters of our hemisphere and hers. For she is a vessel of our own north-west, the fairing of her sheer-plan, the laying-down of her keel, her launching from whatever slip-way, her port of departure, all are of us and ours, together with her ship's complement, the 'many men, so beautiful'.

From her position on the Line she makes a great, and what seems to be a very un-shiplike, leap forward 'like a pawing horse let go', and the Mariner, the only living human creature aboard her and standing on his two feet, is flung forward to the rotting deck-planking in a swoon.

Now indeed she gathers way and accelerates to seraph-speed

which no mortal frame could endure except under seraphic protection. This is afforded the Mariner by his being prone and unconscious on the deck. The seraphs continue and further the effect of that prevenient fall by deepening the coma of the slumberer.

North and still north, league after league the vessel speeds over the Atlantic towards the waters of Arcturus—it is as though the Stella Maris herself added her celestial attraction to the controlled acceleration of this seraph-sped cog and her seraph cogswain.

But, again by celestial prevenience, the acceleration is retarded and the vessel moves at normal speed, 'as in a gentle weather', whereby the Mariner regains consciousness and immediately the full weight of his ordeal returns with all its attendant horrors; nor can he pray.

It will be recalled that it was by the gift of prayer that earlier in the poem the evil spell began to be broken.

Now, not even that is allowed him. *Deus meus, Deus meus, ut quid dereliquisti me?* seems the only echo we hear from that grim deck.

But the returned agony is of very short duration, for the stanza immediately following the one descriptive of this total dereliction, begins 'And now this spell was snapt' and a brief marginal gloss reads 'The curse is finally expiated.'

We are not told how or why nor does this agree with later developments, but the proximate effect is one of release, and, if not one of triumphant gayness, at least there is a sense of reassurance.

We have passed yet another rubicon. For the present writer it recalls, in some sort of way, what certain enclosed religious communities who say the Night Office in choir experience in the early hours of every day when they pass from the three long, unlit Nocturns of Matins to the lights and censing and sung Benedictus of Lauds.

But every reader will have his own analogy for what I am trying, with some difficulty, to express. It really amounts to this: however often we read the poem and so know quite well what is going to happen next, we are taken by a half-credulous surprise.

So was the Mariner. For suddenly, extremely suddenly, he becomes aware that the ship has made a very familiar landfall. Soon she is standing in towards the port of her departure. Now she clears the harbour-bar and now the Mariner is ashore, back in his *patria*, 'mine own countree'.

There follows the act of confession to the Man of Contemplation, the 'Hermit good', the anchorite who, like so many of those actual Celtic solitaries of our North Atlantic seaboard, had for his habitation a wooded place by the sea-margin.

But here Coleridge, rather endearingly I admit, does allow romantic convention to have its way, at least for three lines.

> 'He hath a cushion plump:
> It is the moss that wholly hides
> The rotted old oak-stump'.

These lines are, I think, the only ones in the whole poem that strike an artificial, wholly conventional and somewhat comic note. We are reminded of those friars that turn up at convenient moments in Shakespeare's plays, looking like elderly gentlemen in dressing-gowns, and I doubt if Wardour Street and actors are wholly to blame, I think that already, even in Shakespeare, the sense of Man-the-Sacerdos had gone.

It happens that the episode of the shriving of the Mariner by the anchorite-priest raises difficulties which many readers must have felt.

In a vague way these difficulties have bothered me for a very long time, but of more recent years in a more defined manner, and as the shriving episode is crucial to the poem's structure it would seem necessary to try to clarify the matter.

You and I habitually refer to 'Confession', we seldom if ever use the more technical but more exact and illuminating term, the Sacrament of Penance, we leave that to catechists and manuals. But the deep and deliberate involvement of the poem in this business of 'penance' compels us to recall the more exact term.

It goes without saying that in considering the words used and what they signify in this great poem of the Romantic Revival we must allow not only for 'poetic licence' but for the licence of that particular poetic tradition and epoch. But no matter how much rope we pay out in that regard we still seem to be in difficulties, and if we can't cast off neither can we seem to make fast.

As soon as the Mariner steps ashore he seeks and obtains absolution from the anchorite. Indeed with his first glimpse of the holy man in the pilot's skiff, he says hopefully to himself

> 'He'll shrieve my soul, he'll wash away
> The Albatross's blood'.

So it is impossible to dissociate the episode from the ordinary processes of contrition, confession, absolution, penance.

A penance can be virtually nominal, minimal or maximal depending upon a number of factors. It is not the extreme severity of the Mariner's so-called 'penance' that constitutes our difficulty.

The ordeal imposed recalls that aerial antiphonal colloquy in Part 6 of the poem in which one of the two voices, the voice 'as soft as honey-dew', is heard to say 'The man hath penance done,/ And penance more will do', and now that the nature of the 'penance more' is revealed we see at once that what is imposed is altogether outside the terms of reference of the Sacrament of Penance.

In case we should be in any doubt as to the identification of the life-long ordeal with the penance sacramentally imposed, the poet says in a gloss that having been shriven 'the penance of life falls on him'. It is no part of the job of those who administer this sacrament to impose compulsion-neuroses under the guise of penances, so we are faced with a flat travesty of a sacrament.

This would appear to leave us with one of two alternatives: either Coleridge, for all his unique genius, perception and erudition, was imperceptive of the implications of pastoral theology, or he disregarded what he knew in the interests of the *schema* of his poem.

I hope it was the former of the two alternatives, because no artist is at liberty to distort what he has himself deliberately chosen as part of his *materia poetica*.

Considered from a purely psychological angle the life-ordeal of the Mariner presents no difficulties at all. The recurring and irresistible urge, the temporary releases of tension, might come straight out of the dossier of any modern psychiatrist. Here the poet might seem to be well in advance of his times, though of course the notion of a compulsion laid upon a mortal by the gods or their agents runs through all the ancient deposits with which he was so familiar.

We have then in some fashion to dismiss the hermit as so much stage-property and to dissociate the actualities of the Sacrament of Penance from penance as conceived in this poem.

But as this episode is of cardinal, hinge-like importance to the poem's structure we cannot leave it out of account; that is quite impossible.

For 'penance' we must read 'ordeal' and for Christian confessor we have to substitute some agent of the gods placing a fate upon a mortal.

We can never, of course, *quite* manage this, for we stand within the Christian tradition and so did Coleridge, so that the motif of anchorites and shrivings, no matter how misconceived, belays us (and him) to that tradition.

What I say above about a feeling of not being able to cast-off nor yet make fast, is said with reference to this one episode.

It is evident that this great poem, taken as a whole and in spite of various very differing themes, belongs to the tradition of the wonder-voyages and is evocative of the argosy of mankind and hence cannot avoid evoking the Redeemer, our Odysseus, who in Homer is, at his own command, made fast to the stepped mast.

A good many years back, my friend, Mr. Harman Grisewood, gave me an English translation of that earliest known little book by a Roman of the professional classes who chanced to be a convert to the new religion.

I have it here somewhere among my books but can't find it. But I remember that Minucius is with two friends, one of the old religion of the Roman State, the other, I think, a practising lawyer and a fellow convert. The three are strolling on the seafront on a bank-holiday at Ostia sometime in the first half of the second century. I seem to recollect that they played, or noticed boys playing, that innocent game with pebbles which we call 'ducks and drakes', and that Minucius at some point observes, or makes his lawyer friend observe, that the masts and sail-yards of the square-rigged Roman vessels were an abiding, visible image of the Cross.

Well, Minucius does not bulk large in our tradition, nothing is known of this educated layman except that he was a member of the Church in Rome long before most of his class.

Two centuries after Minucius, among some of the great Greek and Latin Fathers, men, like him, steeped in the Greek and Roman cultural inheritance, there were those who, like him, observing the mast and its sail-yard, pondered the matter deeper. They saw that the ship, the mast, the voyagings, the odysseys and argosies, the perils and ordeals that were part and parcel of classical tradition, could and should be taken as typic of the Church's voyaging. They had a perception of the vessel of the *ecclesia*, her heavy scend in the troughs of the world-waters, drenched with inboard seas, to starboard Scylla, to larb'rd Charybdis, lured by persistent Siren calls, but secure because to the transomed stauros of the mast was made fast the Incarnate Word.

All this: the barque, the tall mast, the hoisted yard, the ordeals of the voyage, has in various ways filtered down through the centuries. It could not very well be otherwise for, after all, there is but one voyager's yarn to tell.

True, many, I suppose most, of the formative theologians and pastoral figures in the Church appear to have had a decided disinclination to admit or at least to employ the foreshadowings and analogies other than those found in the sacred Hebraic deposits.

But in the long run and certainly for us today it is impossible not to see the validity and rightness of Gregory of Nazianzus, of Basil of Caesarea, of Gregory of Nyssa, of Clement of Alexandria, of Ambrose of Milan and of various other less known figures in perceiving that much in the Odysseus saga (and other classical deposits) had correspondences in the voyaging of the Christian soul and in the argosy of the Son of God.

These fourth-century patristic writers, differing in temperament, racial affinity, position and status and in all sorts of ways from Minucius Felix and living in so greatly changed a world from that which the young Roman (though, I understand, a native, like Tertullian, of the Province of Africa) and his friends had known a century and a half back, saw, none the less, amidships the image of the same salvific Wood. And not the yarded mast only, but the planking and timbers composing the vessel, so of the chief timber, the Keel.

It was this idea of the keel that I tried especially to convey in one section of *The Anathémata*, section VI, 'Keel, Ram, Stauros'; in Section IV, 'Redriff', the mast especially; and in other sections, the ship and the voyage.

The keel association is obvious enough, not so obvious as the visually inescapable mast with its cross-yards, but in a more hidden way possibly more moving, for upon that hidden keel all else depends and it is not for nothing that in the concise, strictly factual language of manuals dealing with nautical terminology the keel is defined simply as: 'Principal member of a ship's construction.'

By the time we come to the middle ages proper, the types and foreshadowings or however one cares to express it, were, at least for the great majority, drawn mainly from figures, signs, sacraments of the canonical books of the Old Testament; thus Noah's Ark provided a popular image of the Barque of Salvation. Yet we must not forget that not only did the stream of classical antiquity never dry up and that especially in the monastic houses the writings of the pre-Christian authors were conserved and transcribed, but that the Christian writers, who lived before that classical order had collapsed, were regarded as part of that antiquity, so that there was a confluence of streams. Moreover there was not only a familiarity with the more eminent Christian poets and writers but with the less known authors of all sorts.

All this has become increasingly evident owing to the intensive

and inter-related studies over a wide area. It has been shown that
in some tractate or homily the monastic has used some motif
or maybe embodied a direct quotation (without, as we should
say, giving his source) which is tell-tale of his having been
familiar with the text of this or that barely known or better
known work of pre-Christian Romano-Hellenistic antiquity.[17]

Throughout the medieval period motifs from classical
antiquity were employed by laic literati as plots for tales, poems,
etc. It is said, for example, that the fatal confusion over the
hoisting of the black for the white sail in the Tristan of the
Romances *may* owe something to the story of Theseus, and two
centuries later, Chaucer is full of the heroes and heroines of
antiquity.

Later still, when what is known as 'The Renaissance'[18] got
under full sail and every work of every sort became chock-a-
block with classical allusions, the last thing that appears to
emerge is any notion at all of a deepened sense that basic myth,
such as that of Ulysses, should be taken as typic of the Christian
voyaging and of the argosy of Christ.

Speaking generally, the Christians of the Renaissance, with
their 'New Learning', their refamiliarization with the Greek
texts, seemed very far from perceiving what had been plain
enough to some of the Church Fathers actually living within
that very antiquity which the men of this Renaissance so
assiduously sought to emulate.

When I was in my teens a writer of historical novels made
one of his characters refer to 'Noë, that great admiral'. Whether

[17] For a greater awareness of this continuity a debt is owing to scholars of
our own day, such as, and notably, to the German scholar, Ernst R. Curtius,
and the French Benedictine, Jean Leclercq, and in this island, to Mr.
Christopher Dawson, who has, over the years, again and again indicated the
need to perceive this continuity.

[18] I put it thus because actually 'renaissances' of one sort or another had been
going on through the centuries. Master James of St. George, that Savoyard
architect of Beaumaris Castle in Wales, and of other buildings in this island
and in English possessions in France towards the end of the thirteenth century,
regarded his lay-outs as a return to classical symmetry. I mention this particular
example because to us such architecture seems so utterly 'Gothic'.

this was pastiche or was taken from an actual medieval source I do not know, but it has stuck in my mind over the years as conveying the medieval idea of Noë as commander—in this case of a sea-going vessel. The Arabic word *amir*, governor, commander, ruler, became apparently mixed up with medieval Latin *admirabilis*, by which strange but happy confusion the word passed through French into English.

In the Chester and Townley plays of the Flood and Noë, we get such expressions as 'tent the stere-tre' and 'sette up youer saile' and 'Now to the helm will I hent, And to my ship tent' and 'Help, God, in this nede! As Thou art stereman good, and best, as I rede, of all'.

These convey not the Noah's Ark of our childhood (in my case late Victorian and Edwardian), but a seagoing, masted and rigged vessel, requiring the art of navigation, commanded by an Amir who himself besought the pilotage of the Lord of Voyage and of Haven.

For 'Nowelis flood' in the *Miller's Tale* there is only the burlesque, boring, slapstick, husband-and-wife-squabble motif that fatigues us in the Noë Plays—just as it does in heaven knows how many thousands of stories, novels, plays, jokes ever since.

But in his 'Shipman', Chaucer describes a Master Mariner, who, like Coleridge, came from Devon, from Dartmouth, whose expertise in all that belongs to the art of navigation, theoretical and practical, none could beat, from Hull to Carthage.

By 'many a tempest hadde his berd ben schake', who knew every navigable creek along the coasts of Brittany or Spain and whose cargo-ship was named the *Maudelayne*.

Here, quite fortuitously, no doubt, something of our theme, perhaps, comes through. The Mariner who knew his job, who had voyaged far, the perfect choice of his cog's name—again, I suppose, fortuitous, but with Chaucer you can never be quite sure: he had a wonderful trick of evocation by the casual use of a word or a word or two, often at the termination of a passage, as for example the mention of his Cook's ulcered limb, slipped in between the description of how well that Cook could make thick soup, pies and blancmange.

His skipper was 'a good felawe', a bacchic old tough son of Poseidon, 'Of nyce conscience took he no keep'. But Christ's Barque is not without such, redeemed, of whom the name Magdalen is not untypic.

So that when, after twenty lines descriptive of this able, convivial, but ruthless and unscrupulous ancient mariner, Chaucer's terminal line casually informs us that 'His barge y-cleped was the Maudelayne' we naturally cock our ears.

Milton was obviously intrigued by and used with powerful effect, images of ships and the sea, as when Dalila 'Comes this way sailing, Like a stately Ship . . . and tackle trim, sails fill'd' and earlier in the same poem 'Who like a foolish Pilot have shipwrack't My Vessel'. But throughout his works there is this recurring tendency to draw images from voyagings and vessels. The great thalassic enterprises of the period between 1490 and his birth in 1608 are reflected in his poetry. The then new-charted littorals and uncharted seas crop up pretty often: 'Beneath *Magellan*' and 'Beyond the *Cape of Hope*' and 'th' imagin'd way', i.e. a way round to Cathay or China via an Arctic North-East Passage, presumed to be totally ice-blocked, a topic of the period, to cite but three instances of references to far voyagings and coasts of the great Age of Discovery, and leaving aside all allusions to long familiar coasts, such as 'the *Arabian* shoare' or 'th' Empire of the *Negus* to his utmost Port *Ercoco*' and '*Tremisen*', Chaucer's Tramissene, where his Knight had, three centuries earlier, won three tournaments.

And leaving aside also his countless allusions to, or images of, sites, coasts, lands, rivers, seas, journeyings, personages taken from classical mythology and others from the scriptures of the Old Testament.

With all this wealth of allusion to anabases, and far wanderings in time and space, to odysseys and argosies of one sort or another, to various nautical images, one might have expected from him a recognition, possibly even a kind of anamnesis of the ship: the tree-nailed strakes of the clinker-built hulls, the hidden keel-elm on which all timbers else depend, the great-girthed, cross-yarded mast amidships, the image which those early

Christian writers had been quick to recognize, the visible image of the Wood, to which had been made fast the voyaging Pantocrator.

But whatever we may have expected with regard to such recognition, let alone anything that could, by analogy, be regarded as an anamnesis[19] of sorts, we do not find it.

There is, in his lyric ode to his Irish friend shipwrecked off the coast of lovely Gwynedd, the famous line about the Petrine 'Pilot of the Galilean lake', but that hardly touches our present matter, except for the passing reference to pilotage.

The one occasion that sticks for ever in our mind with regard to his use of the analogy taken from a ship's essential wood is when he evokes the image of the tall tree, selected, felled and fit 'to be the Mast of some great Ammiral'.

And it's the right sort of timber too: soft-wood, shipped from the Baltic. He'd probably seen such, within a couple or three miles of his parents' home off Cheapside, being unladed or stacked or in some mast-pond below London Bridge on the Surrey shore, in the great river-bend towards Deptford and Greenwich. Maybe in Rotherhithe, where, within a hundred and eighty years of the publication of *Paradise Lost*, my mother's father, a mast-maker (and whose sole reading appears to have been Milton, the Bible and the Book of Common Prayer), used to select and work his timber. Sometimes it was American (Oregon) pine, sometimes it was, like Milton's, 'Hewn on *Norwegian* hills'.

But the great poet did not employ his potent image to call up in us or himself the *Crux Fidelis*. Very far from it. His analogy of the great upstanding tree, axed down for a ship's mainmast, has no connection with that tall tree which itself tells the story

[19] I use the word loosely, or rather analogously. For, at least within a Christian context, anamnesis is inevitably associated with the words of Our Lord at the Supper, 'Do this for an anamnesis of me.' Words which, at all events for the central sacramental tradition of Christendom, mean, in a special sense, an effectual recalling. But, by analogy, the word 'anamnesis' can, and in my view, should, be applied to art-works of various sorts in that they seek to 're-present' under this or that mode an existing reality.

of its anguish—'they felled me at the forest-edge'—the saga of its terror but also of its latreutic guerdon, in the most marvellous of Old English poems,[20] the Dreaming Tree that bore up 'the young hero *thaet waes god aelmihtig*' as the carved runes tell on the great *sigbecn*[21] at Ruthwell in Dumfriesshire.

Milton's mast-image is not used to evoke, incant or hold up for us the gleaming *arbor* of the man who, from the Adriatic shore of Ostrogothic Italy came to Merovingian Gaul, and made his hymn which, for fourteen centuries, was to afford liturgic expression of the axial beam of redeemed creation by the image of the beam of a Roman steelyard or balance,[22] also

[20] I cannot read Anglo-Saxon, but there are many words and whole sentences which one can recognize and with some assistance as to the phonetics one can get the feel and rhythm of it. With this much, and recent translations, a pretty good idea of the great splendour of this work can be perceived. For majesty, pathos, true imagination and great marvel it seems unique. It gives expression to the meaning of the Cross as perceived by that mixed Celtic-Nordic complex out of which it sprang. It could not have been written outside that particular fusion of this island in the great age of Northumbrian Christianity (though I understand that the existing MS. is in the Wessex dialect of some two centuries later). However all that may be, it seems to me to surpass, by a very long way, any subsequent attempt to deal with this central matter, in the English tongue.

[21] The term *sigbecn*, 'victory beacon', was used of those high-shafted stone crosses, with their very eclectic motifs: Roman, Byzantine, Syrian, Celtic, Nordic, erected in the seventh and eighth centuries and standing like masts on open sites and suffering the wind and weather of many centuries. The one now housed in Ruthwell Church is inscribed in runic characters with a fragment from *The Dream of the Rood*. I recall with gratitude being informed of this term *sigbecn* by the late R. H. Hodgkin, Provost of Queen's College, Oxford, a man of life-long devotion to that formative period of his people. I note also that he mentions the term in the text (p. 368) of his *History of the Anglo-Saxons* (1935), but the word is, unfortunately, not indexed.

[22] In his hymn *Vexilla Regis*, Fortunatus uses the word *statera* of the beam of the Cross. It requires no knowledge of Latin to see the significance of this image. A glance at the Latin–English dictionary is sufficient. The primary meaning is given as 'steelyard', that balance which is one kind of *libra* or scales.

Should we so choose, we can regard as a Sign of the Cross the Constellation of Libra which is in fixed juxtaposition next the Constellation of Virgo, as our nursery rhyme reminds us: 'The Ram, the Bull, the Heavenly Twins, next the Crab the Lion shines, *the Virgin and the Scales* . . .' which in turn can hardly

by the image of the cross-barred standard to which was bent the purple vexillum of an imperator—an image virtually synonymous with that of the northern stone *sigbecn* of a century and more later, the *lignum* of *'Regnavit a ligno Deus'*.[23]

No, the seventeenth-century English poet used his impressive, possibly the most impressive of his images of comparison, this powerful image of the wood of a tall, wide-girthed, tapering pine, stepped for the great mast of a great ship, in order to dramatize, with brilliant, conscious and startlingly effective artistry, an imagined beam, immeasurably more vast in girth, height, ponderance: the colossal spear-haft in the supposed almighty fist-grip of his god-damned Lucifer.

When those Christians of the Graeco-Roman tradition living in lands bordering the Middle Sea surveyed the cross-yarded wood it imaged, at least for some of them, what it did, apparently, for Isaac Watts (born in the port of Southampton, in the year of Milton's death), the wood on which that 'young Prince of Glory died'.[24]

---

fail to remind us that according to the Fourth Gospel there stood, next the Cross, the Mother.

But it was to the Cross seen as a steelyard that the poet was referring and the dictionary says that while *statera* was primarily used of that weighing instrument, it was used also of the value or worth of anything, so by choosing the right word he evokes the beam that made possible the restoration of the equilibrium of all creation and also the price paid, once and for all.

Hence, in the imagery of the poem, the balance becomes what in fact it is in the Christian mythos: the standard (*vexillum*) of a conqueror and the resplendent Tree.

[23] When Fortunatus wrote this often quoted line of God reigning from the Tree he was no doubt thinking of the actual Crucifixion. True, by his time (sixth century) there were art-works illustrative of Christ on the Tree, but it was not until centuries later, with the development of Gothic architecture, that the wooden rood-lofts in countless parish churches could carry as their central image that of Christ reigning from the Wood and carved in wood, like a mast rising from its mast-thwart at the forward end of the nave—itself a word evocative enough, especially when we remember that in Middle English a ship was called a *nef*, a nave.

[24] Today, Watts's hymn 'When I Survey the Wondrous Cross' has for its second line 'On which the Prince of Glory died', but it is said that originally

As far as I can gather the particular theology of Dr. Watts was as removed as Milton's from the sacramental religion of Clement or Ambrose or Fortunatus or the unknown writer of the Old-English *Dream of the Rood*, but at least he, like them, surveyed, in the wood, the wondrous Cross.

It will no doubt be felt that all this stuff concerning early Christian images of the ship, the mast, the ordeals, the Christus-Ulysses concept, the references to Chaucer or to Milton have little or no bearing on Coleridge's *Ancient Mariner*.

But my view is, and for a long time has been, that, like the Celtic tales of the wonder-voyages mentioned earlier, all these various images of whatever provenance have a bearing on Coleridge's poem, because, as I've already said, the poem cannot escape evoking the whole argosy of man.

To return to the difficulties I feel with regard to the penance imposed by the anchorite on the Mariner, once we accept that

---

the text read 'young Prince of Glory'. Never having seen a copy of that earlier version I do not know how the line scanned, but certainly the emendation that deleted 'young' caused an intrinsic loss and deprived us also of a far-back echo of 'Stripped himself then the young hero, that was God Almighty', of the Anglo-Saxon poem.

Emendations tend to be deprivative, but it would be hard to beat the well-meant emendation that comes to us from the sea, from the Royal Navy. What a pity that code-pennant No. 269, 'expects', was not lost or mislaid aboard the leading vessel of the weather column that October morning outside the Pillars of Hercules some seven years after the first publication of *The Ancient Mariner*. Or, better still, had the 'great Ammiral' himself sharply retorted in plain nautical English, 'Quod scripsi, bloody scripsi', to the bright suggestion which changed the initial proper noun, and still more sharply to the convenient, highly utile reasons of the efficient signals-officer, by whom we lost the crucial verb, 'confides'. I suppose we must consider it fortunate that code-pennants 261 'every' and 471 'man' were to hand, for by these was at least conserved an essential part of that mutilated signal. For his confiding was in his whole sea-borne *ecclesia*: the able seamen who, by definition, 'hand, reef and steer', the personnel of each gun's team, the maltreated little ship's boys who must run to and fro between magazine and gun, and the latest gang-pressed, least able and most wretched deck-hand.

To all these, no less (I suspect more) than to those in command, he meant to address that firm but affectionate, warm but authoritative, semantically impeccable 'confides'.

Coleridge's notion of sacramental penance was misconceived, then we are free to appreciate to the full his psychological insight and, what is perhaps more crucial here, his allegorical intention. For purely as poetic allegory the dreadful and life-long ordeal subserves that allegory with complete logic, just as the logic is subserved by verse the virtues of which need no advertisement.

Cogently, clearly, 'The Mariner whose eye is bright' gives with clinical accuracy an account of his case: the ordeal is inter-mittent, 'at an uncertain hour', it recurs in divers places, 'I pass, like night, from land to land', it involves a kind of Pente-costal gift of languages, 'I have strange power of speech', the tale is never told to a throng of persons but always to a separate individual, recognized by the Mariner as his next unwilling audient, 'The moment that his face I see,/I know the man that must hear me.'

Thus, under whatever compulsion, the cathartic and salvific saga is assured oral continuity. The victim of the ordeal himself becomes its Confessor, the declarer and furtherer of the mythos.

The separate, unwilling listeners to his tale, stunned by what they hear, arise 'the morrow morn' a little nearer Hagia Sophia. True they awaken 'sadder', but that touch could hardly be avoided within the Romantic tradition. Blake might have managed without it, but Coleridge was not Blake.

> The bride hath paced into the hall,
> Red as a rose is she;
> Nodding their heads before her goes
> The merry minstrelsey.

No matter, the ribboned gallant in his wedding best may with his gloved hand seek to hold off the 'grey-beard loon', it is of no avail. He sits on a stone, stock-still as a stone and 'listens like a three years' child' to the crucial re-telling

> 'Instead of the cross, the Albatross
> About my neck was hung'.

The re-telling relentlessly continues and when at last it is over so too is the wedding, and the wedding-feast. True, in the garden-bower the bride and her maids are singing, but now the little bell rings to Vespers the sea-faring folk of the little port.

It is at Vespers that the altar is censed during the singing of the Magnificat, her song who is called the Star of the Sea. The Pole Star was the fixed lode of shipmen of all degrees and kinds, from buscarles to great navigators and Lord High Admirals.

At one period their manuals of seamanship were called the Regiment of the North Star, and the ship's compass was called the Stella Maris as well as the star itself.

I mention these things only because they have a bearing on the motif of the last of the eight full-page illustrations, and then only because I have so often been asked to explain why, in that engraving, a priest is shown censing an altar.

If I have said little of the several other plates it is because I felt that in expressing something of my views as to the poem itself some of the motifs used in the engravings might become more apparent, as will their poverty compared with the great riches of the poem they attempted to illustrate.

The pelican feeding her young from her own flesh in the tail-piece requires no explanation. The Latin inscription of that tail-piece is taken from the Roman Mass, the words being part of what the celebrant says while he is censing the altar after having censed the Oblations: May the Lord kindle in us the fire of his love and the flame of eternal charity. Words which seemed to tally with the third stanza from the end of the poem, and which express a theme that runs like a thread through the whole mysterious weft and warp of *The Rime of the Ancient Mariner*.

1963–4

Index of Names

DJ = David Jones